D0725306

"Event planner Presley Parker is throwing a party at the Winchester Mystery House in San Jose, and you just know all those corridors and secret rooms will be the perfect setting for a murder. . . . Downright fun."
　　　　　　　　　　　　　　　　　—*Contra Costa Times*

"Presley Parker is a delightful event host, and this entertaining mystery captures the ins and outs of planning a séance. . . . Delightfully entertaining."
　　　　　　　　　　　　　　　　　—Mysterious Reviews

"Unforgettable characters, information, and humor all in one divine package. Treat yourself to this one as soon as possible."　　　　　　　　　　　　　—Fresh Fiction

"[A]n entertaining read, full of unique characters and breezy prose. The setting is unique, the structure is smart, and the pacing is quick. . . . Presley otherwise makes for a strong, smart, funny protagonist for whom readers will want to root."　　　　　　　　　　　　　—The Season for Romance

"Presley is a creative, energetic young woman with a wry sense of humor."　　　　　　　　　—The Mystery Reader

How to Crash a Killer Bash

"[Warner] delights her audience with colorful and lively characters, intriguing suspense, and fun party-planning tips. If you're looking for a lighthearted, fast-moving story with enough polish and pizzazz to keep your interest popping to the very last page, look no further than this party-hearty book."
　　　　　　　　　　　　　　　　　—Fresh Fiction

continued . . .

"Exactly what a modern cozy should be: light and playful, a little romance mixed with a little mystery, and thoroughly enjoyable start to finish." —Mysterious Reviews

"The mystery is well plotted, [and] there are plenty of clues and plenty of suspects, letting readers guess along with Presley." —The Mystery Reader

"I highly recommend this book to all mystery readers, cozy [fans] or not. This is a party that you don't want to miss." —Once Upon a Romance Reviews

"The Killer Party series is delightful!" —Meritorious Mysteries

"Presley Parker is a protagonist who readers can't help but like. She's been down on her luck but lands on her feet when she comes up with the idea for an event-planning business. For a mystery series, it's a near-perfect occupation." —MysteriesGalore.com

"Penny Warner has created a wonderful heroine in perilous Presley Parker. . . . With plenty of action on her investigation and several poignant moments, readers will enjoy the perils of Presley Parker." —Genre Go Round Reviews

"The second Party-Planner mystery is a delightful whodunit due to a strong lead and the eccentric cast who bring a flavor of San Francisco to life." —The Best Reviews

"Plenty of motives and suspects . . . a cast of lively characters." —Gumshoe

How to Host a Killer Party

"Penny Warner's scintillating *How to Host a Killer Party* introduces an appealing heroine whose event skills include utilizing party favors in self-defense in a fun, fast-paced new series guaranteed to please."
—Carolyn Hart, Agatha, Anthony, and Macavity award–winning author of *Dead by Midnight*

The Party-Planning Mystery Series

How to Party with a
Killer Vampire

A Party-Planning Mystery

Penny Warner

AN OBSIDIAN MYSTERY

OBSIDIAN
Published by New American Library, a division of
Penguin Group (USA) Inc., 375 Hudson Street,
New York, New York 10014, USA
Penguin Group (Canada), 90 Eglinton Avenue East, Suite 700, Toronto,
Ontario M4P 2Y3, Canada (a division of Pearson Penguin Canada Inc.)
Penguin Books Ltd., 80 Strand, London WC2R 0RL, England
Penguin Ireland, 25 St. Stephen's Green, Dublin 2,
Ireland (a division of Penguin Books Ltd.)
Penguin Group (Australia), 250 Camberwell Road, Camberwell, Victoria 3124,
Australia (a division of Pearson Australia Group Pty. Ltd.)
Penguin Books India Pvt. Ltd., 11 Community Centre, Panchsheel Park,
New Delhi - 110 017, India
Penguin Group (NZ), 67 Apollo Drive, Rosedale, Auckland 0632,
New Zealand (a division of Pearson New Zealand Ltd.)
Penguin Books (South Africa) (Pty.) Ltd., 24 Sturdee Avenue,
Rosebank, Johannesburg 2196, South Africa

Penguin Books Ltd., Registered Offices:
80 Strand, London WC2R 0RL, England

First published by Obsidian, an imprint of New American Library,
a division of Penguin Group (USA) Inc.

First Printing, October 2011
10 9 8 7 6 5 4 3 2 1

To the partyers in my life—my family.
And to party planners everywhere—you know what I'm
talking about. . . .

ACKNOWLEDGMENTS

Thanks to everyone who helped in some way with this book: Colleen Casey, Janet Finsilver, Staci McLaughlin, Ann Parker, Carole Price, Sue Warner, the city of Colma, my wonderful agents Andrea Hurst and Amberly Finarelli, and my incredible editor, Sandy Harding.

"I figured that, if you do a vampire movie in Hollywood, you've made it."

—Christopher Atkins

Chapter 1

It should have been a dark and stormy night, à la Hollywood, but the October moon was full and the sky cloudless. I stood quietly in the cemetery, feeling as if I were viewing a film. But there were no cameras, and this was no movie.

I watched as the tall, pale twentysomething man dressed in tight black jeans and a black chest-hugging T-shirt suddenly appeared from out of nowhere. He seemed to glide toward the wide-eyed, raven-haired young woman who waited for him. She wore a white, flowing dress, sheer and low-cut, that displayed her obviously enhanced breasts. Leaning seductively against a towering headstone, her long hair swirling in the night breeze, she smiled at the man in black approaching her. He held a glass of bloodred wine, his glowing eyes fixed on her.

I felt like a voyeur, but I couldn't take my eyes off this mesmerizing couple.

He offered her the glass, not taking his eyes from hers. There was palpable chemistry between these two people. "This is very old wine. I hope you'll like it."

She wrapped a porcelain hand around the stem, her red-lacquered fingernails tinkling against the glass. "Aren't you drinking?" she asked, her eyes reflecting the bright spotlights. She took a sip.

Staring at her with intense dark eyes, the young man parted his full lips, revealing white teeth that glinted in the light. "I never drink *wine*."

I almost laughed out loud at the familiar line. Count Dracula had said the same thing to Renfield in the original 1939 film. But when the man in black suddenly jerked, as if having a spasm, I gasped. Seconds later he shot up into the air like a rocket and disappeared into the branches of a eucalyptus tree.

"Awesome!" I said, clapping. I could feel my heart racing.

I looked around, certain I'd be joined in a round of cheery applause. But when I saw frowns on the faces of those nearby, I stopped.

"No! No! No!" Lucas Cruz yelled from behind me.

Cruz, as everyone called him, was the eccentric producer/director at CeeGee Studios, located on Treasure

Island. Five years ago, he set up his computer graphics/film company in one of the long-empty Pan Am Clipper hangars on the island. Since then, he'd produced a number of sci-fi and horror films that featured his cutting-edge special effects. One of his films had starred local San Francisco resident Robin Williams as Cosmo Topper in a remake of *Topper*, the popular 1937 ghost film. In spite of Robin's talents, the movie had quickly gone to video.

Cruz had hired me to plan a "wrap party" to celebrate—and publicize—the end of production on his latest horror film, *Revenge of the Killer Vampires*. I'd seen a few clips of the jump-the-shark spoof of vampire flicks that had ravaged theaters around the country. The two "hot" young stars, Jonas Jones, who played the vampire, and Angelica Brayden, the love interest, would no doubt become ET, TMI, and *Gossip Guy* regulars once the film debuted. And I was lucky enough to have just witnessed a preview of the skit from the movie that would be performed at tomorrow night's party.

The wrap party would have been simple enough to host if Cruz hadn't wanted the event held in a cemetery—"for the ambience." After overcoming my initial resistance, I researched the possibilities online and found a *Wall Street Journal* article that mentioned the growing popularity of murder mystery parties, scavenger hunts, and other events held in cemeteries. Hollywood Forever cemetery in Los Angeles projected movies onto its mausoleum walls. Davis Cemetery in

California offered bird walks and poetry workshops. Others presented Shakespeare festivals, family picnics, and even weddings.

The idea behind this: "To nurture warm feelings about the cemetery."

Weird, I thought, but why not?

I made some calls but found San Francisco's few cemeteries unreceptive to the idea. The City had been forced to move many of its cemeteries, due to rising costs of land and lack of space, and those that remained didn't readily open their doors for entertainment purposes. But when I contacted the powers that be in neighboring Colma, I got lucky.

While the historic town of Colma is quaint, with brick-paved roads, ornamental streetlamps, a railroad depot, a retro city hall, and ethnically diverse restaurants, Colma is best known as the final resting place for the who's who of San Francisco's dearly departed. Among its permanent residents are newspaper tycoon William Randolph Hearst; business magnate William Henry Crocker; *San Francisco Chronicle* founder Charles de Young; the infamous, self-proclaimed Emperor Norton; and baseball legend Joe DiMaggio. Even Sheriff Wyatt Earp came to rest in Colma. It's now known as "the City of Souls," and it's also where many deceased former San Franciscans have been "relocated." In fact, now the dead outnumber the living one and a half million to sixteen hundred.

After Cruz paid a hefty rental fee, the city administrator agreed to let us host our party at Lawndale, one of the neglected older cemeteries that had gone bankrupt, thanks to the plethora of the more prestigious cemeteries—sixteen, to be exact—that had opened in the area.

Cruz had quickly found the spot in the cemetery he wanted—a large open-air mausoleum with a patio, surrounded by acres of untended headstones. At the moment, production crew members from CeeGee Studios were working out the logistics of "vampire flight" gone wrong. Two men were trying to retrieve Jonas from the treetop, while others attempted to fix a glitch in the rigging that was supposed to lift the young star up and away in a dramatic disappearing act—but not up and into a tree. It looked as if Jonas, aka Count Alucard ("Dracula" spelled backward), was going to need more flying lessons and a better pulley system.

Still, I was impressed, and I thought the party guests—the primary stars, select film crew, important media, and a few local dignitaries—would be also, at tomorrow night's party. That is, if they weren't too superstitious to enter a graveyard.

I didn't relish the idea of hosting a party in a graveyard—it seemed somewhat disrespectful—but Cruz had promised to make a large donation to the charity organization of my choice. That was something I insisted on when I hosted large parties for clients. This time I'd chosen the American Red Cross. Given the type of party, it seemed appropriate to help out an organization known for its blood drives.

"Watch the trees, for God's sake!" Cruz yelled as

crew members adjusted the young actor's hidden flying gear. "I want him lifted up and over that whatchacallit— that monument there—not flung around like Peter Pan on crack. This is supposed to be thrilling, not embarrassing! Reporters and photographers from TMI, *Gossip Guy*, and Buzz Online will be here tomorrow night!"

Cruz ran both hands through his thinning hair, a habit he had when he was anxious or upset. It was probably why he had thinning hair. Dressed in a T-shirt, saggy jeans, and a hoodie that read "CeeGee Studios," he looked more like a maintenance worker than the man in charge. He wasn't the easiest person to work with, and I sensed I'd regret taking on this job, but in the past he'd helped me out with some of my parties that required unique lighting, background decor, or special effects. Consequently, even though I'd been buried under a pile of party requests since I'd hosted the Séance Party at the Winchester Mystery House, I felt I owed him and couldn't turn him down.

Besides, helping one another is what we Treasure Islanders do.

While Cruz and his crew continued to work on the "disappearing Dracula" glitch, I went over final plans for the party decorations with my own crew. Tonight we were setting up the lighting, unloading the larger props, and doing logistics; tomorrow we'd turn the old mausoleum into a mini-Transylvania.

Delicia Jackson, part-time actress and my office mate on TI, was in charge of the vampire black and bloodred helium-inflated balloons. Currently she was tying the balloons to headstones and monuments in the designated party area. Tomorrow she'd dress for the theme, in a sexy "Vampira" costume. Unlike the star of the film, Angelica, who wore a wig, Dee didn't need fake locks. Her long black hair was perfect for the part.

Berkeley Wong, my events videographer, had already helped Cruz's crew with the atmospheric lighting—headstones with eerie backlights, indirect spotlights, and dozens of candles. He'd be back again tomorrow night to videotape the event.

Duncan Grant, all-around gamer, computer whiz, fan of extreme sports, and Berk's office roommate on Treasure Island, was busy connecting wires behind some gravestones. He'd been thrilled when Cruz had hired him and a few of his friends as movie extras. At the moment, he was hooking up the creepy-voice recordings he'd made earlier on his computer, and placing tiny speakers around the party area. At twenty, with his curly red hair, baggy skater pants, and a black T-shirt that cryptically read "Take Flight," he still looked like a high school kid playing with electronic toys. But these were high-tech playthings. Each time someone walked past a headstone, a disembodied voice said, "I vant to suck your blood," "What a long neck you have," or "Bite me."

Everything was going to be perfect, I promised myself.

"Those are awesome!" I called to Brad, my . . . whatever. I refused to call him "boyfriend." The hunky crime scene cleaner, who also rents office space on the island, had generously volunteered to help out. At the moment, he was setting up Styrofoam tombstones made by the graphic artists at CeeGee Studios. Each marker had been hand painted to look cracked and crumbling, then lettered with funny epitaphs such as, "To follow you, I'm not content; how do I know which way you went?" and "Here lies a man named Zeke, second-fastest draw in Cripple Creek."

"As long as I don't find my name on one of these . . . ," Brad said, securing a fake headstone to the front of a real one with duct tape. Out of his white Crime Scene Cleaners jumpsuit and in black jeans and a black T-shirt, he looked like one of Cruz's creative staff.

I opened a box and began sorting through the garlic "necklaces" I'd be placing on the portable party tables that would soon be covered with red tablecloths. I'd ordered dozens of little wooden crosses and small rubber bats, which I planned to set at each place, along with plastic vampire fangs that doubled as napkin rings. But it was the centerpieces that would catch the eyes of most guests tomorrow night. I'd had mini-coffins made out of Plexiglas that would be filled with red-tinted water and topped with a floating, black rose candle.

I hummed as I worked, probably because I found the surroundings serene and relaxing. While most of the Colma cemeteries had expansive lawns, color spots of flowers, and statues of weeping angels, the grass here at Lawndale had turned brown and the flowers had long ago died. But the headstones were still intriguing, documenting lives often taken prematurely by complications of childbirth, disease epidemics, or wars. Lawndale also had a pet section up the hill called "Pet's Place," reserved for burying animals. Not to be confused with Stephen King's *Pet Sematary*, where the pets actually came back to life after they were buried, this one was filled with tiny headstones featuring names of well-loved cats and dogs, interspersed with the occasional parakeet, gecko, or monkey.

I suddenly sensed someone standing behind me. Half expecting it to be Brad, I turned around and came face-to-face with a grizzled old man in a frayed 49ers baseball cap, wearing dirty overalls and a plaid flannel shirt. His tattered brown boots were caked in mud, his beard caked with bits of dropped food.

Backlit by the work lights the crew had constructed, the man seemed to loom larger than life.

"What's going on here?" The man spat, then grimaced, revealing a row of crooked, yellowed teeth. He swung the beam of a heavy flashlight around the crew. Everyone stopped working and stared at the man— and at the large shovel he held in his other hand.

I was about to explain, when Cruz bounded over, nearly tripping over a cord. "I should ask you the same question, buddy," he said to the man who was nearly twice his size. While Cruz may have had a big bark, I had a feeling this guy had a bigger bite. Those creases in his aging face weren't made by lots of smiling.

"I'm the owner and manager of Peaceful Kingdom, and you're on private property." He spat again, and I realized his lower lip was filled with chewing tobacco.

Reluctantly, I stepped up to take over from Cruz, who had a short fuse to match his short stature. While the big old guy held a menacing flashlight and shovel, I still had some garlic bulbs in my hands, and I knew how to use them if it came to that.

"Hi." I reached out a garlic-free hand. "I'm Presley Parker, from Killer Parties. We're hosting a wrap party for a recently completed film, and we have permission to be here."

"A what party?" he asked, ignoring my hand—thank God—and aimed the flashlight right in my eyes. He reeked of alcohol, tobacco, and dirt.

I shaded the glare. "A wrap party," I said, enunciating. "To celebrate the end of—"

"I don't care if it's a crap party; you cain't have it here!" He gave his shovel a menacing shake.

"I'm afraid we can," Cruz said. The flashlight shifted to his face. "I don't know anything about your Peaceful Kingdom or whatever, but you don't own this place. We have documentation from the city of Colma allowing us to rent Lawndale Cemetery for our event."

"Listen, you maggot, and listen good. My name's Otto Gunther. Me and my wife, Carrie—God rest her soul—we've owned this here cemetery for over fifty years and you're trespassing. So git."

"We're not going to 'git,' Otto," Cruz continued, "but we are going to call the police and have them settle this." He turned to me and pulled out his cell. "Right, Presley?"

I glanced at the others who had gathered to watch the real-life drama. No one looked particularly frightened, but they did seem eager to find out what would happen next—except for Brad, who was nowhere in sight. I looked back at Otto. His angry expression was easily visible in the party lighting.

Or was that an expression of fear I saw behind those bloodshot eyes and rigid grimace?

Otto's hand shook as he held the flashlight on Cruz. "You're trespassing on hallowed ground, people, and you're disturbing the dead. The owl portends that if you're not gone by midnight, Death will follow. . . . Death will follow. . . ."

He turned and vanished back into the darkness.

Cruz looked stunned at the man's own special effect of appearing and disappearing, then shook his head. " 'The owl portends'? That's all I need. A nutcase in a cemetery . . . and a flying monkey in the trees. What else can go wrong?" He was still muttering as he returned to the problem at hand—fixing the vampire's own disappearing act.

I looked into the dark recesses of the cemetery where Otto had disappeared and wondered about the unkempt giant of a man. Where had he gone? And why had he claimed to be the owner of Peaceful Kingdom, whatever that was? At the moment, his kingdom didn't look so peaceful.

Great. I was just starting to relax and now this. Cruz

was right: What else could go wrong at our upcoming Vampire Party? If it was anything like some of my other events—everything.

By midnight, the decorations were in place, Jonas the vampire was able to disappear without a glitch, and rough cuts of the film were ready to be viewed on the side of the large mausoleum. Although I kept looking over my shoulder, I'd seen no more signs of Otto Gunther. At this point I should have been eager for tomorrow night's party. But the threats the old man had made—or implied—had unnerved me. These days it seemed as if every crazy person was ready to shoot a gun for any reason. I'd read in the news yesterday that some guy killed another guy over a parking place in the City.

Of course, in a city like San Francisco, that might have been justified, but still . . .

"I'm pooped. You ready?" came a voice from behind.

I jumped.

"Brad! Don't sneak up behind me like that! Especially in a cemetery." I checked the new Mickey Mouse watch that Brad had given me after I'd hosted a surprise birthday party for Andrew, his brother. "Where have you been?"

"Loading stuff into the SUV."

"So you didn't see that ginormous old guy who stopped by to threaten us?"

"What guy?" He scanned the area.

"Never mind. Just don't sneak up on me again. Don't you watch horror movies?"

"Nope. Just crime dramas and police shows. Horror movies give me nightmares."

I felt my tension melt away with him standing next to me. "You're kidding, right? I didn't think anything scared you. Except the maggots you sometimes clean up at your crime scenes."

He crossed his muscular arms over his muscular chest, almost causing me to have a muscle spasm. "I'm not afraid of maggots. I just hate them."

"Horror movies are only make-believe, you know," I said, teasing him. I happened to love them.

"That doesn't stop Freddy from invading my dreams, the way he does in those Nightmare on Elm Street movies." He shivered.

It could have been that the cold was seeping into the cemetery—or not. I was sure Brad could take down Freddy, Jason, and Michael Myers more quickly than a kiss from a vampire, but it was fun to see this vulnerable side of him.

"Well, let's get out of here before that old guy comes back with a killer backhoe," I said, referring to the mysterious Otto. "We've done all we can here tonight, and it looks like everyone else has packed up and left. We'll finish the rest tomorrow."

"You got somebody watching over all the stuff we're leaving behind?" Brad asked.

"Oh yes. Cruz brought a couple of his security guards, and I hired Raj for extra security. He's around here somewhere. . . ." Scanning the darkness, I spotted my favorite TI security guard, Raj Reddy, shining his trusty flashlight into the dark recesses of the cemetery. No doubt he was searching for illegal gravediggers from Dr. Frankenstein's lab.

"Who's there?" Raj suddenly called out from several yards away.

I followed the beam of his flashlight as he swung it back and forth through the rustling eucalyptus trees, trying to penetrate the darkness.

Uh-oh. Was Otto back?

I spotted a small circle of light in the darkness, about eight to ten feet up in the air. The tiny, intense beam seemed to hover over a headstone, as if suspended in midair, then to bounce to the next, defying gravity.

This was not Raj's flashlight beam—not unless he'd learned to levitate. For a moment, I thought it might be one of Lucas Cruz's special effects. But Cruz and his gang had already left.

And this wasn't in my party plan.

Neither was the scream that followed.

Chapter 2

PARTY-PLANNING TIP #2

To make sure your Vampire Party has "atmosphere," find the perfect venue. An abandoned cemetery is ideal, but if there's not one available, consider renting an old castle, run-down mansion, or simply turn your backyard into a "graveyard," with Styrofoam headstones personalized for your guests.

"Did you hear that?" I said, backing up against Brad. I was shivering, and not just from the cold cemetery air that seemed to slice right through my San Francisco State University hoodie and jeans.

"Sounded like a scream," he said. "Where did it come from?"

"Look! What is that?" I whispered to him, and pointed toward the small but intense beam of light. It suddenly appeared to turn in my direction. Then it disappeared.

Brad wrapped an arm around me. "I'm sure it's nothing. Some kids fooling around in the cemetery."

"But that light. It was bouncing around in mid-air. . . ."

"Hey, you don't believe in ghosts, remember?" Brad gave me a squeeze.

Had I said that? At the moment, I believed in everything from aliens to zombies.

"Who's going there?" Raj called out again, his flashlight waving back and forth in the darkness like a metronome on speed. Or was it just his hand shaking?

Brad released me and headed over to Raj, who was about ten feet away. Realizing I was alone, I quickly followed.

"See anything?" Brad asked as we all stared into the shadowed night. In spite of the few remaining party lights left on and the full moon, the darkness was thick and oppressive.

"Not anymore," Raj said. "It seems to have—"

"There it is again!" I shouted. This time the light bounced along in another part of the cemetery, off to our left. Raj swung his flashlight beam in an attempt to pinpoint it.

Before he could get a bead on it, we heard another scream. If the first one was playful, as Brad suggested, this one sounded urgent.

Next came a loud thud, followed by a string of words that would have been bleeped on Jerry Springer's show—all in a matter of seconds.

The three of us rushed over in the direction of the sounds. These were definitely human noises, I reminded myself as we neared the location. Raj shined his light around until he spotted a figure on the ground a few feet away.

It was the body of a man.

He lay on his stomach, arms and legs askew. I could tell, even in the dim moonlight, that he wasn't breathing. His chest wasn't moving.

Brad started to kneel down when suddenly the body coughed. The man rolled over and sucked in a large gulp of air. Brad sprang up.

Raj shined the flashlight on the young man. In spite of the cold night air, he wore knee-length baggy shorts and a thin T-shirt that read "Traceur." On his head was a band with a small headlamp, and on his feet were a brand of athletic shoes I didn't recognize.

Raj focused the beam of light on the young man's leg. It was covered in blood. As we stared at him, he opened his eyes.

"You okay?" I asked, stepping forward.

"Got the wind"—the young man puffed—"knocked out of me."

"Tore up your leg pretty well too," Brad added, kneeling down to examine it. The guy had scraped the skin off his shin, which caused a lot of bleeding and probably hurt like hell, but the injury looked superficial.

"I'm okay." He sat up; then, with Brad's help, he slowly stood, putting his weight on his strong leg. "Lark?" he called out. "Spidey?"

Lark? Spidey? I frowned. Did the guy have a head injury as well?

A young girl, maybe eighteen or twenty, materialized out of the darkness. Raj ran his flashlight over her. She had short black hair and even shorter, precisely cut bangs. Her eyes were lined in black, and she sported a lip ring, eyebrow ring, and a tattoo of a bird on her left hand. Much like the young man, she also wore a headlamp, short baggy pants, athletic shoes, and a black T-shirt that read "Take Flight." I had seen the same shirt on Duncan Grant. Although Duncan was kind of a geek, he loved extreme sports, everything from Geocaching to skateboarding.

Another young man appeared behind the girl, this one with a shaved head and a tattoo of a spiderweb around his neck. He was dressed much like the other two, including the headlamp, but he was barefoot. His shirt read "Know Obstacles, Know Freedom."

"Fall again, Trace?" the girl said, smirking more than smiling. I guessed this was the Lark referred to earlier.

"It's nothing. Just a scrape," the-guy-who-must-be-Trace said, still favoring his hurt leg.

Spidey the skinhead just laughed.

"Who are you guys?" I asked, completely baffled by their presence in the cemetery so late at night. "What are you doing here?" I hugged my hoodie closer to my chest, partly to protect myself from the cold, partly from the intruders.

The three looked at one another; then the girl called Lark said, "We're not hurting anything." She ignored my other questions.

"You're trespassing," Brad said.

"So are you," the bald one called Spidey said, cocking his shaved head.

"Actually, we have permission to be here," I replied. "So, you want to tell us why you're running around in a cemetery at this hour?"

The guy called Trace grinned. "We're not vandalizing the place, if that's what you mean."

"Then what are you doing here?"

"They are doing some kind of satanic thing," Raj said. "I read about this in *People* magazine."

Spidey suddenly jumped up on the vertical headstone next to Raj. He looked a little satanic, backlit by the moon. A second later, he leaped to another headstone, then another, and another. All the markers were of varying height and thickness, each one taller and more challenging than the next. But Spidey seemed to have no fear of falling. He leaped so gracefully, he could have been on wires, like Jonas Jones earlier—only with a better pulley system.

Finally he reached a mausoleum that had to be at least eight feet tall, with a crumbling facade of Roman columns and birds with broken wings. But instead of jumping down from his high perch, Spidey lunged at the even higher structure, barely grasping one of the birds. And instead of falling, as most human beings would have, he used the bird as leverage to flip himself up and on top of the domed monument—all in a flash of an instant.

This guy was crazy, pure and simple.

Trace turned to us. "Parkour," he said.

"What?" I said, thinking he said my name. "Do I know you?"

"Par-*kour*," Trace repeated, emphasizing the last syllable.

To my surprise, Brad nodded. "Cool. What kind of shoes do you use?"

I looked at him. Was this really a time to talk about shoes? Granted, shoes told a lot about a person—I'd combined my experiences working my way through college as a shoe salesperson with my degree in abnormal psychology to quickly read people. But what did shoes have to do with this?

Trace slipped off the shoe, the one from his hurt leg, and handed it to Brad. "KO Parkour," he said, as if that meant something. "Weighs only nine ounces. Perfect combination of traction and design. One piece, not too thick, good arches, killer grip. Forty bucks."

Brad whistled at the price. Was that good or bad?

"Good thing they're cheap," Trace went on. "I have to get a new pair every couple of months." He was obviously proud of these strange-looking shoes.

"You don't like Waterpros or Slams?" Brad asked.

"Nah, too expensive. But Lark wears Nike Darts or Dunlop Volleys."

They might as well have been speaking Klingon.

"And Spidey, you go barefoot?" Brad asked the other guy.

"Yeah, dude, I like the freedom of movement and the feel of the surfaces."

I had a feeling Spidey was missing a few Twinkies from his lunch box.

"What are you all talking about?" I said, shaking my head at this bizarre, middle-of-the-night discourse.

Brad turned to me. "It's a sport called parkour. People who practice it are called traceurs. Duncan's been talking about getting into it."

"Parker? Tracer? I still have no clue what you're talking about."

"Par-*kour*, like *your*," Lark said, rolling her dark-lined eyes. "It's kinda like skateboarding, without the skateboard. Go on YouTube and type in 'parkour' if you really want to know."

"Actually," Trace said, "it's much more than that. It's a philosophy that combines movement with the environment. A traceur has to overcome any obstacles that get in the way—mental or physical." This guy was the smart one—and obviously the leader of the pack.

"So it's like running an obstacle course," I said, summarizing.

"Sort of," Trace conceded. "But the idea is to run as if you're being chased, or you're chasing someone. And it's not just running. It's jumping, climbing, rolling, balancing, grabbing hold or hanging from something—any kind of movement that will help you get from point A to point B, using only your body."

"And the mental part?" I asked.

"Parkour can help you find out what you want in life, then give you the drive to go after it," Trace explained.

"It's sounding like some kind of religion," Raj said.

"It's more a spirituality," Trace responded. He tried to step on his sore leg and winced. "You get what you put into it."

"You need to bandage that," I said.

He shrugged. Tough guy.

"Do you have competitions?" I asked, growing curious about this sport I'd never heard of until tonight. I wondered if there might be a party theme in it.

"No. It's not competitive. It's more social. It's fun to get together for a jam, and try new places. Most traceurs jam at the mall or a park. But the cemetery is especially challenging. There are lots of obstacles to overcome, with the headstones being so narrow and uneven and sometimes far apart."

I was getting distracted from the task at hand—not uncommon with my attention deficit hyperactivity disorder, or ADHD. I checked my watch, noticing that none of the three young people had watches. "Well, it's getting late, I'm freezing, and I have a party to set up tomorrow."

"Party time!" Spidey said brightly. "Dunk told us about it. That's why we're here, dude. Scoping it out."

"Duncan told you about it?" I asked, surprised. Was he friends with these guys?

"Yeah," Spidey said. "We got to be extras in the film, so we figured we'd come to the party."

"It's a *private* party." Raj emphasized the word "private." "By invitation only. We are having security guards here tonight, so please move along and do your parking somewhere else or you may be arrested. We don't want anything disturbed before the party."

The three looked at one another conspiratorially. What was behind that look?

"Well, try not to disturb anything," Brad said to them.

They nodded, but those odd grins on their faces made me question their sincerity. These kids seemed harmless enough, but anyone who runs around in a graveyard after midnight can't really be too normal.

Oh. That would include me, wouldn't it. . . .

After I checked on the party area one last time, I waved good-bye to Raj and followed Brad to his Crime Scene Cleaners SUV. His car was bigger than my little red MINI Cooper, and therefore held more party stuff. And he'd volunteered to help out, unless a call for a crime scene cleanup came along. You never knew when a dead body would pop up and require Brad's specialized services.

On the drive back to the City, I did most of the talking, planning the final party details and working out the logistics. I knew Brad had tuned me out when I finally asked him a question about the sport of parkour that required a response.

"Huh?" he said, glancing at me before taking the off-ramp to Treasure Island.

"Nothing," I said haughtily.

Brad patted my leg. "Sorry. My mind was wandering."

"No kidding. Where to?"

"Your bedroom," he said, grinning at me.

"Ha! You know I never sleep with anyone before a party. Too much on my mind."

His smile dissolved. "Anyone?"

I smiled mysteriously.

"All right, so what did you say?"

"I just wondered how you knew so much about that sport—parker . . . I mean, par-*kour*. I'd never heard of it."

"I get around," he said just as mysteriously.

"Did you ever . . . clean up . . . after a parkour mishap?"

"Naw. Those guys are pretty hardy. They get a lot of skinned knees and a few broken bones, but doing par-kour doesn't usually kill you."

"Did you ever try it?"

"Once."

I raised an eyebrow as we pulled up to my condo carport. "Really? Where? What happened?"

"It was a long time ago. I was at this girl's house one night—in her bedroom, actually—and her father came in. So I climbed out her window, leaped onto a tree branch, swung to another branch by the backyard fence, stepped on the top of the fence, tightrope walked along the top until I saw a doghouse on the other side, jumped down and landed on it, and finally hopped to the ground."

"No scrapes or bruises?"

"A bunch. But I didn't feel them at the time."

"Adrenaline?"

"Alcohol."

"I see. And you call escaping from a girlfriend's bedroom 'parkour'?" I added finger-quotes to the last word.

"Sure. Running away from something and over-coming obstacles along the way. It's pretty much the same thing. In fact, I may have invented the sport." He gave me a smug glance.

I opened the passenger door of the SUV. "Did it *mentally* help you achieve your goal?"

"Sure. I learned a lesson."

"Really? And what was that?"

"Don't disturb a sleeping dog by jumping onto its house. And don't wander around a strange backyard in the dark where there might be a swimming pool."

I laughed out loud. "You didn't!"

"I did. Fell right in. The family called the cops, and I had a nice, wet ride home in a police unit."

"Serves you right," I said, and leaned over to kiss him good night.

"I'd do it all again if it were you up in that bedroom." He put his hand on my cheek and kissed me again. Longer. Deeper.

I'd had a witty retort, but had completely forgotten it by the time that last kiss ended.

Under Brad's watchful eye, I let myself into my condo, locked the door, then listened as he drove off for his own home on neighboring Yerba Buena Island. My three cats, Cairo, Fatman, and Thursby, tried to quell my loneliness after he left, but having the warm furry coats brush against my ankles wasn't the same as snuggling with Brad. I might as well have let him stay over. I wouldn't be getting much sleep thanks to pre-party jitters—and that kiss.

I told the cats about my day as I fed them, then changed into my cat-covered PJs and got ready for bed. Anxious about the event the next day, I made some hot, soothing cranberry tea and lay back on the couch to watch the news. There was not much happening at one in the morning. No earthquakes. No terrorist attacks. No celebrity meltdowns or returns to rehab.

The city was as quiet as a cemetery.

I fell asleep on the couch and slept like the dead.

I woke up the next morning, my cranberry tea cold, my cats on my legs, chest, and hair, and the TV still on. Stretching out the kinks after sleeping crookedly, I glanced at the time on the wall clock—a little after seven a.m. At least I hadn't overslept. After all, I had a party to prepare for and only twelve hours to complete everything—on five hours' sleep.

I picked up the remote to turn off the morning news, when a photograph of a young man appeared on the screen. I turned up the volume and listened to the reporter's voice as I stared at the face.

I'd seen that face only hours ago and recognized it immediately.

It was the hairless, tattooed, barefooted guy in the cemetery last night who called himself "Spidey."

My gut wrenched. Was he dead?

Chapter 3

PARTY-PLANNING TIP #3

Vamp up your Vampire Party invitations! Fold a sheet of black paper in half, cut out a coffin shape, leaving one side on the fold so the coffin "opens." Write the party details inside with bloodred ink. Then close the coffin with red sealing wax.

I sat up too quickly, wrenching my neck in the process, and rubbed the muscles with one hand while turning up the volume with the TV remote with the other. I caught the female news announcer in midsentence.

"... *the body of a young man found last night at the old Lawndale Cemetery, the apparent victim of a fall. Friends of Samuel Valdez, also known as Spidey, said the twenty-year-old man was strong and agile, and often did physical stunts in unusual places. When asked why Valdez was in the cemetery alone late last night, his friend Thomas Allen, who calls himself 'Trace,' said, 'I have no clue.' He declined further comment. Anyone with any information regarding the death of Valdez is urged to call the San Francisco Police Department.* . . ."

I didn't hear anything that followed. The voice in my head was screaming, "But he wasn't alone! His friends were there! How could this happen?"

And why had Trace lied about not being in the cemetery with him?

I reached for my cell phone to call Lucas, but the phone rang the moment I had it in hand. I looked down at the caller ID: Brad.

"Brad! Did you hear—"

"Presley, I have some bad—"

We spoke over each other, then stopped. I waited for half a second to see if he would continue. When he didn't, I said, "That poor kid. I just heard it on the news. . . ."

"Yeah. Wonder what happened . . ."

More silence. Finally I said, "I need to call Lucas Cruz. See if he's heard anything. And ask him what he wants to do about the party tonight."

"You think he'll cancel?" Brad asked.

"I doubt it. He's pretty self-centered. But I'd like to give him the option. After all, someone died at the party site last night, and it seems to me he might want to consider postponing the event—or selecting another venue."

"Let me know your plans. I got called to do the cleanup, so I'll be out at the cemetery."

Oh my God. It hadn't occurred to me that Brad would be asked to clean up after Spidey's death. But of course they needed a crime scene cleaner, since cemeteries prefer to have the bodies under the ground, not

on top. I guessed that the city of Colma would be foot-
ing the bill on this one.

I wished him luck, told him to call if he found anything else, and hung up. Next, I phoned Lucas Cruz.
When he didn't answer, I left a message asking him to
call me. At this hour in the morning, without a jolt of
caffeine, I couldn't think whom else to call, so I jumped
in the shower and tried to wash away the images I kept
conjuring up of Spidey's death.

I dried off, dressed in jeans and a long-sleeved
T-shirt that said "Boo" on the front in celebration of
upcoming Halloween, and made myself a steaming
hot latte with extra caf. I would need the jolt to help me
focus during the sure-to-be-chaotic day ahead.

After giving my cats a thorough back-scratching
and a healthy bowl of gourmet cat food, I hopped into
my MINI Cooper, planning to head for my office a few
blocks away on Treasure Island. On impulse, I took a
quick turn and pulled up to CeeGee Studios, Lucas
Cruz's film studio nearby. The production company
was housed in a giant hangar that once stored Pan Am
Clipper ships of the thirties and forties that both flew
and sailed. I'd never actually seen one—only photos—
but my grandmother was one of the first female stew-
ards on board. I knew this because my mother liked to
remind me of that every time she came to TI. An ama-
teur historian, Mom knew a lot about San Francisco's
rich history, and she loved to share that knowledge
with whoever would listen—which was usually me.

As for Granny, Mom said she flew on one of the first

and largest "flying boats," called the China Clipper, back in the late thirties. "The Clipper was one of the first true intercontinental airlines, with the luxury and style of the *Titanic* crossed with the Concorde," Mom said, using her docent voice. "Your granny used to talk about the multicourse meals, which were considered extravagant back then, as well as the beautiful china and silverware." Granny loved that the spacious lounge areas made the ship feel more like a hotel than a plane or boat. Having ten crew members for seventy-five passengers added to the luxury—if you could afford it. The cost of travel to the Orient at the time: nearly fifteen hundred dollars.

But according to Mother, Granny's favorite story was about the time she met Humphrey Bogart while he was filming *China Clipper*. She carried around Bogie's autographed picture until she died. Mom said she loved her job, but she was fired only two years later when she married. That was a no-no for stewardesses back in the day.

I knocked on the steel door of CeeGee Studios and waited for someone to open up. Security was tight at CeeGee, to discourage curious tourists from interrupting filming, and while there were no signs announcing CeeGee's occupancy, there were plenty of NO ADMITTANCE placards. I rapped again, to no response, then punched Cruz's private cell number on my phone once more, hoping to talk to him before I headed into work.

He answered on the fourth ring.

"Yeah?" he said bluntly.

"Lucas? It's Presley. Did you hear—"

"Yeah, yeah," he said, cutting me off. "I heard, and I'm sorry about the guy, but he was stupid to be in a cemetery in the middle of the night. As they say in showbusiness, the show must go on, so if you're thinking of canceling . . ."

I was taken aback by his callousness, but then, that was Lucas Cruz. Nothing got in the way of his "art."

"No," I said, "not if you don't want to cancel. I was just checking—"

"Then I'll see you later." Click. End of call.

I felt stupid talking to him on the other side of the door when I knew he was inside—his classic Corvette was parked in the slot marked NEVER, EVER PARK HERE—but at least I had my answer. Apparently, the slogan was true; the show would go on.

I returned to my MINI and drove the short distance to the parking lot at Building One, also known as the Administration Building, where I shared an office for my Killer Party business with Delicia. The Art Deco architecture of the C-shaped, two-story building and oversized human figures that lounged at the entrance greeted me silently, a reminder of their heyday at the 1939 Golden Gate Exposition.

Building One was among only a handful of remnants that survived the fair. The rest of the "Magic City" was demolished when the navy took over in 1941 and turned TI into an active military station. When the navy departed, the four-hundred-acre, man-made island was left with a pier and a harbor, nearly a thousand housing units, almost a dozen barracks-style facilities, a public elementary school, and a clinic. But the "treasure" was gone—the name came from the gold-laden fill dirt that was barged down the Sacramento River Delta from the Gold Country—replaced by toxins left over from the military. And now, with the threat of an earthquake that could lead to liquefaction, the island needed a hundred million dollars for redevelopment and shoring up.

I sighed as I headed for my office. All this meant that someday soon I'd have to move away from my quiet—and inexpensive—little island in the middle of the San Francisco Bay, with its hundred-million-dollar views. For now, though, Cruz's wrap party would give me a big chunk of money to cover my mother's care at her downtown facility, and my condo and office rent for a few months.

If nothing else went wrong.

My office door was open when I arrived. I assumed Delicia had beaten me to work—not usually her style—but it wasn't Delicia inside. Duncan Grant sat twirling in my office chair, his chin resting on his chest, his eyes not moving from the spreadsheet I'd devised for tonight's party. He wore the same clothes he'd had on last night, including the shirt with the parkour reference. His wild red hair was uncombed, and he obviously hadn't showered. I could tell something was very, very wrong.

"Duncan?" I said, stepping in cautiously. "What are you doing here?"

He looked up and I saw his red-rimmed eyes. Had he been crying?

"Did you hear . . . ?" he said, nasally.

I blinked, not sure what he was talking about. "You mean that young guy who was killed last night at the cemetery?"

He looked down at his bitten nails and nodded. "Spidey."

"I forgot—you knew him, didn't you?" I dropped into Delicia's desk chair opposite him. "I'm so sorry."

"Yeah. He was a good friend of mine from Balboa High. We hung out."

I leaned in. "Are you okay?"

He ignored my question. "I hooked him up—and a couple of other friends—for some walk-ons in Cruz's vampire movie. It was epic—they loved it."

I remembered he'd mentioned that last night.

"He was teaching me parkour," Duncan continued. "I was supposed to hook up with him at the cemetery last night, after I finished setting up the sound system. He was going to show me some cool moves." He paused to sniff, then continued. "But I was too wiped out and flaked. Now he's . . ."

Duncan couldn't finish the sentence. He rubbed his eyes with his thumb and index finger, pushing back tears.

I reached across the desk and touched his arm. "I'm so sorry, Duncan. I'm sure it was a tragic accident." Not knowing what to say, I did what I always do—I rambled. "There was nothing you could have done. He must have fallen doing that parkour thing—"

"He couldn't have fallen!" Duncan's outburst was swift and loud. "He was the best! He could practically walk on air. He was going to show everyone tomorrow night. . . ."

Duncan looked up at me and shut his mouth.

"What are you talking about, Duncan?" I asked.

"Nothing." He looked down at his freckled hands. His voice quieted.

Delicia appeared in the open doorway. "Are you okay, Pres?" She glanced at Duncan. "I heard someone yelling. . . ."

"We're fine, Dee. Thanks," I said. "Will you give us a moment?"

She silently backed out and disappeared.

I got up and moved around to Duncan, who was wiping his damp cheeks. I rested a hand on his bony shoulder. "Was Spidey planning to crash the party tonight?"

He sniffed and nodded. "When they found out they hadn't been invited, they decided to come anyway, show off their skills. They were part of the movie and they should have been included."

"But Lucas was inviting only the stars and a few others. I'm sure he didn't mean to hurt their feelings—"

"Lucas Cruz is a jerk. If it weren't for him, Spidey would still be alive."

"What do you mean, Duncan?"

"Listen, I gotta split," he said, interrupting me. He stood up and headed for the doorway. "I only stopped by to tell you, I don't think I can help you tonight."

"Duncan, wait! Where are you going?"

"To clear my head. I need to be by myself."

He stood at the doorway for a moment, rubbing his curly red hair, then strode through the expansive lobby and out the building's double glass doors. I wondered where he was going. And what I could do to help him when he returned.

Delicia poked her head around the doorway. "Safe to come in?"

I stood back to let her in. "Poor guy. A young man was killed last night at the cemetery, and he was a friend of Duncan's."

"You mean Spidey?"

My jaw nearly dropped to the floor. "You knew him?"

"I met him a couple of times. And those other two—Trace and whatshername . . . Lake?"

"Lark," I said. "How come I've never met any of them? Or even seen them before last night?"

She shrugged. "We've gone to a couple of raves together. The one called Trace? He's hot, but he's with Lark. Spidey's pretty cute too, but kinda strange."

Wow. The younger set had a whole secret party life I knew nothing about. I felt a little jealous that they hadn't invited me, even though I was seven or eight years older than all of them.

Dee read my mind. "We'd invite you, but you're always busy working . . . or with Brad."

I supposed that was true. I'd become somewhat of a workaholic since taking on this event-planning business. But I knew it was the only way to make a success of it. And I preferred spending what little downtime I had with Brad than going to something like a rave. The last thing I wanted to do after hosting a party was party.

"Well, I wish I could make Duncan feel better," I said. Even with my background in abnormal psychology, I still felt awkward expressing condolences.

"He'll be okay," Dee said, plopping into her chair and switching on her laptop. "He just needs time. His friends will help. They're a pretty tight group."

"Did you know he was interested in some sport called parkour?" I was suddenly amazed and embarrassed at how little I knew about my coworkers.

"Is that when they climb and jump and flip over stuff? Yeah. I saw Spidey and them do it one time at a mall. Even the girl. It's pretty awesome. Except for the bruises and scars and stitches and stuff. Wouldn't catch me trying it."

"Duncan said he was learning how."

Dee laughed. "Trying, maybe, but he's hardly the type. I mean, I know he loves extreme sports and all, but he doesn't have the body for it. You need muscles and grace. Duncan's too bony and clumsy. I doubt if he'll stick with it. He's better with his electronic gizmos than the physical stuff."

Deep down I hoped Duncan wouldn't stick with it. I knew he was something of a daredevil—always trying the latest thing, whether it was a computer game, a new high-tech toy, or an extreme sport. The kid had no fear, just like his friend Spidey.

I only prayed Duncan didn't end up like him.

My cell phone rang. I recognized my mother's ring tone since I'd personalized it for her—"It's My Party" by Lesley Gore. She used to sing it all the time while prepping for her own events.

"Hi, Mom."

"Presley, darling, how's the Vampire Party coming? Need any help? I once hosted a Halloween party where everyone had to come dressed as a character from an old horror movie—Frankenstein, Dracula, the Wolfman. It was a hoot. And a hit."

Mother had told me this every day for the past couple of weeks. With early Alzheimer's, she still had good long-term memory, but she was quickly losing her short-term recall. She remembered her Halloween party in vivid detail, but not that she'd already told me.

"That was a great party, Mom. You let me help you decorate the old Crocker mansion. Then I had nightmares for a week afterward."

"We did do it up, didn't we?"

I could almost hear her memories through the phone.

I interrupted them. "I'm about to go over to the cemetery now and finish setting up everything. Still lots to do, as you probably know. I'll be by to pick you up late this afternoon for the party, so be ready."

"I will, dear," she said. "I have the perfect costume." Then she hung up the phone without a good-bye.

Although I missed teaching abnormal psychology at San Francisco State, if it hadn't been for my mother, I wouldn't be in this event-planning business, and I wouldn't be able to afford her care facility. For that I was grateful, and I realized that, as the former Party Queen of the City, Mother lived somewhat vicariously through me. I tried to include her in either preparations for the parties I knew she'd enjoy, or simply by inviting her to attend. But she was unpredictable—she'd once posed naked at the MoMA to protest the lack of nude older women in art—and I often prayed she wouldn't make a party foul at one of my important events.

I grabbed my purse and a box full of vampire teeth I'd ordered from Oriental Trading Company. It was amazing how many available party decorations tied into a vampire theme—fake fangs (plastic or gummy); fake blood (liquid candy); fake garlic necklaces (scratch 'n' sniff); and tiny coffins (filled with tiny candy bones), just to name a few. I had to admit, this was one of the most bizarre parties I'd ever hosted. It was also one of the most fun.

Now if there just weren't any mishaps . . .

Right. What was I thinking? When did I ever host a party where something didn't go wrong?

Chapter 4

PARTY-PLANNING TIP #4

*Combine your Vampire Party with a wild "wake,"
such as a "Last Rites Bachelorette Party" so the bride-
to-be can say sayonara to singlehood, or a "Stake in
the Heart Divorce Party" to help the divorcée wave
bye-bye to the bastard!*

I arrived at the cemetery in the late morning, but still
before the rest of my crew—except for Brad, who'd
been called for the cleanup. His SUV was parked along
one of the narrow inroads, so I knew he hadn't left yet.
Recalling the news of Spidey's awful fall and accidental death, I shuddered to think what Brad had had to
"clean up." I couldn't imagine doing his job.

Especially if I'd met the victim that previous evening.

The October air was cool, a welcome reminder that
fall had arrived. I headed over to the party area to check
how things had survived overnight. Thanks to the security guards, including Raj, the decorations, gadgets,

and electronics we'd set up were still in place. I sent the tired-looking men home and told them when to return.

The rental tables would be arriving soon. Once they were in place, I could add more decorations—red tablecloths that looked as if they dripped blood; black ceramic plates with antique, unpolished silverware; and plastic pewter-colored goblets that featured gargoyles and bony fingers. Meanwhile I had plenty of other details to see to—fake cobwebs, tarnished candelabra, rubber bats, and hooting owls to add to the atmosphere.

As if partying in a real cemetery weren't enough.

The event would be held on a patio the size of a baseball diamond. Bordering it on three sides was an open-air, six-foot-high cement and marble structure filled with personalized niches from top to bottom. A small shallow fountain in the center of the patio had long dried up after years of disuse, but Lucas Cruz had his set designers clean it up and rig a hose inside the old spout. The pool was now filled with shimmering blue water and decorated with fake moss.

I was in awe of how much illusion a movie studio could create. Need a fountain? Here you go. Talking gravestones? No problem. A flying vampire who vanishes in the night? You got it.

While I studied the lay of the land—the party area, that is—someone tapped me on the back.

Startled, I nearly stepped into the pond—and would have if a strong arm hadn't caught me.

"Jeez! You gotta quit sneaking up on me like that!"

I hissed at Brad. He looked like the Marshmallow Man, standing there in his white Crime Scene Cleaners jumpsuit.

"I know," he said, trying to stifle a laugh. "You're cute when you're scared. Your eyes flare."

I ran my fingers self-consciously through my bobbed brown hair. "You're not going to love it when I pee my pants. Stop creeping up on me like that."

"Aw, come on. Usually when you're scared, you like to snuggle." He reached out and took me in his arms.

I pushed him away and glanced around. "Stop that. Not here. It's not . . . professional. What if some bereaved person sees us?"

"Pretty unlikely, in this deserted cemetery."

"Well, you interrupted my train of thought. I'm trying to figure out where I want the tables in this what-do-you-call-it area." I waved my hand around the large cement patio.

"Mausoleum," Brad said.

"I know what it's called," I said.

"You'd better know this stuff if you want to sound professional," he continued. "A mausoleum is a building, like a monument. It's usually made from concrete, granite, and marble. Like the Taj Mahal. This one here must have a cost a fortune, back in the day."

"Now you're an expert on cemeteries?"

"I know a little. I find them fascinating. Tombs, sarcophagi, burial vaults, coffins, urns, crypts, catacombs. There are lots of different ways to inter the dead."

"TMI," I said, for "too much information." "Let's

just get this party over with and pray we don't have to buy any extra tombs or crypts or whatever you want to call them." I was thinking of Spidey when I heard the distinctive click of a rifle being cocked. We both froze, then slowly turned around.

"Otto!" I said, recognizing the old man from the previous night. He still wore the same dirty overalls, plaid shirt, and muddy boots. I hoped my friendly tone would soften him a little.

Instead, he raised the weapon and looked at me with rheumy eyes.

"I tol' you people to git," he said, punctuating his last word by spitting a wad of something disgusting on the cement floor. I could smell his alcohol-infused breath from where he stood, about five feet away.

Brad held a hand up. "Hey, listen, old man. Put the gun down."

Otto did just the opposite. He raised the gun higher so it was aimed at Brad's broad chest.

"I told you sumpin' bad was gonna happen if you didn't leave, and it did, didn't it."

"Wait a minute," Brad said. "Did you see what happened out here last night? Did you see that kid who fell to his death?"

I was surprised Brad had the presence of mind to ask the question, what with that gun pointed at us. My question would have been more along the lines of "Is that thing loaded?"

"They don't want you here." Otto indicated the distant headstones with a sweep of his other hand. "And I

don't neither. This here's private prop'ty, and yer trespassing."

We were getting nowhere with this guy. He was repeating himself, not making sense, and this time he
had a gun to back up his words.

Brad continued, speaking slowly and deliberately.
"Otto, please listen. It's important. Did you see what
happened last night? Did you see the kid fall?"

Why was Brad pursuing this? Otto was obviously
intoxicated, and most likely brain-damaged by the alcohol he'd no doubt consumed over the years.

Otto ignored Brad's questions. Instead of answering
them, he continued to mumble. "And the next time
someone comes to my cemetery in the middle of the
night, they'll meet the same fate. The owl portends . . .
and Death responds. . . ."

Portends? Was this guy channeling Shakespeare?

"Drop your weapon and be reaching for the sky,"
came a voice from the side. Brad and I both turned to
see Raj as he stepped out from his hiding place behind
the mausoleum wall. In his hands he held a small gun,
aimed directly at Otto. He looked official in his uniform and was scowling at the old man, but I could see
his hands trembling.

After I registered the fact that Raj had not gone
home—and was wielding a gun—I turned to Otto.
He'd disappeared.

Raj came running over, lowering the gun he held in
both hands, just as on TV. "Are you all right, Ms. Presley? Mr. Brad?" The weapon still wobbled.

"What are you doing here, Raj?" I said, having sent him home earlier.

"And what are you doing with a gun?" Brad asked, shaking his head.

"I decided just to take a little nap in my car," Raj explained. "As for the gun, it's not real." He gave it to Brad to examine. "You know I'm not licensed to have a real weapon. I got this one from the film studio. In case I ever needed it."

Brad rolled his eyes and handed back the realistic-looking weapon.

I grinned. "Pretty clever, Raj."

"Only you could get yourself killed that way," Brad added. "And now you've scared away a person of interest."

"'A person of interest'?" I said, stunned at his lack of fear from having been held at rifle-point only seconds ago. "Otto was holding a gun on us!"

Brad shook his head. "He wasn't going to shoot us. That old thing was an antique. A Winchester. Probably from the late eighteen hundreds. You could tell by the octagon barrel and full magazine and butt plate. Didn't you see the rust? If it had gone off—and that's pretty unlikely—it probably would have blown up in his face. Or at least burned his hands."

I looked at Brad, stunned at this information.

"You know a lot about guns, Mr. Brad?" Raj asked, his dark eyes wide.

"A little," he said, shrugging.

Brad seemed to know a little about a lot of things.

He never ceased to surprise me with his knowledge, especially when it came to elements of crime, which I found oddly suspicious, except for his having been a police officer in the past, until a tragic accident ended his career. It was something he didn't like to talk about.

I turned to him. "Do you think Otto saw something last night?"

Frowning, Brad glanced around the cemetery, most likely looking for the strange old man. "Well, he was probably around here somewhere last night, since he keeps popping up like the undead. He could have seen the kid fall, or . . ." He left the sentence hanging.

"Or what? You don't believe that stuff he said about 'owls portending' and 'Death responding,' do you?"

"Easy with the finger-quotes," Brad said. "You'll put an eye out."

"Answer the question," I insisted.

"No, not necessarily 'Death,' " he said, using finger-quotes to mock me, "but he might have seen someone or something he thought was Death. And if he did, then maybe there was someone else here with Spidey last night who hasn't come forward."

I thought about Spidey's two friends, Trace and Lark. They'd been here with him last night, but that wasn't mentioned in the news story on TV. Why would they just leave him alone in the cemetery like that? Or was someone else with them too? Someone who hadn't come out of the shadows like the others?

Before I could ask myself any more questions, my attention was drawn to the sound of an old beat-up

VW bus. Painted in a ragtag style in green, tan, and red, it pulled up next to my MINI Cooper on the narrow lane, whimpered, and stilled.

Out stepped my wandering coworker, Duncan Grant. The last I'd heard, he wasn't planning to help me with the party tonight. Had he changed his mind? Or was he here to see the spot where his friend had died?

"Duncan!" I said when he approached. "Where have you been? I've been worried about you. Are you all right?"

He shrugged and rubbed his curly red hair. "I'm fine. Just needed a little time to myself. What do you want me to do?"

"I didn't think you were coming back. But if you're sure you're up to it, *uh*, would you check all the wiring, make sure the voice recordings are working, that kind of thing?" It was probably better to keep him busy than leave him to his thoughts about Spidey's death.

He nodded, lacking the enthusiasm he usually had for electronic party tasks.

"You're sure you're okay?" I persisted.

"Yeah. I just hope . . . I hope they bury Spidey soon. . . ." His voice drifted off.

I frowned, puzzled, not sure I heard him right. "What did you say?"

"Nothing," he said. "It's just a stupid superstition. Never mind." He headed off to do what I'd asked him.

When he was out of earshot, I looked at Brad. "What was that all about?"

"There's an old superstition," Brad said softly, "that if you take too long to bury the dead, the deceased person will find another person to take with him." He gave me an odd look.

I shivered at the thought. "You're kidding. You think Duncan believes that?"

"A lot of people have superstitions about death and cemeteries."

"There are more?"

"Sure. Don't bury your loved one in unconsecrated ground. Don't step on a dead person's grave. Don't move a corpse once it's buried."

I remembered what I'd read about Colma when researching this place for the party. Most of the cemeteries in San Francisco had been moved here because of cheaper land. So much for that superstition. And what was supposed to happen if you moved corpses anyway?

"Oh," Brad said, "and you should put a stone on the grave, to keep the dead from rising up."

I remembered seeing several graves in the Jewish cemetery with stones on them as I drove around the area and I mentioned it.

"That's different," Brad said. "In the Jewish tradition, you leave a stone on top of a grave when you visit, to honor the deceased's memory."

"I remember when I was a kid, a friend of mine told me to hold my breath when passing a cemetery or the spirits would enter my body when I inhaled. I held my breath so long, I nearly blacked out."

Brad laughed. "You seem to have overcome that one. Here you are, holding a party in a cemetery."

"Yeah, well, that guy Spidey wasn't so lucky, was he?" I reminded him.

"No, but it's foolish for anyone to be out alone in a deserted place in the middle of the night. If someone had been there with him, he might have been able to get Spidey to a hospital and may have saved his life. Maybe then he wouldn't have died from a head injury—"

I felt the blood drain from my head. "He bled to death?"

Brad stopped as soon as he realized he was spooking me out. Woozy at the image, I reached out for him, then sat down on a nearby fake headstone. That was probably not a good idea, what with all the superstitions about graves, but if I hadn't, I might have keeled over.

"Sorry about that," Brad said. "I shouldn't have said anything. . . ."

"No, no, it's okay." I took a deep breath, let it out slowly, and stood up, holding on to Brad's arm. "I didn't know the details. On the news, they said only that he fell."

"Presley!" I heard my name being called from the periphery of the party area. Duncan waved at me. I let go of Brad and headed over to where Duncan stood.

When I reached him, I noticed he was holding the foot of what looked like a fat dead bird. It dangled from his fingertips.

"One of the owls we rigged up isn't working," he said. "It fell off the tree."

Owl?

I felt a shudder, as if a spirit had passed through me. What was it Otto had said about an owl?

Oh, yes. That Death would respond.

Chapter 5

PARTY-PLANNING TIP #5

Party-crashing paparazzi can be a problem, especially if you're hosting a high-profile event. Beef up security at the door, and check invitations and IDs to prevent unwanted guests from spoiling the fun. Otherwise you may find embarrassing—and litigious—pictures on sites such as TMI and Gossip Guy.

Knock it off, Presley! I told myself. *That's just superstition.* If I didn't watch myself, I'd soon be tossing salt over my shoulder and avoiding Thursby, my black cat, fearing he might cross my path.

But curiosity overcame logic, and I headed for my notebook computer, which was locked in my MINI Cooper's trunk—I never go anywhere without it. I popped open the latch and pulled out the computer, then sat on the passenger side of the car with the door open and logged in. The connection wasn't strong, but after a few moments the search engine Mozilla took me to "superstitions + cemeteries," where I found a bunch of sites listing common beliefs about eerie graveyard etiquette. The warning about the owl appeared near the bottom of one list:

If you see an owl in a cemetery after midnight, that owl portends Death will follow.

The old man was right—at least about the superstition. I read on to see if there might be other superstitions I needed to know about, in case Otto returned with more warnings. But, like Brad, I found myself growing fascinated about cemeteries in general.

"Presley!"

I'd been so engrossed in an article about safety coffins from the nineteenth century—the ones fitted with bells to prevent premature burials—that I didn't realize several more cars had pulled up along the narrow street that led to the cemetery. Delicia, carrying a helium canister and a bag of balloons, waved as she approached my car. I turned off the computer and locked it in the trunk, then greeted her.

"Hey, Dee! You made it."

Behind her came Berkeley, already videotaping the scene with his camera.

"This is hella awesome," Berk said as he swept the camera lens around the party area. The forefront of fashion, he wore skintight, ankle-length jeans, a striped sweater with pushed-up sleeves, and black-and-white-striped Chuck Taylor's on his feet. I know it's a stereo-type to assume all gay men have such an envelope-pushing sense of fashion, but Berk certainly did.

"It's freaking sweet!" Dee exclaimed. "I thought it looked cool last night, but you've done so much more. I feel like a real zombie walking among the dead! On the other hand, Dee had her own sense of fashion. Today she wore a low-cut peasant top, a short flowered skirt, pink tights, and black ballet shoes. And she man-aged to carry it off.

"I guess that's good," I said, not completely sure that zombies and vampires mixed that well. I wondered how the invited guests would dress, since costumes were required. It wouldn't be long before I changed into my own costume—a long black dress and long black vest. Subtle, to the point of being nearly invisible, it was perfect for a party planner who wanted to re-main in the shadows.

Moments later the rental tables arrived, along with the party tents. I spent the next hour micromanaging, which mostly entailed a lot of pointing, but it was ex-citing to see the whole party backdrop come together. By late afternoon, nearly everything was in place, and the cast members, including stars Jonas Jones and An-gelica Brayden—who seemed to be inseparable—had arrived to rehearse their lines for a mini-performance from the film. All we needed was Rocco with the food and we'd be ready to welcome the first guests.

"Parker!"

"Presley!"

"Pres!"

I heard my name called from three different directions and headed to Lucas Cruz first, since he was the one paying for all this.

"Are you sure you didn't leak anything to the media?" Cruz said to me through a set of vampire teeth. "Sure" sounded more like "sir," and "anything" came out as "anyfing." He had changed for the party and was now dressed as a "Vampire Director," sporting a long black cape with the words "Bite me" on the back in giant white letters. He'd tucked his thinning hair under a wig of slick, black hair, and had even painted his nails black. But he still wore his ragged black tennies on his feet. I'd never seen him without them.

"I thought I saw some paparazzi lurking around the cemetery earlier," he added. "You know I gave *Gossip Guy* an exclusive. They're helping to foot the bill for this party, not to mention a few other expenditures, so I don't want anyone else inside."

"I haven't seen anyone who looks like press," I said, not that I'd know a paparazzo from an Ansel Adams.

"Well, make sure Ryan Fitzpatrick from *Gossip Guy* is given the red-carpet treatment. He has carte blanche at the party, understand?"

"Gotcha," I said, tempted to salute him. I made a mental note to keep an eye out for someone named Ryan Fitzpatrick. It wouldn't be too hard, as long as he had a big old camera with him.

I headed over to my second summons, this one from Angelica Brayden, the starring actress. She too was in costume—the one from the film—a long flowing black dress, low-cut to allow her perky breasts to distract men from making eye contact with her. Her makeup was expertly done—bloodred lips against pale skin and heavily lined, smoky eyes, thanks to the makeup artist still applying shadow to her lids. And her long black wig was firmly in place. She looked drop-dead gorgeous and seemed to know it. An African American man, tall and lean, and also drop-dead gorgeous, sat nearby on a fake gravestone, watching her. Dee would have called him hot. If he was wearing a costume for the party, it amounted only to black slacks, a black turtleneck, and black Vans.

"Angelica, you look beautiful—and scary at the same time," I said, and meant it.

She offered a practiced demure smile I'd seen her use on Jonas and a couple of other men. Jonas, in particular, had seemed to be the one bitten by a vampire and under Angelica's spell. The man in black continued to stare at her, expressionless. Maybe he wasn't as easily seduced by her flirtatious charms.

"So, what can I do for you?" I continued.

She dropped the smile. "I'm starving! Can you get me something to eat before I faint?"

I glanced around for Rocco, my caterer, and saw that his truck had just arrived—thank God.

"I'll see what I can do."

She turned her attention back to her makeup artist, dismissing me without another word. I looked at the man in black as I headed away, and realized he hadn't taken his eyes off Angelica. Was he some sort of body-guard? I wondered. She didn't even seem to be aware of his presence.

I made my way over to Dee, my assistant, who'd summoned me from the middle of the party area. She was fiddling with Berk's outfit, a costume that seemed more suited to *The Rocky Horror Picture Show* than a vampire film—white shirt, black blazer, short black pants, and black-and-white-striped tights. At this point, I didn't care what he looked like, as long as he was prepared to videotape the event.

Dee, as usual, looked adorable, as only a short, slim, and curvy young woman could. She was dressed as Vampira, the one-time hostess of a TV horror show. Her cleavage would vie with Angelica for the attention of the men at the party, and I worried about those who fell under her spell. And they would, without even a bite on the neck.

"Presley! Don't you think Jonas looks wicked hot?" she said softly, indicating the star who was now prac-ticing his swing over the party area, something like a goth Peter Pan.

"I wouldn't kick him out of bed," Berk said, smiling naughtily.

"You're kidding. That's what you called me over for?" I looked at each of them in disbelief, then tapped my watch. "This party is going to start in less than an hour and you're both ogling the movie star? Snap out of it!"

Dee giggled. "No, that's not why I called you over here. I'm worried about Duncan."

I looked around for him. "Where is he? I saw him here earlier."

"I know. Me too," Dee said, "but I haven't seen him for a couple of hours."

"Neither have I," Berk added.

I bit my lip. Great. Now that he was back, I needed him to help with the computerized background music. If he'd disappeared again, Lucas would have a fit.

"Okay, tell Raj. Then see if you can find Duncan yourselves. He may be out wandering among the graves, maybe where his friend was killed last night. But don't get lost!"

They nodded and went to find Raj.

I moved over to the food station where Rocco was setting out sandwiches shaped like tiny coffins and mini-headstones. His bat-shaped cookies were to die for—I'd tasted one of his earlier mistakes—and the bloodred punch with floating wax teeth looked as if it had come directly from the mortician's lab.

"Absolutely awesome!" I said to Rocco, who only nodded. Rocco considered himself an artiste, and he had the temperament and his own local cooking show to prove it. He had come dressed in his chef whites, but had spattered his jacket with blood—hopefully made from red food coloring.

I snitched a sandwich for Angelica when Rocco's back was turned, and I fled before he could catch me. I just hoped she kept her mouth shut about her "source."

As usual before a party, I walked the area to make

sure nothing had been forgotten and everything was working properly, from the disembodied voices Duncan had installed that seemed to rise from the gravestones to the rubber bats that were to flutter around in circles overhead. It wasn't long before night began to shadow the cemetery grounds.

In spite of the tranquil, parklike setting that most cemeteries provided, Lawndale Cemetery was more like a crowded churchyard, with crumbling, untended tombstones spaced closely together. I stopped to study some headstones and marveled at the ornate carvings. One in particular displayed frightening designs of skulls and skeletons. Another monument featured a life-sized angel draped in agonizing despair over the top, suggesting eternal damnation rather than eternal rest.

Spotting a few guests entering the party patio, I entered work mode and began overseeing the service of drinks and appetizers. But a scuffle at the entrance to the party area called my attention away from the tasks at hand, and I headed over to see what the problem was. Lucas Cruz appeared to be arguing with a scruffy, burly man wearing a safari vest and holding a large camera. I figured he was a paparazzo, but was this the one I was supposed to be looking for? The one who was supposed to get the red-carpet treatment? Somebody named Ryan Fitz-something? If so, why was Lucas Cruz yelling at him?

A small crowd of staff and crew members had gathered around the two men. I squeezed between them to see what the problem was.

"Get the hell out of here!" Lucas shouted, his face red with rage.

"It's a free country!" the other man said, spouting what was probably his mantra.

"This part isn't!" Lucas returned, louder. "I paid for it!"

"I'm just doing my job!" came the angry retort.

They were acting like schoolchildren. I sensed this banter would go on all night if someone didn't stop it.

And that would be my job.

I moved over to Susan Serpa, Cruz's assistant, and told her to go find Brad, the security guards, and anyone else who might be able to get this soon-to-ignite war ended before there were any casualties.

Then I said, "What's going on?" My words were drowned out by the continued shouting. So much for my taking charge.

Brad appeared seconds later and stepped up to the task, elbowing between the two men. Although the paparazzo was big, his girth was mainly fat, while Brad was all muscle. As for Cruz, he looked like a scrawny teenager next to these guys.

"Hey! Knock it off!" Brad said with authority. Speaking of a take-charge demeanor, Brad had it. It was part of the reason I liked him.

But I was getting distracted.

Lucas started in. "I want this leech, this parasite, this piece of trash out of my sight! I have a restraining order against filth like this scumbag, and I won't have him anywhere near me or my party!"

Scumbag took counterpoint. "That order applies only in San Francisco, not in Colma. And I have as much right to be here as anyone."

At that point, Lucas reached up, grabbed the man's camera strap with both hands, and jerked him close enough to spit on him with every word. "I swear to God, I'll kill you if you don't get out of my face!"

Brad pulled Lucas off, while Raj and another security guard who'd just arrived restrained the camera guy. Susan, the quivering assistant, simply stood by, nearly in tears. The rest of the audience looked on in silence. Some were seemingly shocked by the impromptu performance. Others appeared amused.

"Get him out of here," Brad said to the guards, now standing between the two men. "I'll call the police. They can handle this."

The words seemed to zap the steam from the paparazzo's bravado. He backed off, shaking loose the grip of the guards. With a last daggered look at Lucas, he turned and stomped off toward a beat-up Toyota double-parked in the narrow lane.

"What was that about?" I asked Lucas as he pulled himself together in front of the onlookers. "I thought you wanted me to give your *Gossip Guy* reporter the red carpet?"

"That wasn't Ryan. That was some jerk from TMI. Name's Bodie Chase. He wrote a story last year that was full of lies about me. And that was after he'd followed me in my car and nearly got me killed. I got a restraining order against him. He's not supposed to be within a hundred yards of me."

"Well," Brad said, "he's gone now. The threat of calling the police seemed to do the trick. I don't think he'll be back."

I caught Brad's eye and nodded a silent thanks. He winked at me in response.

As the group broke up, I glanced around to see if there had been any damage to the party props. Everything seemed in place, and the guests were back to eating, drinking, and mingling. I was about to check on Lucas, to see if he had calmed down, when I caught a glimpse of Angelica Brayden. The star was here. But instead of making her way to the party, she stood unmoving—and without her bodyguard—in the cemetery several yards away, peeking out from behind a tree. She'd apparently had been watching the scuffle from a distance. But unlike the others who had witnessed the scene, her expression, lit by moonlight, was neither shock nor amusement.

Angelica looked terrified.

Chapter 6

Angelica caught me staring at her. She blinked several times before turning away and heading back to the party, leaving the eerie shadows created by the moon. I had only seconds to wonder what had terrified her so much, because more guests were arriving and the area was getting crowded. I headed over to make sure Raj remained at the entrance to check invitations and IDs against the guest list. I didn't need any more unwanted party crashers.

The guests had gone all out when it came to costuming. I recognized several familiar faces, including Robin Williams, a local resident—of San Francisco, not Colma. He was dressed in the customary black, with a wild black wig, pale makeup, and glitter covering his face and arms. The words "Team Edward" were emblazoned on the back of his long-sleeved T-shirt, along with a photo of Robert Pattinson, the young actor who played Edward Cullen in the Twilight movies. Robin had done a film for Lucas Cruz a few years ago, and I'd seen him at other parties, as well as around the Treasure Island studio.

This time he'd brought his pal, Davin Green, the mayor of San Francisco, who, wearing a werewolf outfit, had come as "Team Jacob." Seeing the handsome mayor out of his expensive tailored suits and looking like a furry canine made me laugh. I hoped Berk was getting all of this on videotape.

I spotted several versions of vampires in attendance: Bela Lugosi's Dracula, Nosferatu, and the guy from *True Blood*, several sexy Buffy the Vampire Slayers, a handful of ghosts—Casper, George and Marion from the movie *Topper*—and a couple of zombies from *Night of the Living Dead*, and *Blacula*, channeled by Willie Brown, the former mayor.

This party was going to be a hoot.

Brad had left to pick up my mother over an hour ago, and I was relieved to see they'd finally arrived. I guessed the traffic had been bad—or Mother hadn't been ready and kept Brad waiting. He wore his Crime Scene Cleaners jumpsuit, which he thought fit the theme perfectly, while Mother had dressed as Anne Rice, with a short black wig, a black lace gown, and a jeweled cross on a chain around her neck. She held a copy of *Interview with a Vampire* in her hand, in case no one figured out who she was. She looked absolutely stunning. But then, parties were her life.

I blended into the background, nicely dressed as a mourner in my black cocktail dress. I'd added a black cloche hat with netting and wore my black Mary Janes for practical comfort. I'd worn the outfit once before at an Over-the-Hill Wake Party I'd hosted for long-time local TV personality, Ross McGowen, who'd wanted to put the "fun" back in "funeral" for his sixtieth birthday. Fun had been an understatement at his milestone bash.

As I circulated through the party, I heard the theme from *Batman* playing in the background—not the one from the TV show, but the one from the movie composed by the guy who used to be in Oingo Boingo. Thank goodness Duncan had pulled it together and was on the job. I hurried over to the DJ's spot and found him pressing buttons on his computer, his ears covered by large headphones.

"Sounds great!" I semishouted, trying to pierce through the noise of conversations and music.

He pointed to his ears, indicating he couldn't hear me.

I nodded, gave him a thumbs-up, and mouthed, *Thank you*.

He shrugged and returned his attention to pushing buttons.

I was glad he was here—and not just to help out and play the music. I hated to think of him sitting at home alone, depressed about his friend's death. He'd disappeared for the last couple of hours before the party, but he was back now, and that was what mattered.

Someone tapped me on the shoulder.

"Have you seen Ryan yet?" Lucas Cruz said, still speaking through vampire teeth. "Seen" had come out as "theen."

"Who?"

"Ryan Fitzpatrick? The reporter from *Gossip Guy*?" Lucas scanned the crowded patio. "He was supposed to come early, take pictures, do some videotaping for his show. Have you seen him?"

Since I didn't know what Ryan Fitzpatrick looked like, I said no, but that I would check with Raj, who was guarding the entry. I walked over and, as expected, found Raj in the midst of scanning a guest's ID with his flashlight. The man was fumbling through his jacket pockets.

"I have it here somewhere," he said. He'd made no attempt to dress in costume. Instead, he wore a long-sleeved white T-shirt under a Sharks Windbreaker, and saggy jeans. He'd accessorized with wire-rimmed glasses, a hemp backpack, and on his feet were loafers, no socks.

The main accessory that caught my attention was the large camera around his neck.

"Are you Ryan Fitzgerald?" I asked.

"Fitzpatrick, yes," he said, now digging into the pockets of his jeans. "I seem to have lost my invitation . . . and can't remember where I put my ID. . . . Wait! Let me check my wallet." He withdrew a tattered denim wallet that looked as though it would fall apart in his hands if he added one more dollar bill.

He opened the wallet and thrust his driver's license toward the guard. "See?"

Raj shined his flashlight on the card, then on the man's face. Although I didn't watch his Hollywood gossip segments, I recognized him from TV. Thirtysomething, he had his hair covered with a Giants baseball cap, and, when he smiled, he flashed ultrawhite teeth that everyone in show business seemed to sport these days.

"Sorry," I said to Ryan, "but we're being overly cautious. We had an incident earlier with another paparazzo—"

"I'm *not* a paparazzo," the man said as he snatched the ID back and crammed it in his wallet. "I'm a professional photographer and reporter for the nationally syndicated show *Gossip Guy.*"

"I apologize," I said, "but, as I was saying, another . . . photographer . . . tried to sneak in and take pictures, so we're just making sure that everyone is on the guest list."

Ryan Fitzpatrick cocked his head. "Who was the other photographer?"

"I forget his name. Someone Lucas Cruz knows."

"Bodie Chase?" Ryan hissed.

"Yes, I think that was his name."

Ryan glanced toward the party area. "Where is he?"

"Gone. My security guards removed him from the premises, and he left after we threatened to call the police."

"Good riddance. That creep is the kind of 'wedding *faux*-tographer' that gives us professionals a bad name." He didn't need finger quotes with the venomous way he said "wedding *faux*-tographer." The derogatory slap was clear.

I glanced at the man's Sharks jacket and Giants cap and wondered what his definition of professional attire was.

"Besides," he continued, "I'm supposed to have an exclusive. After all, my producer is helping to pay for all of this." He straightened the camera around his neck. "Now, if you'll excuse me, I have work to do."

"Sure," I said. "I'll tell Lucas you're here. He's been looking for you."

I doubted if Ryan heard my last words. He'd already waded into the sea of costumed attendees, no doubt hoping to get a scoop for the "nationally syndicated show."

Hey, I thought, suddenly realizing what this meant. My party might be featured on national TV!

I was almost giddy with excitement about the possibility of my fifteen minutes of fame—and I hadn't even had a glass of wine yet. If this Vampire Party made the entertainment news, I could get calls for parties from Hollywood to New York. Before I knew it, I was caught in a full-on fantasy, pondering questions such as what would I wear? What would I say? And would I need an emergency Botox treatment?

I was in the middle of imagining my outfit—

something dressy but not pretentious—when I heard an odd sound during a short music break. It came from the cemetery area beyond the party patio—and sounded like someone crying.

Several guests, drinks in hand, had wandered off the patio and over to some of the nearby headstones, no doubt to ponder the names, dates, and circumstances of those who had departed. But the sound of a sob had come from another direction, deeper into the cemetery. I took a few steps and squinted into the moonlit darkness to see if I could find the source. I wondered if it might be Duncan, still upset about losing one of his friends.

Moving stealthily among the headstones, I spotted a man in the shadows, his back to me.

"Duncan?" I called as I neared the figure.

The man spun around. Behind him stood a woman he'd apparently been embracing.

It was Jonas and Angelica. The look on both their faces was the same: guilt.

"Oh . . . *uh* . . . ," I stammered, feeling awkward about the obvious intrusion. "I'm sorry. . . ."

"It's okay . . . really . . . ," Jonas said softly. "Angelica was just upset and . . ." He looked at Angelica to finish his sentence.

Instead of responding, Angelica gathered her long skirt and abruptly ran past me, back to the party. I thought I saw her wipe her cheeks as she fled.

I looked back at Jonas.

"Is she all right?"

Jonas sighed. His shoulders slumped. From his body language, I thought he was about to admit something about their intimate embrace. But the words he said weren't what I expected.

"Angelica's being stalked."

"What?" I asked, not sure I had heard him correctly, he was speaking so softly.

Jonas bit his lip and nodded. "Yeah, someone's been following her, texting her, calling her, sending pictures. The son of a bitch. She's terrified."

"Has she called the police?"

Jonas frowned. "She doesn't want the police involved."

"Why not? Doesn't she realize having a stalker could be extremely dangerous? You have to convince her to let the police know."

He shook his head. "We can't."

"We?" I repeated.

"Angelica and I . . . we're . . ." He didn't finish his sentence.

"Oh my God," I said. "You weren't just comforting her. You two are actually . . ."

Jonas looked away, obviously uncomfortable.

"Involved, yes. So you can see why we can't go to the police. The paparazzi would jump on a story like this. All the sordid details, exposed for everyone to see. No. No way."

"But what's so wrong about the two of you having an affair? That's pretty common in Hollywood these days, stars filming a movie together falling in love.

Look at Brad and Angelina. Surely that can't have a negative effect on your careers."

Jonas looked at me with those pained dark eyes. No wonder Angelica had fallen for him. He was handsome, sensitive, and cared about her reputation. But even in the dim moonlight I could see there was something more behind those eyes.

"What is it, Jonas?" I asked. "What's wrong?"

He frowned. "Angelica is . . . married."

Oh boy, I thought as I made my way back to the party, leaving Jonas alone at his request. Angelica was secretly married? According to Jonas, the man I'd guessed was her bodyguard was actually her husband. No wonder that photographer guy from TMI wanted to crash the party. He must have had a suspicion that something was going on. I could only hope Ryan Fitzpatrick from *Gossip Guy* was clueless about the potential scandal and stuck to snapping pictures of the happy, costumed guests. If he started asking the wrong questions, this party could be in serious trouble.

But I had questions. Was Angelica's husband trying to protect her? Or was he suspicious that she might be involved with Jonas? The way he hung around and stared at her creeped me out a little. Was he just being watchful because of her stalker? Or was he trying to catch her in a compromising position?

"Ladies, gentlemen, and bloodthirsty vampires," a voice boomed over the loudspeaker.

I spotted Lucas Cruz at the microphone, trying to

gather the guests into a semicircle around the party patio. "Fang you very much," he continued, using a really bad Transylvanian accent. "We have a special surprise for you—a reenactment from my new film, *Revenge of the Killer Vampires*. Please, give it up for the two talented stars of the movie, Jonas Jones and Angelica Brayden!"

A roar of applause nearly deafened me as the eager—and no doubt inebriated—guests welcomed the entertainment portion of the party. Lights flickered ominously, the music turned brooding, thanks to Duncan, and a hush came over the crowd. Two blue-tinted spotlights suddenly lit up, one focused on Angelica, the other on Jonas, giving their skin a sickly cast.

Consummate actors, neither showed any signs of the real drama that had played out only moments ago in the cemetery. There were no tear stains on Angelica's pale cheeks, no concern on Jonas's unlined brow. They were just two people seemingly—and actually—attracted to each other as they stood face-to-face among the movie-prop headstones.

As in rehearsal, Jonas recited his memorized lines and offered his glass of red wine to Angelica. She took the glass, then cocked her head, exposing her long slim neck. It was the scene everyone was waiting for—the bite on the neck.

Jonas leaned in. . . .

The crowd held a collective breath as he bared his fangs and . . .

All hell broke loose.

From out of the darkness about half a dozen bizarre figures seemed to fly on to the scene. They all had black eyes, white skin, red lips, and wore ragged, bloody-looking clothes. One guy's hair stuck out in all directions, another had longish green hair, while still another had shaved one side of his head, leaving the rest of his hair hanging in his face. A few had bleeding wounds; some had ugly scars; knives, or cleavers protruded from the foreheads or arms of others.

Blood dripped from their mouths and chins.

One of the party guests screamed, setting off the others. They clustered together, not knowing which way to go, trapped by freaky-looking zombies on all sides. One woman had spilled her drink on her outfit, startled by the freaky intruders. Another man cowered behind his date.

I glanced around for Lucas or Brad or Raj, but instead caught a glimpse of Angelica, who stood frozen in her spotlight, looking terrified once again. There was no sign of her bodyguard/husband, but Jonas was there, holding her clutched to his chest.

Suddenly, with a jerk, he was wrenched from her and became airborne.

The pulley!

But this wasn't part of the rehearsed scene.

I watched helplessly as Jonas flailed in the air, hanging only by the wire he'd been attached to before taking the stage area. Kicking his legs and flapping his arms, he looked crazily comical, not at all fearsome or frightening the way Lucas had intended—except maybe to Angelica, who watched in horror as he swung overhead, frantically trying to grab on to a nearby tree limb.

Meanwhile the invasion of the living dead was in full force. Bodies leaped from headstone to headstone like mutant monkeys. It was hard to tell the girls from the boys, with all of them dressed in similar costumes and makeup, but I thought I recognized at least two of the people: Trace and Lark—the young man and woman I'd seen the previous night—the night Spidey died.

What were they doing here? They'd known about the party, but we'd specifically asked them to stay away. Still, this parkour event seemed planned, not spur of the moment. Was it some kind of antiestablishment demonstration? Were they trying to make a point?

I hustled over to Duncan, who stood transfixed, watching the traceurs seemingly fly from monument to monument, dazzling—and frightening—the party crowd.

"What's going on, Duncan? What are they doing here?"

He shrugged, but I could tell he knew more than he was letting on.

"Duncan! Tell me. What's this all about?"

"I don't know, Presley. Honestly. I told Trace I couldn't be involved, since I was working for you. But I guess they decided to do it anyway."

"Do what? Ruin the party? Why?"

Duncan looked at me. "Don't ask me. Ask . . ." He scanned the crowd, then nodded toward a very irate producer who was trying to chase after the grave-leapers.

"Cruz? What does he have to do with this?"

"I guess you'll have to ask him."

Chapter 7

PARTY-PLANNING TIP #7

There's nothing like a surprise guest to liven up your party. For a vampire theme, consider hiring a local actor to "crash" in costume and give the party a feeling of authenticity. Then, to raise the level of excitement, invite fake paparazzi.

I couldn't ask Lucas Cruz what was going on, because at the moment he was running around like the proverbial movie mogul with his head cut off, trying to get Jonas down. The security guards, once they'd shaken off their stunned reactions, were chasing the zombie traceurs who continued to leap from gravestone to monument like risen spirits.

I looked around for Brad, thinking if anyone could put a stop to this, he could. But I found him standing in a corner, watching the theatrics. I gave him a "WTF" look, then suddenly knew why he wasn't reacting.

Sirens filled the air.

Brad held up his cell phone and smiled. He'd called the cops—on my party.

I guessed he didn't really have a choice. At least they'd scare away the interlopers—or should I say interleapers. This was no time for playing with words. I had a party to rescue.

Three Colma police squad cars pulled up and six officers jumped out. It must have been a slow night in the City of Souls to warrant three units. Brad greeted them at the entrance to the party and gestured toward the zombies, whose numbers were diminishing.

As the officers fanned out, shining their flashlights into the dark cemetery that surrounded the party scene, the crowd began to relax and conversation picked up again. Apparently, the police had added even more entertainment to the event. Delicia and Rocco caught my signal to pour more drinks, but when I looked in the direction of the DJ's turntable, I saw that Duncan had disappeared from his spot. I headed over to Berk and asked him to fill in as DJ. I just hoped he hadn't brought along any of his underground rap music and would stick with the lineup I'd prepared.

By the time the cops left, thirty minutes later—with no arrests—the interruption seemed to be nearly forgotten. The guests were back to mingling while enjoying Rocco's chocolate graves, aka red velvet cake covered in chocolate icing and topped with a Ghirardelli chocolate headstone. The flowing red wine helped.

"Interesting party," Brad said, sneaking up behind

me. "But then, when you're in charge, they're all interesting."

I slugged down half a glass of merlot. "Yeah, well, at least no one died this time," I said. "Can't always say that, can I?"

Brad opened his mouth to reply, but I cut him off. "Don't answer that. It's a rhetorical question."

He didn't. Instead, he asked, "How's Cruz? Last I saw him, he was telling some of the guests the leapers were all part of his party plans. That guy will take credit for anything."

"I'm sure he was just trying to calm them down. And besides, what's a party without a little drama?" I took another swig of wine and licked my lips.

"So where are the stars?" Brad asked. "They seem to have disappeared along with the traceurs."

I glanced around. There was no sign of either Angelica or Jonas.

Uh-oh.

Were they off consummating their secret affair?

I blushed. Where had that thought come from? Too much wine? Before I started daydreaming about what it would be like to do it in a cemetery, I said, "I don't know. Duncan has vanished as well. Probably ran off with his grave-walking friends. I thought I recognized Trace and Lark under that zombie makeup, but when I tried to ask Duncan about the party crashers, he just shrugged and said, 'Talk to Cruz.'"

Brad's knitted brows told me he was as puzzled as I

was. "I guess you'd better ask him then, after he's done holding court."

I nodded. "I'm a little worried about Duncan. Losing his friend Spidey, and then this invasion of the body snatchers. I'm sure he knew about it. I wonder if he knew about Angelica and—"

I clapped a hand over my mouth.

"Jonas," Brad said, finishing my blurted sentence. "Yeah, you'd have to be blind not to see they've got something going on."

I stared at him in awe. "You knew?"

"It's obvious. The way they avoid each other except when they're doing a scene together. Even then, they rarely make eye contact even when they're running their lines. So you suspected it too?"

"No . . . actually, I saw them—by accident—over there"—I pointed—"in that secluded section of the cemetery. At first I thought it was just Jonas, but then I saw Angelica with him. When I got to them, she was crying; then she ran off. That was when Jonas admitted they were having an affair. Believe me, I was stunned."

"You know she's married, right?"

I stared at him. How did he manage to know everything? "I suppose that was obvious to you too?"

"You didn't notice that guy hovering around her, watching her every move?"

"I thought he was her bodyguard."

Brad harrumphed. "Tall and lean? Doesn't exactly have the bodyguard build, now does he?"

How naive was I? "I suppose you also know she has a stalker."

Brad was silent. He blinked several times, then cocked his jaw.

"You didn't know!" I said. "I can't believe you didn't know this too!"

"How do *you* know she has a stalker?" Brad said.

"Jonas told me."

"What did he say?"

"Just that Angelica's been getting texts and e-mails and phone calls and stuff like that . . ."

Brad crossed his thick, bodyguard arms over his chest. "Have they called the police?"

"Jonas said Angelica doesn't want to involve the cops. It might get out to the media—that she's married. But none of this is my business anyway. I'm just the party planner, remember?"

"Yeah, but what happens at your parties doesn't always stay at your parties, if you get my drift. . . ."

I didn't. I was too busy trying to figure out what, if anything, this had to do with the party crashers who had come and gone. And why things like this always seem to happen to me.

Around midnight, as the party began to wind down and the last guests finally straggled off with their party favors—photos taken of them in their vampire costumes standing between Jonas and Angelica—I began my favorite part of an event—the cleanup. While most people dread the aftermath, I love it because it gives me a chance to think about the highlights of the party, how it all miraculously came together, and what I'll do next time to make it even better.

In this case, probably not host it in a real cemetery.

I was popping balloons when Lucas Cruz came over, drink in hand. He, like many of the last guests, was a little tipsy. But it was his party, and he could drink if he wanted to.

"Great party, Presley," he said, slurring my name.

"I hope you enjoyed it, Lucas," I said as I packed up a box of garlic necklaces. "Sorry about that mishap with the party crashers."

"No sweat." He waved it off as if it were a pesky fly. His drink nearly became airborne. "I just told everyone it was part of the event, and they bought it."

"Well . . . good. If you're happy—"

"But," he added with an evil glint in his eye, "just wait until I get my hands on Duncan."

That was my cue. "Yeah, about that. Duncan said to ask you about those traceurs—the parkour guys? He seemed to imply that you were responsible for having them here. Did you arrange for them to come and frighten the guests a little more?"

Cruz looked at me as if he'd just discovered I was the Bride of Chucky. "Good God, no! Why would I do that?"

"*Uh* . . . maybe to add a little more drama. Get your name on the news. After all, that reporter from *Gossip Guy* was here. Maybe you thought it would make good TV. I just wish you'd let me know, that's all."

"That's ridiculous!" Cruz huffed. "The party was going to be great as planned, especially with that scene between Jonas and Angelica, and his taking off in the air as he was supposed to do. I didn't need a bunch of thugs running around adding to the theatrics. Where did you get such an idea?"

"Like I said, Duncan told me to talk to you."

Cruz laughed. "Traceurs. You mean poseurs, don't you? Bunch of kids thinking they have superpowers and can walk tall buildings like Superman. I know who they are. They're a bunch of punks who aren't grateful playing extras in my film. They wanted to come to the party too."

"That's what this is all about?"

Lucas's face flushed. "Look. I needed some extras for the movie, and I asked Duncan if he had any friends who might be interested."

"And he offered Trace, Lark, and Spidey?"

Lucas looked exasperated. "I guess those are their names. I only used them a couple of times. They were paid the standard rate. They should have been grateful. But when they found out I was having this wrap party—I suppose Duncan told them—they expected to be invited! As if I would invite extras to the wrap party. No way."

It was beginning to make sense. "So they crashed the party, hoping to ruin it for you."

"I suppose. But I'll tell you this—Duncan Grant will never work in this town again."

With that cliché, Lucas staggered off to check on his own staff, also busy collecting their gadgets and gear.

By half past midnight, almost everyone had cleared out and gone home. Delicia offered to drive my mother home, so Brad stayed and helped me with the final packing up.

"Great party," Brad said, zipping up his black leather jacket. "In spite of a few glitches."

The night had grown colder and I zippered my own hoodie over my black dress. "Well, as I said, there were no real dead bodies—only the costumed kind. Can't ask for more than that."

Just as I finished loading the last box of plastic coffins into Brad's Crime Scene Cleaners SUV, I heard a low shriek coming from up the hill, where the pet section of the cemetery lay. Brad and I looked at each other. He pulled out a flashlight he kept in the SUV and shined it into the darkness. With all the party lights removed, the only light came from the moon and what looked like a trailer up on the hill.

Brad headed in the direction of the sound.

I grabbed his arm. "Don't!"

"What, are you suddenly superstitious?" he whispered. "Someone's out there. They may need help."

"It might be a wild animal. With rabies," I said, trying to stop him from rushing into danger. I thought about Spidey and shivered. I had a bad feeling about this, but I wasn't about to stay by myself. Grabbing on to one of his jumpsuit belt loops, I trailed behind him, trying not to trip over the uneven ground and chunks of broken headstones.

"It came from over there," he whispered, and

pointed up the rise, still in the direction of the pet cemetery. "Listen . . . I hear someone. . . ."

It was true. I also heard someone. Mumbling? Or ranting. I had a hunch who it was.

As we neared the pet cemetery, where the property seemed better kept than Lawndale's, I saw a figure sitting cross-legged at the crest of the hill. He was chanting something I couldn't make out, repeating words over and over and rocking his body back and forth. Finally, I caught a few words that sounded like "pestilence, death, pestilence, death."

Brad shined his light on the man.

"What's he saying?" I whispered to Brad.

I felt him shrug. He called out, "Hey, mister. You all right?"

Otto Gunther looked up, his face a mask of terror and pain in the beam of Brad's flashlight.

"Leaving a grave open all night brings pestilence and death to everyone . . . everyone . . . everyone . . . ," he mumbled.

"What are you talking about, Otto?" I asked as I took a few steps closer. As we neared him, Brad shined his light around Otto, no doubt checking for signs the old man might be hurt. I got another chill, thinking of Spidey. But Otto's plaid shirt and overalls showed no signs of blood, nor did his face.

We stepped up the small rise that marked the front boundary of the pet cemetery and noticed a mound of dirt. Otto, I realized, was sitting at the edge of what looked like an open grave. The piled dirt looked fresh and moist in the beam of light. The hole was big enough for a large dog.

The back of my neck tingled as I peered over the edge.

Inside the freshly dug grave was a curled-up figure wearing a white mask and black cape—Dracula.

I gripped Brad's arm, wanting to look away from unable to stop staring into the grave.

Brad glanced around the nearby grounds using his flashlight and picked up a long dry branch that had fallen from a rotting oak tree. He stuck it into the grave and slowly, carefully, hooked it under the mask. With a flick of his wrist, the mask flew off, revealing a blood-covered head.

I gasped.

And then I recognized him—the paparazzo from TMI who'd tried to sneak into the party.

Apparently, he'd returned. Or maybe he never left.

Either way, how did he end up lying in a pet grave?

Chapter 8

Brad and I looked at each other, then back down at the obviously dead body. No one walked away with a head wound like that. I don't know how Brad kept his party food down, but mine was churning in my stomach like the Mad Tea Party ride at Disneyland. I held on to Brad's arm until the spinning passed.

To distract myself, I looked at Otto. He still sat there, chanting his mantra: "Pestilence, pestilence, pestilence . . . death, death, death . . ."

Something glinted at his side—his shotgun.

Oh God. Had Otto shot the paparazzo? The guy had certainly threatened he would. Had he actually done it?

But wouldn't we have heard the shot?

I tapped Brad to get his attention and nodded toward the gun. He caught my drift and stepped over to Otto. With a swing of his foot, he kicked the gun out of reach. I took a deep breath, switched on my iPhone flashlight app, and looked into the grave again, wondering if there were any gunshot wounds.

"Brad. Look," I said, indicating the body.

Brad stepped over and knelt down, shining his flashlight over the dead man. After a quick examination, he focused the light on the guy's head.

"No gunshot wounds," he said.

He stood up and glanced around the area. I wondered what he was looking for. We'd already found Otto's gun. Then Brad spotted something a few feet away and walked over, his flashlight leading the way. When he stopped and looked down, I followed him.

A shovel.

I remembered Otto had had a shovel with him earlier.

Brad shined the light on the back of the blade, revealing a smear of red.

Blood.

He stood up, pulled out his cell phone, and dialed 911.

In less than ten minutes the cemetery was once again crawling with Colma cops. One of the officers tried to question Otto, who continued to mumble incoherently. Two others interviewed Brad and me separately. I don't know what kinds of questions he got, but mine from the female cop named Annie Wong were mostly routine:

What was I doing in the cemetery? (Having a party . . .)

Did I know the deceased? (Only that he tried to crash the party.)

Did I know the groundskeeper? (Met him last night when he told us to leave his property.)

Did I see anything unusual? (Nope.)

Did I know anyone who might have wanted the victim dead?

Lucas Cruz quickly came to mind.

There was no way I was going to give up Lucas at this point. I was certain he'd never kill anyone, especially not for just crashing a party. He channeled his anger through his visceral films.

"Not really," I finally replied, wondering what Brad would give as an answer to that question.

Officer Wong flipped her notebook closed. "That'll be all, Ms. Parker. We'll call you if we need anything more."

"Not so fast, Parker," came an all-too-familiar voice from behind me.

"Oh great," I mumbled, and turned around. The tall, good-looking man was dressed more for a dinner date than a crime scene investigation. That tailored suit did not come off the rack and those Italian shoes didn't arrive via UPS from Shoe World. "Detective Melvin. What are you doing in Colma? Isn't this a bit out of your jurisdiction?"

"Are you kidding, Parker?" Detective Luke Melvin said. "I wouldn't miss this for the world. When I heard you were involved, I had to come. You know how much I enjoy investigating crimes when you're the primary suspect." He actually winked at me.

God, I really wanted to muss up his overgelled hair, but I was afraid he might arrest me for assault.

"Sorry to disappoint you, Detective, but I'm not a suspect, and I had nothing to do with this. In fact, it didn't happen during my party."

"If that's true, it'll be a first," Melvin said, shooting his cuffs.

Brad sauntered over, and the two old friends gave each other some kind of complicated hand jive. "So they called you in?" Brad asked, avoiding my daggered stare.

"I was just telling Parker here, it's a standing order," Melvin said. "Anytime her name appears, I want in." He flashed a perfect white smile at me and I wondered if he'd had his teeth sharpened as well as whitened. Well, he could just bite me.

"Look, Detective, I'm too tired to engage in witty repartee with you tonight. Arrest me or let me go home. The other officer has my statement. If you want more, call me in the morning."

I glanced at Brad, who tucked in his chin, not wanting to get involved in the dislike-hate relationship between his cop friend and his "girlfriend."

Physically and emotionally exhausted, I headed for the SUV to wait for Brad. I watched as the EMTs loaded the covered paparazzo's body into the waiting ambulance. Next came Otto, in handcuffs. He was put in the back of a police unit, looking bewildered and frightened. In spite of his earlier anger and his superstitions, I suddenly felt sorry for the old man.

Brad followed a few minutes later.

"You want to crash at my place?" he said, starting the engine.

"I think I'll just go on home, if you don't mind," I said. "Rain check?"

"Sure."

He drove me to my condo in silence, both of us thinking about the evening's events. There had been two deaths in the same cemetery in two nights. Were they related? I had no idea what a parkour kid could have in common with a paparazzo.

"Sleep tight," Brad said after he pulled into my condo carport on Treasure Island. He leaned in and gave me a gentle kiss. "I'll check on you tomorrow."

I slipped out of the passenger seat, then leaned in through the window and asked Brad, "What's going to happen to Otto?"

Brad shook his head. "We'll see."

I headed for my door with a nagging feeling in the back of my head.

Even though I was exhausted, my thoughts raced as I prepared for bed. By the time I dropped my tired body onto the mattress, I'd come to one conclusion: The deaths of Spidey the night before and the paparazzo tonight had to be related. But how?

I had to find out more about the two guys.

I knew Spidey was a friend of Duncan's. He enjoyed doing parkour. He was an extra in Cruz's film. He was at the cemetery the other night with two friends, Trace and Lark.

And he had supposedly fallen from a gravestone, hit his head, and died—alone.

I knew even less about Bodie Chase, the paparazzo. Lucas Cruz hated him for some reason. Chase had tried to sneak into the party, most likely to take unflattering pictures and gather embarrassing information on the film's stars. He'd been run off the property, but apparently had returned later, in the form of Dracula. The mask had hidden his identity at the party.

And it looked as though he'd been hit over the head with Otto's shovel and dumped into an open pet grave.

So, what did they have in common, besides being dead and having head injuries?

Could they have known each other? It was a long shot, but not impossible.

Lucas Cruz jumped to mind again. He hated Bodie Chase and had a restraining order against him. But had he hated him enough to kill him? Angelica Brayden and Jonas Jones also had a reason to get rid of him if he found out their secret. Not to mention Angelica's husband—what was his name?

So how did any of this tie in with Spidey? None of it made sense.

Unless Lucas Cruz had a grudge against Spidey too. Cruz hired him as an extra in his movie. Maybe Spidey found out something during the filming that Cruz didn't want made public?

Oh my God—*what was I thinking*?

Why was I trying to make a case against Lucas Cruz? While he wasn't exactly a friend, I knew him well enough to know he wasn't a killer.

Didn't I?

"Enough!" I said to my cats, who had nestled onto my bed. I switched off the light, bid them good night, and closed my eyes for some much-needed sleep.

Solving a possible double homicide could wait until morning.

I woke the next morning to the sound of my doorbell ringing. Rolling over and covering my eyes from the sunny bedroom window, I stole a quick peek at the clock radio.

Nine!

I shot up like a rocket and double-checked the time. Nine oh one to be exact. That couldn't be right. I never slept late. Too much to do.

Throwing a robe over my cat pajamas, I walked to the front door and peeped through the hole. Brad stood on the porch, lattes in hand, along with a white bakery bag. I started to drool just looking at that bag.

"These are getting cold!" he called through the

door. I unlocked the three locks and yanked open the door.

Instead of stepping inside, Brad looked me up and down as I stood in my rumpled robe, PJs, and punk hair. He laughed, then leaned in and gave me a quick kiss.

"You're just now getting up? No wonder you didn't answer your phone."

I pulled the door wide for him to enter. "Hey, I had a rough night, remember?"

He made his way to the small wooden table that divided the tiny kitchen from the tiny living area and set down the coffees. "But you never sleep this late. Are you sick?"

Hmm. I felt my forehead. Maybe I *was* coming down with something. At least it wasn't bloody, I thought, remembering last night's discovery.

"Here. I brought you some medicine." He put the white bag on the table and tore it open, revealing six fresh beignets, covered with powdered sugar.

My eyes just about popped out of my head. "Beignets! Where did you get them? Is there a secret Café du Monde hidden somewhere in the City that I don't know about?"

I sat down, snatched one, and took a big bite—then I coughed, sending the white powder billowing into the air. In my hurry to fill my mouth with the crispy sweet confection, I had snorted a blast of powdered sugar. I must have looked like a desperate coke addict.

"Simmer down there, girl. You're supposed to eat it, not inhale it."

"Sorry," I said, wiping my mouth with a napkin. "I haven't had a real beignet since my mother hosted a Mardi Gras party years ago and flew them in from New Orleans. Where did you get them?"

"Brenda's. On Polk. Near the Tenderloin."

"I've never been there." I took another bite, then said, "Zzs ur da di fur!" Translation: "These are to die for."

Brad laughed at my bad manners. "You'll have to try the chocolate ones. They're filled with hot Ghirardelli chocolate. And the crawfish ones."

I was about to lick my lips at the image of a chocolate-filled beignet when he said the word "crawfish." I made a yuck face instead. "Stop talking. Let me enjoy my beignet."

Once we'd had our fill of the donutlike treat, I brought up the subject that had been on my mind since last night.

"Did you talk to Detective Melvin? Any news about the dead guy?"

Brad wiped his mouth. "No. But they questioned Otto last night."

"Do they think he killed that paparazzo? And Spidey?"

Brad raised his hands. "Whoa, there! Who said anything about Spidey being murdered? His death was an accident, remember?"

I decided to keep my mouth shut and not argue the

point. But I still had a hunch the deaths were related. I just hadn't figured out the connection yet.

"Okay, then Bodie Chase. But why would Otto want to kill him? Just to get him off his property?"

"I didn't say they'd arrested him for murder. I just said they questioned him. After giving him a chance to sober up a little."

There I went again, jumping to conclusions. As a party planner, when I had a problem, I needed to solve it quickly; hence my tendency to make snap decisions. Apparently I made murder accusations much the same way. It was a good thing I was a party planner and not a cop.

"So, did they learn anything from him?"

Brad pointed to his upper lip, indicating I had something on mine. I licked it off with my tongue. Powdered sugar. Yummy.

"No, the guy pretty much rambled about the same stuff he said when we were there. Sounded like a bunch of superstitions to Luke. They're keeping him on a twenty-four-hour psych hold before they release him."

"What about the shovel? That was blood on it, right?"

"Yep. Forensics matched the blood on the shovel to Chase. He was definitely hit over the head with that shovel. And they found prints on it."

I perked up. "Great! Whose?"

"Whose do you think?"

"Otto's," I answered, deflated.

"Bingo."

"Brad, do you think Otto did it? Actually swung that shovel and whacked the guy? He doesn't seem coherent enough."

"I agree. And as I said, he hasn't been officially arrested."

I took a last sip of my latte and stood up. "I have to get dressed. I'm sure there are a million party things waiting for me at the office. You have any plans today?"

"Nothing yet. But the day is young."

He no doubt meant that soon there would be crime scenes to clean up, and his workday would begin. He crumpled up the pastry bag and threw it into my recycling bin. "I'll see you back at the office."

"Thanks for the breakfast. I loved it." I kissed him. His lips were sweet with residual sugar.

After he let himself out, I headed for the shower. As the warm water sprayed my body, I thought about poor Otto. It sounded as if he'd been through a lot. Now he might lose his freedom. And while I was glad I could stop suspecting Lucas Cruz of being a murderer, something still bothered me.

Had Spidey's death really been accidental?

Or was Otto involved in some way?

It was the only connection I could make at the moment. But as Brad had said, the day was young.

I hopped into my red MINI Cooper and drove the short distance to Building One, which now housed my

Killer Party business. My first office had been demolished when the barracks building burned down on the island, and the second barracks had been condemned. My new office was much nicer, but the rent was higher too. I'd been coerced in to hosting a party for the Treasure Island Development Agency in exchange for a discount on rent. That and the income from last night's Vampire Wrap Party would help keep my mother and me afloat for the next few months.

The door to my office stood open as I crossed the large Art Deco Building One lobby. Delicia must have come in early, I thought, until I remembered I was coming in late. I peered in and found her sitting at her desk. My desk chair was also occupied—by a downcast Duncan Grant.

I looked at Delicia. She rolled her eyes.

Uh-oh.

"Duncan!" I said cheerily. "What are you doing here?"

The young man made no effort to get up. Instead, he pointed to my computer screen.

I leaned over to see what he wanted to show me. It was an article from the *San Francisco Chronicle*, dated six months ago.

Nineteen-year-old David Krumboltz, described as a "good kid," died last night from injuries sustained in a fall from an eight-story parking structure in the Mission District. Krumboltz, who'd lettered in cross-country running at Balboa High School, planned to compete in the sport at San Francisco State University, where he was a student.

"This is not a homicide investigation," Detective Luke Melvin told reporters. "We're just trying to determine how the accident occurred." Krumboltz's friends said they believed parkour, an urban sport popularized on the Internet, is to blame.

"Parkour is all about running and jumping from one point to another, like rooftops or fences, and doing it as quickly and with as much finesse as possible," said a friend of Krumboltz's known only as Trace. "David was totally into parkour."

I stopped reading and looked at Duncan.

"This guy died doing parkour?" I said, stating the obvious.

He met my eyes. "Yes, it's possible to die doing parkour if you're leaping and jumping around eight-story parking garages."

"So why are you showing me this, Duncan?"

"Because, you usually *don't* die if you're just tracing on a bunch of headstones. Even a fall from a six-footer wouldn't kill you."

"Unless you hit your head wrong . . . ," I started to say.

Duncan stood up, shoving my desk chair back with a violent kick of his foot. "That's just it. Spidey *didn't* fall. That was no accident. Whoever killed that guy at the cemetery last night probably killed Spidey too."

I frowned at him, puzzled. "How did you know about the guy from last night?"

"Helloooo?" Delicia interrupted. "It's been all over the TV news. And so is Killer Parties, by the way. Your phone has been ringing off the hook."

Oh God. This wasn't the type of media attention I wanted to promote my party business.

Duncan moved to the doorway, his eyes red with frustration. Or was it rage?

"Somebody killed my friend," he said. "I'm going to find out who it was. And kill him."

Chapter 9

"Oh great," I said, reopening the door and plopping into my recently vacated chair. "Now Duncan's decided to become a vigilante."

"Let's hope he doesn't get ahold of a gun," Dee said. "With his lack of coordination, he's apt to shoot himself in the nuts."

"Nuts?" Brad stood in the doorway, his hands cupped protectively around his manhood.

"Yes, nuts," Dee reiterated. "That guy may be a genius when it comes to gaming and computers, but he can't walk five steps without bumping into something."

I shot her a look. "Dee! Stop it. We all have our strengths and weaknesses. Besides, Duncan is all talk, I'm sure." At least, I hoped he was.

Brad entered the office and opened a folding chair that leaned against a wall. He turned it around and sat in it backward, crossing his muscled arms over the top. Every time he did that, a jolt shot up my spine.

I tried to recover. "*Uh . . .* we were talking about Duncan," I said. "He's upset about his friend's death. He doesn't think it was an accident."

"How come?" Brad asked.

"I'm not sure. I don't think he has any evidence. He showed me this article"—I pointed to my computer screen—"about a kid who died doing parkour. But his fall was from an eight-story building, not a five-foot headstone. He seemed to imply that Spidey wouldn't have died by falling."

"That's all he has to go on?" Brad asked.

"Unless he knows something we don't."

"Like what?" Dee asked. "The only connections he has with the police are through you, Brad. Did you tell him anything?"

"Nope," he said.

"Because there's nothing to tell, right?" I said.

"Nope," he repeated.

I stopped. "What do you mean 'nope'? Brad Matthews, did you learn something from Detective Melvin that you haven't told me?"

"Whoa, there, girl detective. I just found out myself."

I leaned in, eager to hear his news. "Found out what?"

Brad raised an eyebrow in an attempt to appear mysterious.

I gave him a light slap on his arm. He probably didn't even feel it. "Talk, mister!"

"Well, the forensics report says the official cause of Spidey's death was blunt force trauma to the head that caused massive hemorrhaging."

"And . . . ?"

"It doesn't say it was caused by the piece of gravestone they found lying on the ground under his head, even though the stone was soaked with blood."

"So what does that mean?"

"When I did the cleanup—"

"You found something!"

He grinned.

"What? Tell me!"

He shifted in the chair. "Well, if Spidey tripped and fell accidentally, then hit his head on that broken piece of gravestone, there wouldn't be blood anywhere but on his head and on the ground where he fell, right?"

I nodded. Then it hit me like a ton of headstones. "You found blood splatter!"

"*Spatter*. It's called spatter. But yeah, when I was cleaning up, there were streaks of blood a few feet away, on another headstone."

"And the police missed it?"

"Like the rest of us, they assumed Spidey's injury was caused by hitting the stone. An accident. They weren't looking for spatter. Even when I found the blood, it was dry and I didn't think much about it, figuring it had probably been there awhile. In fact, I only mentioned it to forensics when I remembered it a few hours later."

I sat back, a little disappointed in his revelation. "But that could be anyone's blood. And it could have been there a long time."

Brad nodded. "Still, they sent out a tech to check and make sure."

I leaned in again. "And . . ."

He shrugged. "DNA tests haven't come back yet, but they just learned the type. It's the same as Spidey's—B negative—which is pretty rare. Only two percent of the population has B neg."

My toes tingled in anticipation of the possibilities. "So if it turns out to be Spidey's blood, and there was a blood splatter—*spatter*—only a few feet away, that could mean someone might have hit him, causing Spidey to lose his balance and fall to the ground. . . ."

"It could."

"And send his blood flying," I continued, thinking aloud. "Possibly with the same shovel that was used on Bodie Chase, the paparazzo." I thought for a moment, then had an idea. "What if the shovel-wielder put that piece of headstone under Spidey's head after he fell, to make it look like that was what caused the head injury?"

"You mean, staged the crime scene," Brad summarized.

"Yes. The killer could have lifted Spidey's head and smashed it down onto the stone to cover the shovel wound. . . ."

"Stop!" Dee cried, covering her ears. "You're gonna give me nightmares!"

I looked at Brad. "Are they doing a DNA test on the paparazzo?"

Brad nodded.

"Has it come back yet?"

"Nope. But when it does, we'll know two things: one, whether or not the blood on the shovel is the paparazzo's blood—"

"And two," I continued for him, "if there's any evidence of Spidey's blood on that shovel as well. Which would mean Duncan's suspicions are right: that Spidey *was* murdered. Most likely by the same weapon used to kill Bodie. And probably by the same person."

Brad stood up and refolded the chair. "Those are big ifs, Presley. These things take time, and right now there's no solid proof. We'll just have to wait and see what Luke finds out from the tests."

Patience isn't one of my strong suits. There was no way I was going to sit idly by and wait for Detective Melvin to feed us bits of information at his whim.

Besides, there was the little matter of Spidey's pal and my sometimes employee, Duncan Grant. He didn't seem to care about stuff like DNA. He was already convinced his friend was too talented at parkour to fall and may have been murdered.

Maybe I had better visit the cemetery and see that blood spatter myself.

In order to give Duncan some time to chill before I questioned him, I made a few party-related phone calls—one for a gay-rights activist group in the Castro that wanted a YMCA theme party. The fund-raiser for the GLBT—Gay Lesbian Bisexual Transgender—group would include having guests dress as one of the characters from the Village People. And, of course, they wanted it held at the local Y. I couldn't wait to get started on the cowboy/police/construction worker/biker decorations for this one.

When I finished taking care of business, I went looking for Duncan. He wasn't in his office, nor was his beat-up VW in the parking lot, but I had a hunch where to find him. I picked up my purse and told Dee I'd be back around noon. When she asked where I was going, I answered, "The cemetery."

"Why are you going back there?"

"Time to raise the dead," I said mysteriously, and headed for my car. It took me twenty minutes to get to Colma in the light traffic. The usually congested Highway 101 South was almost always a parking lot in the morning and late afternoon, but at the moment cars moved along, and the hills stacked with box-shaped, pastel houses flew by.

The freeway turned into Junipero Serra Boulevard,

then El Camino Real, and moments later I saw the expanses of green cemetery lawns ahead. As I entered Colma, I noted all the multicultural restaurants—Thai, Filipino, Mexican, Brazilian, Nicaraguan—mixed in with the stores that sold monuments, floral arrangements, and other accoutrements for the dead.

The grand cemeteries, with names like Woodlawn, Greenlawn, and Cypress Lawn, sculpted in colorful bushes and flowers, offered an instant feeling of peace. Some had mini-castles that housed the administrative offices and chapels, nestled among the immaculate grounds, dotted with occasional ponds filled with geese and ducks.

I read the usual warning signs as I passed them: DO NOT FEED THE BIRDS, NO PICNICKING, and UNLAWFUL TO DRIVE THROUGH A FUNERAL PROCESSION. Good to know. Turning onto Eternity Drive, I drove past the Asian cemetery with its red monuments, the Jewish cemetery where Wyatt Earp lay, and the Italian cemetery, home to Joe DiMaggio, and continued around to the neglected Lawndale cemetery. I could see crime scene tape still encircling the open grave on the small rise.

Duncan's old VW was parked by the entrance.

I parked the MINI next to his car, got out, and filled my lungs with the smell of eucalyptus, pine, and a fragrant flower I couldn't identify. Not immediately spotting Duncan, I sensed I'd find him where Spidey's body had been discovered.

I was right. He was lying on top of a grave next to

the spot, his head resting against the headstone. His eyes were closed, earbuds in place, and he slowly nodded back and forth to the music of his iPod. I heard the muffled sound of a Beatles song, "Hey Jude."

He didn't see or hear me as I approached.

Not wanting to startle him, I gently tugged on one of his earbuds. In spite of my cautious efforts, Duncan jumped. He pulled out his buds and sat up quickly, as if expecting to defend himself against a killer he was certain was lurking among the headstones.

"Hey, Duncan," I said. "It's just me. Didn't mean to scare you."

"What are you doing here?" Duncan asked, sounding almost resentful at the intrusion. He folded up his knees and wrapped his arms around his legs, withdrawing into a protective shell.

"I wanted to talk to you."

"How did you find me?"

"I tried to imagine where I'd go if I were you. This seemed the most logical place."

He turned his face away and watched an elderly couple walk along one of the paths. I couldn't decide if they were mourners or just curious tourists. With all the famous names here, I had a feeling this place drew quite a few of the latter.

"Duncan, Brad found something when he was cleaning up the scene. I thought you might want to know." Was I feeding the fire? Or helping someone who wanted to find the truth?

He looked at me. "What?"

I stood up and glanced round, curious to see if I could find the blood spatter. In the daylight, it wasn't difficult. I found a nearby worn headstone with half a dozen burgundy drops streaked across the front and side. The inscription wasn't easy to read, thanks to weathering and the passage of time. I could barely make out the words.

DAVID MITCHELL
    1891–1961
WRINKLES SHOULD MERELY INDICATE WHERE
SMILES HAVE BEEN. —MARK TWAIN

I peered at the small, dark red lines, some as long as three inches. Gesturing at the headstone, I said, "Duncan, come look."

Duncan leaped up and bounded over, then knelt down and examined the marks.

He looked up at me, his eyes wide. "It looks like blood."

"That's what Brad thought."

Duncan turned his head away from me and wiped at the tears that had formed in his eyes.

After Duncan composed himself, I walked him back to his car and he drove off, promising to wait for more news and not to do anything rash. To keep him busy and distracted, I asked him to design a new Web site for Killer Parties, my company. That way he wouldn't have time to get into trouble. Meanwhile, I had a few ideas I wanted to follow up on.

I returned to the spot where Spidey had been found. I knew Brad had cleaned up the site thoroughly, and the forensics team had probably done a complete search of the ground where Spidey's body had lain. But I wondered if they'd thought about where Spidey might have been just before he fell from—or was knocked off—a gravestone.

After checking the area to see if anyone was watching—the old couple had disappeared—I stepped up on a short headstone in my Mary Janes and promptly fell off. Removing my shoes, I tried again in bare feet and had better luck with traction, and my toes curling over the sides to aid my balance. With my arms extended, I found myself able to step from one short headstone to another, as long as they were within a leg's length away.

This is kind of fun, I thought as I tried for a taller headstone. I would have been mortified if anyone had seen me, but at the moment it felt exhilarating. I wanted to shout, "On top of the world!" but didn't.

And then I got cocky. I misjudged the distance to the next headstone, and as I stepped out, I twisted my ankle. I dropped like a rock to the ground, hitting my right knee and elbow in the process. As I lay there imagining how stupid I must look, I felt a sharp pain along my arm and leg. I sat up and carefully pulled up the torn sleeve of my long-sleeved T-shirt. A long ugly scrape ran down my arm. Tiny dots of blood appeared, and I gently lowered the sleeve to help blot the bleeding and protect the wound.

I checked my throbbing leg. My jeans had torn at the knee, revealing another bloody gash. Stretching out my leg, I held on to the closest headstone and pushed myself up, one-handed, to standing. I hoped no one could hear the curses coming out of my mouth every inch of the way.

Idiot.

What was I thinking, playing around on headstones like one of those athletic kids? That would teach me.

Maybe.

And then it occurred to me. Spidey had had a gash on his head, supposedly from hitting a piece of gravestone as he fell to the ground. But what about his elbow? His knee? Nobody fell off something without at least trying to break the fall—as I just had. Spidey would surely have had some scrapes, gashes, or blood on his arms and legs, if he'd lost his balance and fallen.

I pulled out my cell and called Brad.

"Crime Scene Cleaners," Brad said.

"Did Spidey have any marks on his body, other than the head wound?" I asked.

"What?"

I repeated the question.

"Where are you?" he asked.

"Please, Brad. It's important. Can you find out if Spidey had any defensive marks on his body, as though he was trying to break his fall?"

"I suppose—"

"Great. Call me back when you know. Thanks." I hung up before he could ask any more questions. If my hunch was right, there would be no defensive wounds on Spidey, only old scabs from any previous falls he'd had.

That would add credence to the possibility that Spidey had been murdered, just like that party crasher last night. He could have been hit over the head with the shovel and knocked unconscious while on top of the tombstone, and so he wouldn't have been able to break his fall.

And that would mean there was a killer still running loose.

Possibly right here in the cemetery. If that was the case, it was time to be like Wyatt Earp and get myself the hell out of Dodge.

Chapter 10

I drove back to the office, rehashing my conversation with Duncan. I hoped he'd take my advice and stay out of trouble, but he was young and impulsive, and I had a hunch he was going to do some snooping on his own. I felt I had to help him look into Spidey's death just to keep him safe.

Duncan seemed to think Lucas Cruz was suspect, even though there didn't seem to be any evidence to support that. But something was going on between Lucas and Duncan . . . and it wasn't good.

I pulled into the Building One lot on Treasure Is-land and parked the MINI, noting that Brad's SUV was also there. Duncan's VW van, however, was not. I wondered where he'd gone.

My office door was locked and the room was empty when I arrived. Dee had written "AAA. BBL." on the dry-erase board hanging on the wall. I'd quickly learned her texting code, which she also used on "While You Were Out" memo pads, phone texts, and other communication media. This one meant, "At an audition. Be back later."

I dropped my purse on the desk and walked next door to Brad's office. He was sitting at the computer, frowning at whatever he was reading on the screen. I felt a chill run down my spine, thinking he might have found something having to do with Spidey's death. Stepping around behind him, I peered at the screen.

He was checking sports scores.

"Darn it," he said. "The Sharks lost again. They should never have traded their goalie."

I stood back and stared at him.

He looked up. "What?"

"Nothing. I assumed you were helping me figure out what happened to Duncan's friend Spidey and that photographer. I didn't know you were too busy reading about baseball."

I turned to leave. Brad grabbed my hand.

"Hey, not so fast. First of all, it's hockey, not baseball. And second, don't you want to hear what Luke said about the blood type?"

I spun around and eyed him suspiciously. "Okay, what?"

He leaned back and crossed his hands behind his head. "He said . . ."

"What? Stop teasing and tell me!"

"Well, the police confirmed that the blood from the spatter on the gravestone and the shovel are the same, meaning it's almost certain that Spidey was hit with the same shovel that killed Bodie Chase."

I let out the breath I'd been holding. "Wow," I whispered. "Then Duncan was right. Someone did murder his friend."

"Looks like it. Luke's looking into all the possibilities. He'll find out what happened."

"You have a lot of confidence in Detective Melvin, don't you?"

"You don't?" he said, still holding on to my hand.

I said nothing, but my mind raced. Having Detective Luke Melvin on the case didn't make me feel great. While he was a smart cop, he moved at a ridiculously slow pace, and he didn't always jump to the same conclusions I did when it came to ferreting out a killer. Brad had explained in the past that the police were cautious in order to prevent mistakes. But with ADHD, I couldn't wait forever to make a case. Plus, I wondered if Duncan's comments about Lucas Cruz had any merit.

"He's okay. We butt heads a lot," I said, and again turned to go.

He didn't let go of my hand. "Hold up! Where are you off to?"

I glanced at my watch. "Lunch?"

"Is that an invitation?"

I shrugged, pretending to play hard to get. Ha! That ship had sailed soon after I met Brad.

He grabbed his black leather jacket. "My treat," he said. "Where to?"

"*Hmm*. I know just the place," I replied mysteriously. "The food is good, it's all you can eat, and it's free. Plus we can walk there."

Brad eyed me suspiciously. "Are we going fishing off the pier? 'Cause I'm a kind of catch-and-release guy."

I smiled and led him out of his office. "That's because no one's ever used the right bait before."

"Lucas?" I said into my iPhone as we stood outside the CeeGee Studio doors on Treasure Island. I knew he was in because his yellow Porsche was parked in the NEVER, EVER PARK HERE slot. He'd answered on the fourth ring with a curt, "Yeah?"

Looking completely baffled as to why I'd brought him here when I mentioned lunch, Brad listened to my side of the conversation with Cruz.

"Presley," Cruz said. "I heard about that scumbag Bodie. Can't say I'm sorry he's gone, but what a way to go—ending up in an open grave. You heard who dunnit yet?"

"Actually, I wanted to talk to you, Lucas. I'm right outside the studio. I thought I'd pick up my check. Got a few vendors who want to be paid. Will you let me in?"

I heard him call to his assistant, Susan, to open the door. "See you in a few," he said, and hung up.

Moments later, the metal door opened and we were greeted by Susan, who wore jeans, a long-sleeved "Vampires Do It Forever" T-shirt, and her perpetual look of anguish. I wondered what it was like working for this creative genius.

Then again, I didn't really want to know.

"He's in his office," Susan said, letting us in. She pointed, but I knew the way. Sniffing the air, I turned to Brad and said, "Pizza!" Then I led him over, under, and through pieces of stage equipment—ladders, cameras, dollies, golf carts, cords the size of pythons. I felt as if I were on an obstacle course.

When we reached the catering table just outside Lucas's office, I stopped, waved my hands as if I'd just magically produced the bounty, and said, "Ta-da!" Two beefy guys in jeans and T-shirts were helping themselves to slices of meat-laden pizza, completely ignoring the huge bowl of Caesar salad and platter of cut-up veggies. I had a feeling nothing green ever touched those plates. I recognized the caterer's logo— Pizza Hacker. They were famous for their gourmet pizzas and door-to-door service.

"Help yourself," I said, nodding toward the paper plates. "I want to talk to Cruz a few minutes, but I'll join you when I'm finished. Save me a slice of the Margherita. But be sure to try the Crowd Pleaser. The fig-and-caramelized onions are to die for."

Brad just shook his head in disbelief. "This is our lunch date?"

"Sure. As promised—good food, all you can eat, and free."

"So, you come here often?"

"Only on pizza day. Raj lets me know when Pizza Hacker is catering; then he lets me sneak in."

I left Brad—speechless, but hopefully hungry—standing at the buffet table, and headed over to Cruz's office. I knocked.

"Enter!" came the voice on the other side.

Cruz was at his desk, talking on his cell phone and gesturing dramatically as he spoke. He was a talk-with-his-hands kind of guy, and wouldn't be able to stop himself even if locked in irons. I wondered if most film directors were like that.

I glanced around the familiar office as I waited for him to end his heated conversation, shamelessly eavesdropping on his side—"I don't know how he found out about it! . . . I had nothing to do with that! . . . I'm sorry too, but he had no business being at the party!"

It wasn't hard to figure out that he was talking about the renegade paparazzo killed last night. News like that can spread faster than an Internet virus on this tiny island.

I pretended not to listen and studied the walls of Lucas's office, scanning posters of his films, including *Return to Alcatraz* (with Seth Green), *The Haunting of the Painted Ladies* (Robin Williams in a cameo role), and *Earthquake in the Hood* (starring a bunch of rappers who become heroes after an earthquake takes down the City).

Dozens of awards lined the top of a wooden bookshelf crammed with books about Ray Harryhausen, Manga, and "steampunk," which Cruz explained was a subgenre of science fiction where technology of the future is mixed with technology of the past.

Zing, I'd gestured, shooting my hand over my head.

"Think of H. G. Wells and Jules Verne as cyberpunks," he'd added, which helped a little.

When Cruz finally hung up the phone, he seemed to have forgotten about me. He stared down at his desk, as if looking for the answer to an unasked question.

"Lucas?" I said, bringing him back to the moment.

"Sorry, Presley. This whole dead paparazzo thing is cluttering my mind. Where were we? Oh yes. You want to be paid."

He pressed a button on his desk phone and said, "Kay? Do you have Presley's check ready?"

"Yes," the voice on the speakerphone squawked in response.

"Would you bring it to my office? She's here now." He clicked off.

"Thanks, Lucas. I hope you were . . . satisfied with the event."

"Aside from bookend deaths, it was great. Actually, the publicity can't hurt either, as long as that Gossip Guy does a decent job reporting about the film. The local news is supposed to show video from the wrap party tonight, then interview me on the set afterward. Which reminds me, I gotta get some film clips ready."

There was a knock at the door. Cruz called out, "Come in!" An older, heavyset woman entered, holding an envelope. "Here you go," she said, handing it to her boss. She smiled at me and backed out of the office, closing the door behind her.

Cruz passed the envelope to me without checking it. "Thanks again, Presley." He stood up to leave.

I followed suit, then added, "Lucas, do you have any idea who might have killed that paparazzo?"

His usually animated face went blank, like an actor on cue.

"No idea," he said, meeting my eyes and forcing a smile. "As I said, I'm not sorry he's dead. He was a scumbag and a leech, digging into other people's business for a buck. If he fell into an open grave on my watch, I wouldn't pull him out, that's for sure."

"What about Duncan's friend, Spidey? Any idea what might have happened to him?"

Lucas blinked several times, a very different reaction than the one to my previous question. What was behind those blinks?

"He fell, didn't he? That was what I heard."

I didn't want to give away too much information, so I said, "Possibly. Although it's also possible he was hit on the head first and fell."

He stood quietly for a moment. "Murder?"

I shrugged, watching his body language as he

dropped back into his seat. It was almost as if his legs had given out from under him.

"Are you all right, Lucas?" I said, genuinely concerned.

"He . . . that kid . . . he threatened me," Lucas mumbled, "when he found out he and his friends weren't invited to the wrap party."

Whoa, I thought. "What did he say?"

"He said he'd tell the tabloids something . . . something that would ruin the film."

"Like what? Did he know something?"

"No! Nothing! I told him to go— Well, I told him to get lost. There was nothing that little punk could do to hurt my movie."

Thinking aloud, I said, "So you'd been threatened by Spidey . . . and Bodie . . . before the party . . . and now they're both dead."

Lucas looked at me, the color draining from his face. "Oh God, Presley. The police are going to think I killed those two guys."

"Did you get me some pizza?" I asked Brad as we left the building.

He opened a grease-stained paper sack and showed me my lunch. As we walked back to Building One, I filled him in on my visit with Cruz between cheesy bites—that both Spidey and Bodie had threatened him.

"Any news from Melvin?" I asked, then took another bite of pizza.

"As a matter of fact, he called while you were with Cruz."

My mouth was full, so I let my raised eyebrows ask, *What's up?*

"Otto's been released."

I swallowed, nearly choking. "Really?"

"Not enough evidence to hold him yet. All circumstantial at this point."

"Wow. Even though his fingerprints were on the shovel?"

"It was his shovel. There are apt to be a bunch of his prints on it."

I sighed, feeling a mixture of relief and confusion. "Do you think he's innocent?"

"Let's just say I don't think he murdered those two guys. But with his being in the cemetery all the time, I think he saw something. I'm just not sure we'll get it out of him, with his rattled brain."

I nodded. "Any evidence of defense wounds? Anything on the DNA test?"

"No defensive wounds on his arms. And Luke's pushing the DNA test. Said they should have the results later today or tomorrow. They used outside testers—and have, ever since the lab was involved in that drug scandal last year."

"What scandal?"

"One of the technicians skimmed the cocaine evidence."

"Jeez. You can't even trust your own staff in your own police department."

"SFPD is a corporation just like any other business. Mostly good guys, with the occasional bad apple." We headed up the steps of Building One. "The DNA lab wasn't involved, but it was so backlogged, they started using outside labs. They usually get faster results—three to five days rather than weeks. Forty-eight hours if it's pushed. And believe it or not, it's cheaper."

"Let me know as soon as you find out, okay?" I said as we approached my office. The place seemed deserted, and I heard the footfalls of my Mary Janes echo through the cavernous lobby. "I'd like to let Duncan know we're working on this as fast as possible, so he doesn't take matters into his own hands."

When we reached the door to my office, Brad pulled me close and gave me a pizza-flavored kiss. I pushed him back and glanced around. The place was empty, aside from the security guard at the front desk, who was reading a magazine.

"What?" he said. "What's wrong with a little affection between two people?"

I felt myself blush. "Not here," I whispered.

"Why not?" He pulled me in again and held me around the waist.

"Because. It's not professional. And everyone will know."

"You think they don't know already?" He grinned. "And so what if they do?"

I let him kiss me again, then twisted out of his grip and unlocked my office door.

"See you tonight?" he said as I entered.

"Can we eat in, at my place?" I asked. "Lucas is going to be on the local news tonight. And I'm hoping Killer Parties might be mentioned."

"Sounds good. I'll bring dinner. Not pizza. Maybe popcorn for dessert."

I reached for his arm as he started to back away toward his office. I pulled him inside, closed my office door, and kissed the surprise off his face.

Chapter 11

PARTY-PLANNING TIP #11

When composing your guest list, make sure your invitees are compatible. For example, if you're hosting a Vampire Party, you may not want to include serious wolfman or zombie fans. Otherwise you may have a nasty gang fight on your hands.

I went home early to avoid the distractions of work and found myself amid the distractions of murder. My background in abnormal psychology had made me hyperaware of people's quirky traits and how close so many "normal" characteristics bordered on abnormal.

While most people are temporarily distracted by a police siren or a call from a child, few completely forget what they're doing. Likewise, most people tend to line up plates in the dishwasher or make the beds just so, but only a handful require the therapy needed to stop obsessive-compulsive excessive hand-washing. And while there are many people who believe that cute guy or girl over there is giving them the eye, most don't become paranoid and think they're being stalked.

It was a fine line we walked along that continuum between normalcy and mental illness. My ADHD is just this side of profound, so with a little help I can function well in society. In fact, sometimes ADHD gives me an edge. I can multitask, accomplish things quickly and efficiently, and I pick up subtleties that others miss. I don't have a mental illness; I have a disorder.

When I had taught my abnormal psychology class about an illness or disorder, I had listed the patient's characteristics to show my students the overall picture. Then I had tackled each trait individually. I did much the same thing for a party—listing all the details in order to create a plan, then addressing each point. Just like the diagnostic tools used in psychology, the *Killer Party-Planning Guide* I'd created for upcoming events worked well in other applications as well—like solving a crime. So, after feeding my cats and changing into shredded jeans and the "How to Survive a Vampire Party" T-shirt Cruz had given me, I whipped out my party-planning pad and sat down on the couch with a glass of merlot.

Starting at the top, I worked my way down through the checklist, first filling in information about the party, then adding what I knew about the two murders.

Theme: Vampire Wrap Party
Location: Lawndale Cemetery

Host: Lucas Cruz, producer, CeeGee Studios
Date/Time: October 22, seven p.m. to midnight

Under the Guest List category, I put down the names Lucas Cruz had given me, including the major actors on the film, Angelica Brayden and Jonas Jones, some of the crew, a few people in the film industry, and Ryan Fitzpatrick from *Gossip Guy*. Below the guest list, I inserted two subcategories, Victims and Suspects.

Victims:

1. Spidey, October 21 (night before the party), sometime after midnight.
2. Bodie Chase, October 22/23, night of the party, during or after the event?

Under those two entries I added the following:

Suspects/Motives:

Suspects. *Hmm.* Well, certainly all the guests at the party. But if I had to single out a few who might have had a motive . . .

Lucas Cruz?

- He'd omitted Spidey from the guest list, and Spidey later tried to interrupt the party setup with his friends, Trace and Lark. Maybe Spidey came back and threatened him, and Lucas then killed him.
- He'd argued with Bodie and told him to leave

the party, saying he had a restraining order. Maybe Bodie had threatened him. . . .

- His movie would no doubt benefit from the scandal—but that was hardly a reason to commit murder.
- Was there something going on between Angelica and Lucas? Jealousy over other men? The need to protect her from the big bad world?

But I knew Lucas Cruz, and he just didn't seem the type to kill anyone. He channeled his anger by yelling at his staff and staging violent scenes in his movies.

Otto Gunther?
- The old man tried to run everyone off "his property," including the parkour guys and the movie people.
- He had the murder weapon—the shovel.
- He had some kind of mental illness or deficiency, probably alcohol-related.
- Yeah, but did he have the strength to knock down two guys, one physically fit and the other just plain big? And was he coherent enough to carry out the murders?

I liked him better as a witness than as a suspect, albeit an unreliable witness.

So who else? If I wanted any kind of comprehensive and viable list, I had to start brainstorming all possibilities. Such as:

Trace and/or Lark?
- Motive for killing their friend? No clue.

Jonas and/or Angelica?
- Maybe they were afraid Spidey, as well as the paparazzo, saw them together and would expose their secret relationship?

Angelica's husband—what was his name?
- He had a motive to kill Jonas for fooling around on his wife, but why Spidey and Bodie? What was their connection to him?

Someone out to get Lucas? Frame him for murder?
- A competitor? Spidey or Bodie for revenge?

Someone trying to frame Otto?
- Otto saw something he shouldn't have and needed to be eliminated?

Ryan Fitzpatrick from *Gossip Guy*?
- He wanted to knock off the competition and killed Bodie? But why Spidey?

Someone else with some kind of secret agenda?

A random serial killer?
- My brainstorming was turning into a tornado, going around and around at random. The only person I'd left out was the butler.

I set down my pen and pad and finished my wine. It was nearly five forty-five—definitely time for a break and nearly time for the evening news. I poured another glass and one for Brad, expecting him to arrive any minute with dinner. We'd eat while we watched *Gossip Guy*'s interview with Lucas—and hopefully a nice mention of Killer Parties.

A knock at the door. Perfect timing. I paused when memories of answering a door too quickly rushed in, and called, "Who's there?"

"Big Bad Wolf," Brad said, trying to sound gruff. It gave me a tingle.

I let in the Big Bad Wolf. He held two foil bags of fragrant food. "What are we having? Pork?" I asked, thinking of the Three Little Pigs.

"Close. Ribs," he announced, and handed me a bag. "Too big a clue, *huh*?"

"They smell wonderful. And I'm as hungry as a wolf." I carried one bag to the table while Brad brought the other. I had already set our places, along with the glasses of wine, mine half-gone already.

"Where'd you get the ribs?" I asked as we sat down and ripped open the bags. Before me was a feast fit for half a dozen hungry wolves. Not only ribs, but coleslaw, baked beans, corn bread, and honey. I almost visibly drooled.

"Everett and Jones."

"You went to Berkeley to get these?" I nearly shrieked.

"Wouldn't go anywhere else."

The place was a hole-in-the-wall in the East Bay city, mostly takeout, but it was also a gold mine, and when you ordered, you got a choice of three temperatures—mild, medium, and Watch Out! Hot! I'm a chicken when it comes to hot sauce, so I always stick with mild. But Brad had brought all three, and he generously spread the WOH on his own ribs. After his first messy bite, I thought I saw his eyes watering. Tough guy.

We didn't talk for the first five or ten minutes. Instead we made *Mmm* and *Ohhh* noises. I worried the neighbors would think we were having sex, but I frankly didn't care. In fact, I was halfway through the meal when I remembered Cruz was being interviewed on TV. I wiped my hands with a paper towel, grabbed the remote, and turned up the volume on the news channel.

"I hope we didn't miss it," I said, turning my chair toward the TV screen.

"I had my eye on it. Nothing yet."

While I waited for the *Gossip Guy* theme song to start up, I resumed my love affair with the food. By the time we finished everything, there was still no sign of Lucas Cruz or mention of my Killer Party event. We washed up during a commercial and snuggled on the couch with our wine.

While the news announcer did a story on the gentrification of the Tenderloin area of the City, I turned down the volume and asked Brad, "Want to see what I've been working on?"

He took the pad from me and glanced at it. "These are your suspects?"

"So far. Did I forget anyone?"

He shook his head, grinning at my attempt to solve the case on paper. "I'm surprised you didn't write down 'double-suicide' or 'an act of God.'"

"Very funny," I said, snatching it out of his hands. "I'm trying to figure this out for Duncan."

I picked up my pen and went to work on the next item on the list.

Venue (aka Crime Scene):
• Lawndale Cemetery in Colma

I noted the two locations, one among the gravestones where Spidey was found, and the other in a freshly dug grave near the pet cemetery where we'd discovered Bodie. Brad had taught me early on to study the crime scene because it had a story to tell, but I couldn't make sense of either spot. One seemed random; the other deliberate. Meanwhile, Brad was no help, busy watching the sports news segment on TV. I moved on to the next item and filled it in with what I knew.

Decorations (aka Weapons, Clues, Physical Evidence):
• A shovel with blood from both the victims . . . (needs to be confirmed by DNA test)
• Otto's fingerprints on the shovel

- Blood spatter on headstone near Spidey

That was all I had at the moment. I needed more physical evidence. Moving on.

Party Activities (aka What Happened):
- Two people were murdered.
- The first, before the party (possibly murdered).
- The second, after the party (definitely murdered).

So, what did they have in common—besides both deaths having occurred in the cemetery? No idea—yet.

Refreshments (aka Drugs? Alcohol? Poison?):
- Nothing so far.

Favors/Mementos (aka Photos, Videos):
- View Berk's video footage of the party.
- Check the Gossip Guy's photos, videos.

Brad nudged me, and the tip of my pen shot off the side of the pad.

"What?" I said, irritated at the interruption. If he wouldn't help me, he could at least not bother me while I tried to figure it out for myself.

"The segment," he said in a hushed tone. "It's coming up."

I sat up, excited about seeing bits of my party on TV. I wondered if the segment was national. That would really give Killer Parties the publicity I'd dreamed of.

The newscaster waited until the brief lead-in finished, then began her spiel. At the same time, a picture of Bodie Chase filled the screen.

"In developing news, police are investigating another mysterious death at the Lawndale Cemetery that occurred late last night. This time, the police are calling it murder. Bodie Chase, thirty-five, was found dead inside a freshly dug grave, his skull fractured by what police believe was a shovel belonging to a man claiming to be the cemetery manager and custodian. It was the second death at the cemetery in about a twenty-four-hour period.

"Early this morning we reported the death of Samuel Valdez, also known as Spidey, who police believe died from a fall the previous night. He'd been engaging in the popular underground sport of parkour, which involves gymnastic-type movements such as jumping, climbing, and running over objects in public places. But San Francisco Police Department Detective Luke Melvin said they now regard the death as suspicious, in light of this new development.

"Our reporter interviewed one of the party attendees, Mayor Davin Green, who said, 'While I was invited to attend the party, hosted by Lucas Cruz and Killer Parties to celebrate his new vampire film . . .'"

I flashed a quick grin at Brad.

"I questioned the good taste of holding the event on consecrated grounds, and ultimately left the party early, so I can't add anything further."

I felt my face flush with anger at the mayor's words.

"He should talk—the hypocrite! Has he forgotten his 'surprise' wedding on Alcatraz, with a ball and chain theme, of all things. Doesn't he know that other cultures have regular parties at grave sites?"

"Calm down," Brad said. "I want to hear the rest."

The reporter continued. *"We'll have an in-depth interview with CeeGee producer, Lucas Cruz, up next, so stay tuned for* Gossip Guy."

I leaped up from the couch, furious at the way the event had been portrayed and the fact that Killer Parties had been mentioned in such a negative light. My three cats scattered, frightened at their mistress's sudden temper. "What a crock! This is horrible!"

"Hey, they say bad publicity is better than no publicity," Brad said.

I glared at him, livid. "No, it isn't. Bad publicity is bad publicity! That newscaster practically implied that Killer Parties was responsible for two murders!"

"You're overreacting. She didn't imply anything—except maybe bad taste. Which wasn't your fault. Other than that, she was just reporting the facts."

"The facts according to the mayor, which aren't, in fact, facts. They're part of some political agenda. Jeez! I could kill him!"

"Better watch what you say. Words like that could get you into trouble."

I chugged the rest of my wine, refilled the glass, paced the room for a few minutes, ran out of steam, and sat down again.

Brad turned off the TV.

I turned to him in shock. "What did you do that for?"

"*Uh*, it seemed to be upsetting you."

"Please turn it back on. I want to hear the *Gossip Guy* segment." I knew he was trying to help, but I had to hear the rest.

He shrugged and switched it back on.

I sighed and said, "Bring it on, Gossip Guy," to the TV. My expectations had been too high, hoping Killer Parties got some free publicity, and the actual report crushed me. But I needed to hear the rest. Brad put an arm around me, and I took a deep breath as the *Gossip Guy* theme music played against a background of Hollywood-style flashing lights.

The glitz faded and the face of the man I'd met last night, Ryan Fitzpatrick, appeared. Wearing a suit and tie, he was sitting at a desk and grinning as if he'd been found not guilty of a heinous crime.

After a brief introduction, the camera pulled back, revealing Lucas Cruz at the desk next to Ryan. He looked like he always did—jeans and a CeeGee T-shirt—but he'd thrown a corduroy blazer over his shirt and combed his thinning hair. Under the harsh lights, he looked older, and his eyes darted around, as if he were nervous, sitting in front of the camera for a change. It was painful to watch him fidget with his thumbnail as he listened to Ryan's practiced speech.

"Welcome, Lucas Cruz. Thanks for joining us on *Gossip Guy* tonight. Let's get right to it. You hosted a party last night that didn't quite go the way you expected, correct?"

"Actually," Lucas said, looking down at his thumbnail and avoiding Ryan's eyes, "Presley Parker from Killer Parties planned the event. I hired her to help me celebrate the wrap of my new film, *Revenge of the Killer Vampires*, starring those two hot young stars, Jonas Jones and Angelica Brayden. . . ."

"Could he be any more commercial?" I said to Brad. He shushed me.

"But yes," Cruz continued, "we did have a mishap occur after the event was over. Nothing to do with the party, of course."

"A mishap, you call it?" Ryan said, smirking. "The police are calling it a murder—"

"Oh! Well, I don't know anything about that," Lucas said quickly. "As I said, that happened after the party was over—"

"The body was discovered then," Ryan said, interrupting Lucas's interruption, "but it *could* have happened during the party, don't you agree? And in fact, he was *murdered* only a few feet away from where everyone had been enjoying themselves at your event, correct? And, furthermore, you *knew* the victim, isn't that right?" Ryan punched his words with verbal italics.

The color drained from Cruz's face when he realized he was being ambushed, not interviewed. He squirmed in his chair and looked off the set, as if searching for someone to rescue him.

"I—I didn't really know the guy. He was a paparazzo—"

"He was a *reporter* for TMI," came another interruption. "Isn't that correct?"

"Yes, but he hadn't been invited—"

"As a matter of fact, you had him *run off* the property when he showed up unexpectedly, isn't that correct?"

Lucas adjusted his blazer. I could see beads of sweat on his forehead. "It was a private party."

"Let's show some *footage* from the event, shall we?" Ryan, hardly the bumbling reporter he'd appeared to be the previous night, had transformed into a hotshot host full of confidence and smooth talk. He turned to a nearby screen.

There it was, in living color. The camera had caught the ugly argument between Lucas Cruz and Bodie Chase on camera. Cruz stood there calling him names, shoving him, looking ready to punch out his lights.

"Wow!" Ryan said as the clip ended. "You didn't look happy at *all*, did you, Lucas? But wait. We have *more*."

He nodded to the nearby screen again. This time it featured a scene from the visit by the costumed traceurs as they invaded the perimeters of the party. And once again, Cruz was caught on tape threatening them off the property, like some old farmer scaring crows away from his crops.

The screen went black and the camera returned to Ryan and Cruz. If this had been a boxing match, Cruz would have been on the ground with Ryan standing over him, arms up in victory. "Two men are dead, Lucas Cruz. The young man who belonged to a group of extreme athletes and who had the misfortune of enjoying the sport the night before your party. And the reporter from TMI who was just doing his job—like me—and trying to get some footage of the event. What do you say to *that*?"

What Cruz said was bleeped out. I couldn't read his lips because the techs had blurred his mouth using three-second time delay. He yanked off the lapel mic, threw it at Ryan Fitzpatrick, and stomped off the set.

While Cruz had exploded like a volcano, Ryan seemed completely unruffled. I had a feeling the Gossip Guy was used to having his guests throw things at him and walk off the set.

Unfortunately for Cruz, the whole Bay Area—and probably the whole nation—had just watched him lose his cool and attack his interviewer.

Would the police see him as being capable of murder?

Chapter 12

PARTY-PLANNING TIP #12

One of the best ways to liven up a dying party is to videotape the guests. Then play the tape back as entertainment. For example, if you're hosting a Vampire Party, record the guests dancing to "Thriller," acting out scenes from Twilight, or biting one another's necks. That should provide some much-needed laughs.

"Did you see that?" Brad said, sitting up.

"Yeah, pretty childish, stomping off like that."

"No, not that. Back it up."

I looked at him blankly.

"You recorded it, right?"

I shook my head. "I didn't think to. . . ."

Brad grabbed up the remote and pushed RECORD.

"It's too late, isn't it? Why are you recording now?"

"If your DVR works like mine, it'll record from the beginning of the show, as long as you haven't switched channels." He stopped the recording and pushed PLAY. The beginning of the news show appeared. He fast-forwarded until he reached the segment with Gossip Guy and Lucas, then pushed PLAY.

"We've already seen this," I said, not ready to witness the public humiliation of Killer Parties again.

"Just watch."

I took a sip of wine, sat back, and watched the screen, up to the point where Lucas appeared, schmoozing with the party attendees. At that point, Brad suddenly paused the recording.

"Look." He pointed to the right side of the screen.

All I saw was Lucas Cruz chatting up the guests, followed by the invasion of the parkour guys. It was interesting to see his look of pleasure turn to disbelief and finally horror as he realized his party was being crashed.

"Been there. Seen that," I said.

Brad rewound the part and played it again, freezing it once more at the same point. This time he got up from the couch and pointed at something in the upper right-hand corner.

"Oh my God. It's Jonas and Angelica," I said. The couple stood close together in the background, away from the party. From their frowns, they appeared to be having an argument. They didn't seem to know they were being videotaped.

"Look there." Brad touched the screen. A shadow lurked behind a tree just to the left of the pair, seeming to observe them while keeping out of sight.

I squinted at the image, then turned to Brad. "Who is that? Do you think it's her stalker?"

Brad shook his head. "I'm guessing it's her husband-slash-bodyguard, but I can't tell for sure. I'll call Luke and see if their forensics department can enhance the image."

A thought occurred to me. "Hey, maybe her husband *is* her stalker," I said, excited about possibly solving one part of the mystery so quickly.

Brad grinned at my impulsiveness, but I liked things resolved. Unanswered questions and loose ends nagged at me like a hangnail, and I picked at them until I had answers, even if sometimes those answers weren't quite accurate.

We watched the recording a few more times until I imagined everyone at the party to be the lurker behind the tree, including Brad. That meant it was time to call it a night.

"You want to stay over?" I asked Brad, cuddling up to him after switching off the TV. I was exhausted from thinking.

"I don't know. What's in it for me?"

I giggled—I couldn't help myself. "A bed full of cats and breakfast in the morning."

"Thank goodness I took my allergy pills before I came over," he said, smoothing my hair.

"They're for the cats, right? You're not allergic to me, are you?"

"Not yet. But I may need a Zantac before you make breakfast."

I hit him with a couch pillow and ran down the hall, screeching like the victim in a horror movie as he chased me into the bedroom.

I woke up early the next morning, eager to talk to Jonas after seeing the video on *Gossip Guy* the previous night. Maybe he could tell me more about some of the "behind-the-scenes" drama. Brad left after making us an omelet to die for—eggs, sour cream, baked beans, and a little mild barbecue sauce, all leftovers from my fridge. He'd gotten a call from SFPD about a cleanup at an eldercare home—a suicide—and dashed off after giving me a quick kiss and a nether pat.

His latest assignment made me think of my mother. I wondered if she ever got depressed at her care center.

It was time for a visit.

Better yet, an outing, or an "adventure," as she liked to call it. There was no reason why she couldn't come with me as I "interrogated" Jonas—especially since it would be broad daylight. I enjoyed her company, and she visibly benefited from getting away from the "old folks," as she called them. I punched her number, asked her if she wanted to meet a handsome movie star up close and personal, and told her I'd pick her up in an hour.

The care center just off Van Ness Avenue and around the corner from Tommy's Joynt was one of the best in the City—and, of course, one of the most expensive. But I couldn't envision my ex-socialite mother spending her remaining years in a discount facility where the indigent elderly or disabled ended up. Good thing I was making enough money to provide her with her own room in a nice hotel-like facility, with supervised in-and-out privileges and days filled with stimulating activities beyond basket weaving and TV watching.

When I arrived, I found Mother in the craft room, engaged in her favorite activity—scrapbooking. She was dressed in classic, vintage San Francisco clothes—a red St. John knit suit, matching heels, and a hat with netting, which she'd scrunched up to reveal her still-beautiful face. Her makeup was expertly done, albeit a little heavy on the rouge, but referencing her old high school and party photographs, she'd maintained that style through the years. Now, with Alzheimer's, she seemed to have mentally and physically returned to those heydays of flamboyant events, society fund-raisers, and gala gallery openings. The only things missing today were her white gloves. I had a feeling they were tucked safely in her red leather handbag.

"Hi, Mom," I said as I strode over to the table where she was crafting with another older woman. Photographs of herself at various functions were strewn about, along with colorful sheets of paper, scissors, glue, tape, and other scrapbooking implements. She'd tried several times to get me interested in the hobby, but I was too busy working on my business to spend the time assembling old memories. Besides, I didn't have that many memories yet. My mother, on the other hand, had a lifetime's supply. And one day I'd be grateful to inherit her scrapbooks.

"Presley, darling! What are you doing here?"

I gave her a quick hug. "I came to pick you up for an adventure, remember?"

She frowned and blinked several times, then broke out into a smile. "Of course. I was just so wrapped up in all of this, I nearly forgot!" She swept her hand over the papers in front of her, then turned to the other woman at the table. "Oh, darling. This is Helen. She's new at the hotel, and I'm introducing her to all the wonderful things we do here."

Mother called her facility a hotel, and I didn't see any reason to correct her. I reached out a hand. "Nice to meet you, Helen."

Helen mumbled something as she offered me a weak hand before returning to her task—cutting red paper into little hearts. Mother closed up the album she'd been working on. "Well, I must be off now, Helen. I'm going on an adventure with my daughter, Presley." She placed her album in a small cubby that had her name on it, retrieved her red wool coat with the real mink collar, and followed me to the front desk.

Once we were signed out and in my MINI Cooper, she asked where we were going. I reminded her about our planned visit to see a movie star or two.

"How exciting! Who are we going to see? I knew a lot of stars in my day, you know. Everyone from Hollywood came to San Francisco for my parties. Gary Cooper. Bette Davis. I was hired to host a fund-raiser for Shirley Temple's political campaign. . . ." She grew silent, lost in memories—or trying to bring some back.

"Today we're going to see the star from the party the other night—Jonas Jones. And maybe Angelica Brayden too. Do you remember them? They're staying at the Mark Hopkins, your old stomping grounds."

"I don't believe I know them. What picture were they in?"

"Revenge of the Killer Vampires, but it hasn't been released yet. We saw them do a scene from the film at the party, remember? I have a feeling they're going to be major stars."

Mother spent the short drive up steep California Street to the famous Mark Hopkins Hotel reminiscing about the many stars who had attended her parties. She hinted she'd had affairs with a couple of them but declined to be specific. I didn't doubt her for a minute. My mother had married five times—she was a serial monogamist—but that didn't mean there had been only five men in her bedroom. And I'd had five fathers. How many kids could say that?

Driving over trolley tracks and slaloming between cable cars, we passed Grant Avenue and Chinatown, the Twins—Vivian and Marian Brown—Armoire Boutique where my mother often shopped, and the exclusive and practically unmarked men's club, the Pacific-Union. I pulled into the brick driveway of the hotel, at the top of Nob Hill. A valet took the car, and a uniformed doorman held open the heavy door as we headed inside.

The cozy lobby was filled with guests, most occupying the plush couches and chairs under the crystal chandeliers. The luxury hotel had seen as much sensational history as a soap opera. I'd heard the stories from my mother each time we went to the Top of the Mark for a special occasion.

"Mark Hopkins was one of the Big Four, the founders of the Central Pacific Railroad, you know," Mother said, forgetting she'd told me this story a number of times before. "He built his wife, Mary, a forty-room, Gothic-style dream home, but he died before it was completed. After she inherited the property, she promptly married Edward Searles, thirty years her junior. When she died at seventy-three, in 1891, she left her seventy-million-dollar estate to her second husband. . . ."

I half listened as I headed for the elevators on the left. I led Mother into one of two elevator cars that went to the Top of the Mark, and pushed the T button for the nineteenth floor.

"Edward eventually donated the estate to the Art Institute"—Mother continued her lecture as we rode up—"but it was destroyed in the fire, after the 1906 earthquake. A mining engineer named George Smith bought the site, and, in 1926, he built this nineteen-story French château with Spanish ornamentation, reminiscent of the wild Barbary Coast. . . ."

We stepped out of the elevator car and into the glass-walled restaurant and lounge, "the home of one hundred martinis." The panoramic views of the bridges, skylines, and Alcatraz held me hypnotized for a few moments. I wondered what it would be like to spend the night in such an opulent place, then remembered the room rates started at four hundred dollars.

"Where are they?" my mother said, interrupting her lecture.

"Who?" I answered, then remembered why we were in such a stunning place. I glanced around for a handsome young man with pale skin, short black hair, and a body strong enough to handle cables and pulleys without injury. He was sitting at the small curved bar in the back, wearing aviator sunglasses and sipping gold liquid from a short glass.

When I'd called Jonas earlier, using the contact number on the guest list Cruz had given me, I was surprised to find he was still in town, staying at the Mark Hopkins. He'd said something about the police wanting to interview him again before he returned to Hollywood and about having some business to take care of before he left, so he agreed to meet with me when I mentioned I had some news about the paparazzo who'd been found dead.

Heading over, I held out my hand and greeted him.

He turned to me and smiled tightly. "Presley." He glanced at Mom, who'd followed me over, suddenly tongue-tied in the presence of this young and handsome movie star.

"This is my mother, Veronica Parker. Mom, this is Jonas Jones. You remember him from the party the other night?"

She blushed and held out her hand as if she expected him to kiss it. He shook it gently. "Nice to meet you, Ms. Parker. Shall we find a table?" He slid off the barstool and glanced around, then indicated a small black table in the corner, away from the half dozen other midday drinkers. It came with a view of the breathtaking Grace Cathedral below.

I sat down, but Mother remained standing, her cheeks pink. "Presley, dear, I'm going to freshen up. I'll be back in a tick."

"Oh. Okay, Mom. You know where the restroom is? Don't get lost."

"Don't worry, dear. I know my way around this place like the back of my hand. Will you order a Shirley Temple for me?"

As Mother headed for the restroom, Jonas sat down opposite me and took another swig of his drink, which I guessed was whiskey and something.

"So, what's this about the paparazzo?"

The cocktail waitress sidled up and asked what I wanted. "Two Shirley Temples," I said to her, then turned to Jonas after she left. "Did you watch the news last night?"

He glanced out at the view. "Yeah. Gossip Guy—what a jerk. It's as if he's trying to screw over Cruz and our movie."

"Yeah," I said, trying to sympathize with him and gain his trust. "But I noticed something else while I was watching. Something in the background of the footage they showed."

Jonas was a very good actor. His face remained blank, eyebrows raised in interest. But no amount of acting skill could hide the sudden rush of color to his face. "What did you see?" he said evenly.

"You."

He cleared his throat and took another sip. "I'm not surprised. After all, I was at the party."

"But you weren't actually *at* the party in this segment. You were in the background, several yards away, in the cemetery. The same place I'd seen you and Angelica together earlier."

He started to say something, then swallowed the rest of his drink in one gulp and signaled the waitress. "So? I'm sure we weren't doing anything, with all those people around. I doubt anyone saw us. And so what if they did."

"Well, if the police decide to study that video, they may see you together, and no doubt they will enlarge your images. And even at a distance, in the shadows, the looks on your faces were . . . well, odd." He squirmed in his seat.

"How?"

"From what I could tell, you were frowning at each other, as if you were having some kind of argument."

"So? That's not a crime, is it? Two artistic personalities don't always agree—"

"That's not all."

He waited, his face now a blotchy crimson. Tiny beads of sweat had broken out on his forehead. "What?"

"Someone was watching you."

"What do you mean? Who?"

Before I could answer, Jonas glanced at something behind me. This time he wasn't avoiding my eyes. He'd seen something, or someone, that had caught his attention. I turned and followed his gaze.

Angelica Brayden stood in the entry to the bar wearing black tights, a long red top that barely covered her butt, a plaid scarf around her neck, and red Ugg boots. Instead of wearing her long black vampire wig, she had her hair styled short, slinky, and blond. Free of makeup—and even at a distance—she looked as if she'd been crying. The moment she realized I'd spotted her, she spun around and bolted.

"I have to go," Jonas said, leaping up and causing the table to rock.

"Jonas, wait. I have to ask you—did you know the paparazzo who was killed last night, Bodie Chase?"

His hands were trembling. Was that fear? Nervousness? Concern for Angelica? Or did the alcohol have something to do with it?

"Of course I knew him. He'd been hounding Angelica and me since we first arrived in the City to shoot the film. But I have no idea who killed him or that other guy, if that's what you're asking. All I know is, Angelica's in some kind of trouble and I need to go to her. Now."

Mother, who had come up behind Jonas while he was talking, blinked several times as she watched him storm out of the bar.

"What was that all about, dear?" she said. "Did he make a pass at you? I know you. You can be very abrupt when discouraging men from getting close to you, but . . ." Mother rambled on, but I didn't hear the rest of her usual lecture about me and men.

I was too busy wondering why Jonas had overreacted, and what he meant by Angelica's being in trouble.

Chapter 13

PARTY-PLANNING TIP #13

If you need ideas for games and activities at your Vampire Party, here's a twist on an old favorite. Instead of "Pin the Tail on the Donkey," play "Jam the Stake into the Vampire's Heart." Set up a "body" using stuffed clothing, insert a balloon filled with red-tinted water under the shirt, and have guests try to pop the "heart."

"Come on, Mother! Hurry!"

I grabbed my mother's hand and pulled her to the elevators, hit the DOWN button at least nineteen times—there was no way we were climbing down nineteen floors—and got into the elevator car before anyone could get out.

"Sorry! In a big hurry!" I said by way of explanation when several men in suits glared at me on their way out. I pushed LOBBY a dozen times, then hit the CLOSE DOOR button, just as the doors were already closing.

"What is wrong with you, Presley?" Mother asked,

looking at me as if I'd just sprouted pointy vampire teeth right before her eyes. She reached over to feel my forehead—anything that was wrong with me had to be a fever, according to my mother—but I pulled back.

"Nothing, Mom. I don't want to lose Angelica Brayden. I want to talk to her and Jonas, and see if I can get to the bottom of this stalker business, and I may not get another chance. Come on!" I pulled her through the opening elevator doors, across the lobby, and out of the Mark Hopkins, not bothering to wait for the doorman. Glancing up and down the street, I caught a glimpse of Angelica's blond hair and red top. She had crossed the street and was mounting the stairs of Grace Cathedral, one block up. Oddly, Jonas was nowhere in sight.

"There she is!"

I led my mother to the crosswalk, looked both ways, and, ignoring the pedestrian light, darted between a cable car and a honking taxi to reach the other side. Dragging my poor mother behind me, I ran-walked up the four flights of steps to the famous old church. When we reached the top, I let Mom catch her breath while I looked around for Jonas, thinking he'd be right behind Angelica, but I saw no sign of him. Had he not followed her after all? Or had they arranged a rendezvous point?

I was about to turn around when I caught a glimpse of another man standing across the street. He seemed to be watching me. As soon as I spotted him, he knelt down and tied his shoe. Sensing something about him, I waited for him to stand up and continue walking. Instead, when he stood, he whirled around and headed back the way he'd come.

I hadn't seen his face, but with his dark skin, tall, lean body, and black pants and shirt, I was pretty sure it was "the shadow," as I had come to call Angelica's husband.

Maybe Jonas had spotted him too and decided to disappear.

I returned my attention to Mother and finding Angelica. As she entered the church, Mom pulled her veil down over her face and crossed herself. She'd been a Catholic for a while, when married to a man of that faith, and still used some of the rituals no matter what the church. Born a Methodist, she'd also been Jewish, Mormon, and Buddhist, and was currently looking into becoming a Wiccan. That woman had covered all her bases when it came to the hereafter—or wherever.

I followed her inside and paused. Each time I entered the French-Gothic cathedral, the majestic atmosphere took my breath away. Passing the reception-information desk, I gazed at the glowing stained glass panels, tall arched ceiling, and massive pipe organ. Mother went on autopilot and began her docentlike tour of the church, explaining its history and eccentricities once again.

"You know, dear," she began, in a hushed, reverential voice, "the first chapel they built here back in 1849 actually burned down in the 1906 earthquake, just like the Mark Hopkins. The Crocker family—Charles Crocker was one of the four railroad barons—donated the property for the cathedral. When they began work on it in 1928, it took another forty years to complete it. It's the third-largest Episcopal cathedral in America."

"I know, Mother," I whispered, hoping to cut her short. "You told me last time we were here."

Ignoring me, she continued. "Since then it's become an international pilgrimage destination for people from all over the world. A lot of them come to see the two labyrinths. Did you know they're authentic replicas of the ones discovered in France in the twelfth century?"

Of course I knew. She'd told me many times about the "authentic replicas." Truthfully, I was glad she'd brought me here when the first labyrinth was created, some twenty years ago. The first time I experienced it as a child, we'd gone in the evening when a musical group happened to be singing a song specifically written for walking the labyrinth. The whole night had been magical. Walking the thirty-six-and-a-half-foot-long, eleven-circuit design that wove back and forth like a circular puzzle had helped me harness my flighty attention and focus on whatever problem I needed to solve.

"Did you know the cathedral was featured in several films? Alfred Hitchcock filmed his last movie, *Family Plot*, here. Plus," she continued, counting off on her fingers as she listed other movies, "*Bicentennial Man* with Robin Williams, *Bullitt* with Steve McQueen, *Vertigo* with Jimmy Stewart, *The Wedding Planner* with Jennifer Lopez, and *Milk* with Sean Penn, to name a few."

Grace Cathedral was without a doubt impressive,

even without its Hollywood heritage. But I was not
there to gawk or listen to Mother's spiel. Time was a-
wasting. I took her hand and pulled her farther into
the chapel, where a handful of people sat, mostly sin-
gly, among the vast rows of pews that led to the stunning altar covered with a vividly embroidered cloth.

Mother sat down in one of the back pews, obviously
tired from my dragging her around. "Stay here, Mom.
I'll be right back," I said, and headed up one of the
aisles, looking for Angelica. With her bright blond hair
and colorful plaid scarf, she wasn't hard to spot.

I slowed when I reached her pew, not wanting to
scare her off, and slid into the same row, taking a seat
about four feet away from her. I hoped she might be
deep in prayer and not notice me initially.

She didn't, but it wasn't because she was praying.
She was rapidly texting on her cell phone.

I scooted over a few inches, trying to be subtle. No
reaction. I scooted a few more inches. Not until I was
practically up against her did she finally look up from
her rhinestone-studded phone. Her eyes flared; she
recognized me instantly. She stuffed her bling-covered
phone in her huge, multipocketed designer handbag,
preparing to flee. I touched her arm before she made a
move to slide out.

"Angelica, please. I need to talk to you."

I could see the fight-or-flight response in her bear-
ing; then it all seemed to leak away, leaving her shoulders slumped. "The crypt café," she whispered.

She slid out and I started to follow; then I glanced

back to check on Mother. She looked as if she'd fallen asleep in her pew. I hesitated, thinking she might wake up and panic when she didn't see me. But I wasn't about to lose Angelica. I had to take the chance Mom would still be there when I got back. Luckily when she dozed off, she slept long and deep.

I just hoped she didn't snore.

I turned back to look for Angelica. She was gone. I walked swiftly toward the church elevator, wanting to run but knowing it wasn't appropriate in a place like this. I stepped into the open elevator car with one of the Episcopal priests, who said, "Crypt?"

I nodded, smiling.

"Don't worry," he said. "We still call it that, but there aren't any more crypts down there. Just some meeting rooms, our gift shop, and a Peet's café."

I had a feeling he was asked about the term often. As soon as the doors opened, I followed the smell of strong coffee to the tiny café. Angelica was sitting at one of the three tables, staring at her coffee, as if she might want to dive in.

I sat down next to her. She looked up. Without makeup, she was still pretty, but there were bags under her eyes, her skin was sallow, and her eyes were red.

"What do you want?" Angelica asked, getting directly to the point.

I took a deep breath. Where to begin? "I'm trying to find out what happened to Spidey the night before the party, and to the paparazzo after the party. It's starting to look like Spidey didn't die as a result of a fall. He was probably killed. And the police think Bodie, the paparazzo, was hit in the head with a shovel. They found Spidey's blood on that same shovel. I think their deaths are connected. And I think you may know something about them."

She gave a big sigh, as if the weight of the world were on her slim shoulders. "I've been over this with the police, Presley. I told them and I'll tell you—I didn't really know Spidey. He was just an extra on the set. We flirted a little; that's it. Maybe he had a crush on me. It happens. And I've never met this Bodie guy, although I've seen him before. I have no idea why they were killed."

Her words said one thing, her hands another. She was rubbing the palm of one hand with the thumb of the other as if trying to rub out a spot or soothe a pain. Clearly she was anxious about something. She'd quickly passed over the fact that she and Spidey had "flirted a little." How much was a little? And what did it mean?

"Was Spidey—or Bodie Chase—stalking you?"

Her red-rimmed eyes flared again. I wondered if that was an acting technique.

"How did you know about my stalker?"

I had no particular loyalty to Jonas and said his name.

She closed her eyes. "Jonas."

"So it's possible one of them was the one sending you those notes and texts and calling your cell phone?"

"I don't know. Honestly. Yes, someone—I don't

know who—has been sending me . . . stuff. But it comes with the territory. Guys get crushes on actresses all the time."

"Do you have any of the messages on your phone?" I asked, hoping to see how threatening they really were.

She pulled out her cell phone, touched her text messages icon, scrolled through, then turned the cell phone toward me.

I took the phone and read the message: *No matter where you go or what you do, I'll find you and have you.* The message had been sent by someone using the name "Eternal."

I handed back the phone. "Have you tried to trace this?"

"Yes, I have a . . . friend who knows how to do that kind of thing."

"Has he learned anything?"

"Not yet." Angelica returned the phone to her purse.

"Jonas said you were worried."

She pressed her lips together. The hand-rubbing picked up again. "Not really."

Liar.

"You do know that sometimes these stalkers are dangerous, right?" I thought of a couple of actresses who'd been seriously accosted or even murdered by their stalkers.

"Yes, but I'm careful. And I have protection."

I looked around. "I don't see your . . . bodyguard."

She laughed. "Nobody's going to bother me in a church."

I looked at her.

"Except you, maybe," she added, then checked her watch as if she had an urgent meeting to attend. "Listen, Presley, I gotta go. I don't have anything else to tell you." She stood up, rearranged her scarf, and downed the last of her coffee before throwing it into a trash can.

"Angelica, this killer—whoever he or she is—may kill again. If there's anything you can tell me that would help . . ."

"I don't have anything! If anyone knows anything, it's Lucas Cruz. He's the one who hired the extras and then didn't invite them to the party. That was what started all this. And then he had that argument with the paparazzo. So why don't you ask him?"

I was surprised at the bitterness in her voice. Had something happened between Cruz and Angelica to cause her to imply that he had something to do with these deaths?

I tried one last question. "Angelica, I saw you in the cemetery with Jonas—"

She cut me off. "I know. I was there, remember?"

"No, I mean I saw you on the *Gossip Guy* segment last night on the news. You and Jonas were caught on tape, standing in the background. You both looked upset, as if you were having an argument."

Her sallow face reddened. "So? There's no crime in two actors passionately discussing their craft, is there? Now really, I have to go. Like I said, talk to Lucas if you have more questions. Just leave me out of it."

She started to walk away when I called out, "There was someone in the shadows, watching you."

She whirled around. "What are you talking about?"

"Brad and I noticed it last night while we were watching the show at my place. Someone was lurking behind a tree, as if spying on you. It couldn't have been Lucas. He was front and center in the video. Any idea who it was?"

She paused, then shook her head, but I thought I saw the light go off in her eyes, shrouded by fear. I had the distinct feeling she did know.

My guess? Her husband.

I panicked the moment I reentered the cathedral. Mother was not in her pew. I searched the area and asked a few people sitting in nearby rows if they'd seen her, but no one seemed to have noticed the elegantly dressed woman in red with the netted hat. She'd vanished.

I ran out of the front entrance and scanned the area from the top step, searching up and down the hilly street. No sign of her. Someone came up behind me. I turned around to face the priest who'd ridden in the elevator with me.

"Are you all right, miss?" he asked. Apparently I didn't look all right.

"My mother," I said between rapid, shallow breaths. "I've lost her!"

In a calm voice he probably used to address the congregation, he said, "What does she look like?"

I described my mother to him. He nodded solemnly.

"I know the woman you speak of. She comes here from time to time. I saw her walking the outdoor labyrinth just moments ago." He pointed to the right side of the church.

I let out a breath, shook the priest's hand, and thanked him profusely. I'm sure he thought I was an overly dependent mama's girl who needed to cut the cord. Following his point, I headed around the side to the courtyard where I found Mother walking the intricate path and mumbling to herself. As I approached, I heard her say, " 'Then, methought, the air grew denser, perfumed from an unseen censer. . . .' "

I took a shortcut through the winding path and stepped over to her, gaining some irritated looks from the other walkers. Apparently one didn't interrupt another's path.

"Mom! You scared me! I didn't know where you were."

"Oh, darling, I was here. Where else would I be?"

On a cable car headed for Fisherman's Wharf. In a cab traveling to the de Young Museum. In a bar flirting with a traveling salesman. God knew.

I took her hand. "We have to go now, Mom. I think we've had enough of an adventure for today. Let's go get a bite to eat at Tommy's Joynt. Then I'll get you back home."

"All right, dear, but I wasn't finished with my maze walk. You know, walking this path is sort of like solving a puzzle, like those crimes you sometimes try to solve. Only I didn't have a puzzle to solve, so I just re-cited 'The Raven' by Edgar Allan Poe:

> *Clasp a rare and radiant maiden, whom the angels*
> *   name Lenore?*
> *Quoth the raven, 'Nevermore.' "*

My mother was truly a rare and radiant maiden. She could recite poems she'd memorized as a child, something I could never do, yet not remember what she'd done yesterday. Alzheimer's is funny like that.

But she was right about one thing. We were both, in our own ways, entangled in a labyrinth—Mom in her memories and I in a mystery.

Chapter 14

PARTY-PLANNING TIP #14

Make your next Ladies' Night a Vampire Party with a romantic twist to celebrate a birthday girl, bachelorette, or bride-to-be. Fill the room with black and red balloons, scented candles, and posters of Edward and Jacob from the Twilight series. Then have a vampire stripper make a surprise appearance. . . .

After we finished our roast beef sandwiches at Tommy's Joynt, I dropped Mother off, making sure she got into her building safely. She said something about not wanting to be late for her bocce ball class, and I admired the way she stayed busy and physically fit. The variety of activities at the center was the primary reason I'd chosen it. My mother was a social woman and would have been bored silly if she'd come to live with me. At the center she was safe, happy, and still able to join me for "adventures," much like the ones she'd taken me on when I was a kid. Plus, she got to flirt with the men there.

It was nearly two p.m. by the time I got in my car.

Before pulling into the street—and to avoid getting a ticket for using my cell phone while driving—I called Duncan's number. As much as I hated those earpieces that everyone seemed to be wearing instead of earrings, I knew I'd have to get one someday.

"S'up, Presley?" Duncan answered. It still startled me when someone seemed to be clairvoyant and knew I was on the line. Caller ID had its advantages and disadvantages. You couldn't take anyone by surprise anymore.

"Hi, Duncan. How're you doing?"

"Okay. Any news?" He sounded tired.

"Not yet, but I'm working on it. I wondered if you could tell me where your friend Trace lives. I'd like to ask him a few questions about Spidey and his relationship with Angelica."

"He's not going to know anything, Presley. The police have already talked to him. He'd have said something to me if he knew what happened to Spidey. Besides, there was no 'relationship.' Maybe he liked her, but that's as far as it went."

"I know, but I'd still like to talk to him. Is that a problem?" I was sensing hesitancy on Duncan's end.

A pause, then he said, "No. Just don't bug him, okay? He's been through enough. We all have."

"I understand."

"He's at the Towers. You want his number?"

"No, I thought I'd drop by. He's staying at a hotel?"

"It's a dorm at San Francisco State. He's on the fourteenth floor—science and tech floor."

Of course. I should have recognized the name. "I didn't realize he was in college. You guys only mentioned your high school connection."

"Yeah, well, college wasn't for me or Spidey, but Trace wants to become an engineer or something. He's pretty smart. If he's not doing parkour after class, he's usually there at the dorm. Room 1404."

I took down the information, hung up the phone, pulled into traffic, and headed for the university, located near the upscale St. Francis Wood neighborhood on Nineteenth Avenue. A rush of classroom memories kept me occupied along the way, and I realized how much I missed teaching abnormal psychology at the university. For nearly eight years I'd taught three sections of the course, all filled with students eager to learn about the atypical development of a person. They were enthralled by the examples of bizarre behavior I shared. One of their favorites—the psychopathology of Unabomber Ted Kaczynski—kept them asking questions I couldn't always answer, such as how did Ted become a lonely, antisocial murderer while David, his brother, led a successful life as a married attorney who had the courage to turn in his own brother. And each time we discussed a disorder—anxiety, mood, personality disorders—my students were certain they had a form of it. Gotta love 'em.

Except for Lindsay Nicholson, whom I discovered was sleeping with my "boyfriend" at the time. Rob Michaels was a professor in the English department, and we'd been dating for several months when I found out he was cheating on me. She probably fell for him after he read her some of those romantic poems. It had certainly worked on me.

Not anymore.

I pulled up to the Tower lot and found visitor parking, realizing I also missed campus life. In my spare time I'd taken classes in everything from sailing in nearby Lake Merced to film studies. The university has one of the top film schools, with graduates such as Annette Bening, Dana Carvey, and Danny Glover. I'd eventually planned to get my doctorate in clinical psychology, after I got some of the fun classes out of the way, but due to the university downsizing its staff, that was now on hold.

I tried the front door of the building—locked, of course. Opening my purse, I got out my old faculty card and tried to run it through the electronic lock. Nothing. Trying not to act like a loiterer, I lingered at the door until a student finally came out, then grabbed it and slipped inside.

"Excuse me," a voice said. I glanced around and saw a young woman with short hair sitting behind a small reception desk.

"Oh, sorry. I didn't see you there," I said. *Uh-oh*. It was the RA, apparently making sure loiterers didn't try to sneak in through the front doors.

"Do you have ID?" she asked.

I stepped over, got out my wallet, and flashed my faculty card.

"It's from last year," she said, eyeing me.

I looked at it. "Oh, shoot! I must have left the new one in my office. I'm just here to meet with a student. . . ." I tried to appear innocent and hopeful.

"Okay, go ahead. But sign in."

I did. "Thanks," I said, then headed for the elevators.

Zooming by the floors on my way to the fourteenth, I remembered many of them had different themes, such as the science and technology floor where Trace was housed. The dorm rooms were apartment style, with two bedrooms, and two people in each.

I knocked on the door of room 1404 and was surprised when it was opened by Lark instead of Trace. Her dark hair was in a twist at the top of her head, and she was wearing clothes similar to the ones she'd worn doing parkour—baggy shorts and a T-shirt.

"Lark! What are you doing here?" I said, blurting out the first thing that came to mind.

She shrugged and said, "Hanging out. You're that lady from the party. What are you doing here?"

"May I come in? I need to speak to Trace."

She widened the door opening, allowing me to step inside the living area. I glanced around for Trace.

She seemed to read my mind. "He'll be out in a minute. Did he know you were coming?"

I spotted two closed bedroom doors and wondered which led to Trace's room. "*Uh*, no. I was in the area and thought I'd stop by."

"You wanna sit down?" Lark asked, apparently accepting my lame excuse, and plopped herself in a threadbare chair, apt for a college student's dorm room. The only other option was a couch strewn with books, papers, T-shirts, and a couple of beer cans. I opted to tour the living area while I waited, and I checked out the kitchenette that offered a microwave, fridge, and stove top, but no oven. I wondered if they cooked.

Stepping back into the living area, I scanned the walls, lined with posters. Most were of extreme sports figures, but the only one I recognized was skateboarder Tony Hawk. The rest featured guys kite surfing, water surfing, hang gliding, skydiving, snowboarding, and doing what looked like street luge. This was certainly a guy's dorm room.

I finished my tour and turned to Lark. "So, do you go to school here too, Lark?"

"Naw. I'm not into all that school shit."

After a moment of silence, I asked, "Do you work?"

"*Huh-uh.*"

Another awkward silence. "Still live at home?"

Before she could answer, one of the bedroom doors burst open. Trace stood in the doorway half-naked, a wet towel wrapped around the bottom half of his torso, covering him from his pubic hairline to above his knees—not much. His chin-length brown hair was damp and sticking out in all directions.

"Hey," he said, then shook his head like a freshly shampooed dog.

"Hi, Trace. I don't know if you remember me. Presley Parker. I helped with the party the other night. . . ."

"Yeah, yeah. What's up? You don't go to school here, do you?"

I laughed. "No. I wanted to ask you a few questions about your friend Spidey."

"Yeah, okay. I'll be out in a sec. Just gotta grab some clothes. Lark, take care of our guest, would you?" He shuffled off to the bedroom on the right.

She nodded but made no effort to get up.

"Want a drink or something?" Lark asked, leaning her head against the back of the chair. She was obviously not eager to move from her spot.

"No, I'm fine," I said. "So, how are you doing . . . you know, with Spidey's death?"

"Bummed," she said simply.

It was clear I wasn't going to get anything more from her. Fortunately, I didn't have to wait long for Trace. Unlike Delicia who might have taken twenty or thirty minutes to dress, do her hair, and put on her makeup, Trace was dressed in shorts and a T-shirt seemingly in seconds. He was barefoot from the shower and his hair still stuck out, but other than that, he looked ready to welcome company.

He headed for the fridge, pulled out a beer, and hoisted it toward me as an offering. I shook my head. It was a little early in the day for me. He popped the top, grabbed an Oreo from a half-empty bag, and stepped over to the couch. With a sweep of his cookie arm, he cleared the seating area and sat down, then patted the area beside him for me.

Hoping I didn't sit on any wet spots—beer or God knows what—I sat down lightly and turned to Trace.

"So, what's up, Presley Parker? I hear you're trying to find out what happened to Spidey. Any luck?"

I shook my head. "I thought you might be able to answer a few questions."

"I'll try. But I told the police everything I know. Don't know much else 'cause I wasn't there when he . . . you know . . . died."

"Well," I said, "as you probably know, Duncan doesn't believe he fell. He thinks Spidey was too good to lose his balance like that."

"Everybody falls," Trace said. "It goes with the territory." He took a long swallow of beer, then burped. If this guy was grieving, then maybe the beer was helping him cope. But his lack of emotion made me wonder how close they had been as friends.

"So you think it's possible that Spidey fell? Even though it's starting to look otherwise?"

"Like I said, no idea."

"What do you think he was doing in the cemetery after you left? Why didn't he leave with you and Lark?"

Trace tapped his head. "Truthfully, the dude was kinda psycho." I saw him steal a glance at Lark, but she looked away. "Always wanting to push himself, you know? Trying to impress people."

"Girls, you mean," Lark added.

"Anyone in particular?" I asked Lark.

This time she glanced at Trace.

"Trace?" I asked.

He sighed, took a gulp of beer, and said, "Ever since we got to be extras in that movie, Spidey's been wanting to hook up with Angelica."

"Wow. Did he really think she was interested in him?"

Trace tapped his forehead again. "He got this crush on her and wouldn't stop talking about her. Said he'd impress her with his parkour stunts. Said she was always giving him the eye, flirting with him. He was sure she was hot for him. As I said, he was a little psycho." He swallowed the rest of his beer.

I wondered if Spidey might have been Angelica's stalker. It was possible, especially if he was what Trace called "psycho" and obsessed with the actress. He might have had an unrealistic view of himself as some kind of parkour star and saw Angelica as someone who would want to be with a guy like that. I wondered if Spidey knew about Angelica and Jonas. Or about Angelica's already being secretly married.

"Did he ever write her, text her, or follow her, or anything like that?" I asked Trace.

He tossed the beer bottle into a plastic basket. "Other than talking about her nonstop, I have no clue. It's not as if we were together twenty-four-seven."

Lark shot him a look, then glanced at the open bedroom door.

Trace scratched his stomach. "Listen, I gotta go. I want to find out what happened to Spidey as much as anyone. But I don't have any more answers."

I rose to go. Obviously our meeting was over, but I had a feeling there was something in the bedroom he didn't want me to see.

"Just one last question then. Where did Spidey live? I'd like to go see his parents."

Trace and Lark looked at each other again.

"He . . . was homeless," Trace said. "His parents moved back east somewhere when he was in high school. He stayed here. Hasn't been in contact with them for years."

"Homeless?" I repeated, surprised at the news.

Trace nodded, but Lark glanced away.

"Well, thanks for your time."

As I headed for the door, I tried to see inside Trace's bedroom and caught a glimpse of something that made me gasp internally.

On the far wall was a large, full-color poster of Angelica Brayden.

I stepped into the hallway of the dorm and heard the door close behind me. That had been a very odd interview. Well, Trace and Lark might be finished with me, but I wasn't quite finished with them.

One of the best techniques I'd learned in dealing with people who had something to hide—like a disorder they didn't want revealed—was to surprise them with a visit when they least expected it. I doubted if the doorknob had even cooled before I knocked again at room 1404.

Lark answered. As I expected, she was surprised to see me back.

"Forget something?" she said, keeping a tight grip on the door.

"Sort of," I said. "I have to make a few more stops and wondered if I could use your bathroom before I go. I may not get another chance."

No one would refuse a person's request to use their bathroom, would they?

"Trace!" she shouted back into the room. "Presley wants to use the bathroom. You cool?"

"Come on in," Trace called back. Lark pulled the door open reluctantly and pointed toward the room adjacent to Trace's bedroom. "It's over there."

Trace, standing by the bathroom door, moved over, allowing me access, but blocking the view to the rest of his room.

"Thanks," I said. "I'll only be a minute."

I entered the small bathroom and locked the door behind me. The room contained a toilet, shower—no bathtub—and sink with a cupboard underneath and a medicine cabinet above. There was barely enough space for a human being, but then, this was college life.

I ran some water to make it sound as if I were peeing—I knew the walls were paper thin. Then I opened the medicine chest. To my surprise, there were three shelves of women's cosmetics, and only one shelf with men's shaving supplies. I shut off the water and flushed the toilet, then quickly opened the cabinet doors. Inside, I found a pink hair dryer, a black hair dryer, and two hairbrushes, plus three razors—one pink, one black, and one red. I closed the doors and took a last glance around the bathroom before making my exit.

Then I saw what had been right in front of me: On the rim of the sink was a cup containing three toothbrushes—one pink, one black, and one that featured Spiderman.

Trace, Lark, and Spidey.

That could only mean one thing: Lark was living in Trace's dorm room—and Spidey had been living there too.

Chapter 15

I was pooped from playing Nancy Drew. Nancy always seemed tireless in her exploits to find the culprit responsible for stealing a valuable necklace, hiding an important will, or "haunting" a moss-covered mansion. I wished I had her energy, not to mention her ability to solve a crime without any help from the Hardy Boys. At the moment, I had neither Frank nor Joe—nor energy.

Of course, Nancy had to endure chloroform, abduction, quicksand, and being trapped in an attic with her hands tied behind her back and left for dead, with nothing more than a lipstick to free herself. Me, I'd never had to deal with any of the above. But I'd had my share of life-threatening situations, and I didn't relish dealing with any more near-death experiences.

So far, so good. But seeing Trace and Lark had got me thinking. A lot of odd looks had passed between the two of them. Was it possible that Trace—or Lark— killed Spidey? I thought of the poster I'd seen in Trace's bedroom. Or should I say Spidey and Lark's bedroom too? If the two of them were crashing at Trace's place, it was against the rules, and he could be evicted if anyone found out. But that wasn't a reason to kill Spidey.

As for the poster, maybe Trace also had a crush on Angelica, and maybe she was leading him on as well. Maybe Spidey was jealous and threatened Trace—or vice versa. And what part did Lark play in all this? Was she jealous of Angelica and the attention she was stealing from Trace and Spidey?

I reached Treasure Island around four in the afternoon, my head full of more questions. I parked the car in the lot and headed for the office. It was unlocked but empty when I entered. A message Delicia had left on the "in/out" board read: "Duncan's office." She took this "in/out" board seriously if she felt she had to let me know she was only two doors away. I walked the few steps to the office Duncan shared with Berkeley, knocked, and tried the knob. It opened. I peered in. Berkeley was watching a videotape of my Vampire Party.

There was no sign of Dee or Duncan.

"Hey, Berk. Was Delicia here?"

He nodded without looking up from the small camera screen. "She and Duncan left about half an hour ago."

Hmm. She hadn't put that on the message board. I stepped inside. "Did they say where they were going?"

"Nope."

I felt the little hairs at the back of my neck prickle in alarm. Were they out trying to find a killer? "Did they say anything at all?"

Berk finally looked up, apparently realizing the annoying office neighbor wasn't going away anytime soon. "No, Presley. As soon as I walked into the office, Dee got out of my chair and headed out. Duncan followed her."

I wished Berk and Duncan had one of those message boards. I'd have to get Dee to take care of that.

"So, you have no idea where they went?"

Berk rolled his eyes at me.

"Okay. I get it. You don't know."

He returned to viewing the tape.

"Don't suppose you've seen anything in that videotape that might give us a clue about Spidey's death. Or about that paparazzo?"

"Not yet. But I'm keeping an eye out. Duncan asked me to. And I assumed you'd want to know if anything hinky showed up."

"Hinky?"

"Yeah, you know, weird . . . or suspicious."

I suppressed a smile. Berkeley was always the hippest guy in the room. I couldn't keep up with his footwear, let alone lingo. I glanced down at today's shoes: plaid high-top PRO-Keds.

"Cool shoes," I said, heading for the door. "But plaid?"

"Argyle. Like the Norwegian curling team wears."

"Really? They look more like something one of my dads might buy."

"It's hip to be square, Presley."

Of course. "Well, let me know if you see anything, will you?"

He nodded.

On my way back to my office, I knocked on Brad's door. I heard a muffled "Come in," and opened the door. Brad sat at his small metal desk, frowning at his laptop screen.

"Hi," I said, glad to see him. "What are you working on?"

He gestured toward the screen. "Just got an e-mail from Luke."

I sucked in a breath. "About the DNA test?"

He nodded. "It's definitely Spidey's blood on the shovel and the gravestone. And Bodie's blood is also on the shovel. Whoever killed these guys used the same weapon—the shovel."

I sat down opposite Brad, relieved at the news, only because it proved my—and Duncan's—suspicions. Not only was Spidey murdered, but he was almost definitely killed by the same person who murdered Bodie.

Now all I had to do was put on a fresh frock, gather my chums, jump into my roadster, and figure out whodunit. That was what Nancy would do.

"Did the detective find anything else—other fingerprints on the shovel? Hairs? Any of that forensic-type stuff?"

"Nothing else. Lucas said the guy probably wore gloves or wiped it clean, and maybe a cap."

"Why's he so sure it was a male?" I asked.

"It's pretty unlikely a female could hit those guys hard enough to kill them."

"But maybe she could have hit them hard enough to cause them to lose their balance or stun them, then finished the job—Spidey with the stone and Bodie with another bash to the head."

"Possible. But it would take a lot of strength to kill someone with just a shovel."

I tried to picture a woman swinging a shovel at a guy moving along the tops of gravestones. It wouldn't be an easy trick to take him down—unless it was a complete surprise. Maybe she tripped him first. As for the paparazzi, a surprise attack would be the only way a woman would have an advantage. And she could have lured the men into those dark, isolated spots. . . .

"How about you?" Brad asked, breaking my train of thought. "Where you been?"

"Oh, I went over to the dorm at San Francisco State to see Spidey's friends, Trace and Lark."

He raised an eyebrow of concern. "By yourself?"

"Of course. Nobody's going to kill me in a college dorm, not with all those students around."

He didn't look so sure. "Learn anything?"

"I didn't find a closet full of bloody shovels, if that's what you're asking."

Brad laughed.

"But I did catch a glimpse of Trace's bedroom, and there's a huge poster of Angelica Brayden on his wall. Someone there is a big fan. He mentioned that Spidey had had a crush on the actress, and Spidey thought Angelica liked him too, although Trace didn't seem to take that very seriously."

"Interesting. You believe it?"

"I don't know. Trace could have had a crush on Angelica too. He also indicated that Spidey was not all there." I touched my forehead, as Trace had done. "I tried to find out more about Spidey, such as where he lived, but Trace said he was homeless. Then I got suspicious and wondered if Spidey might have been crashing at the dorm. So I told them I had to pee and checked out the bathroom cupboards and medicine chest."

"And?" Brad asked, grinning.

"I'm pretty sure Spidey—and Lark—are living there, staying in his bedroom. Their toiletries were there—a girl's hair dryer, three razors, and a Spiderman toothbrush. If Trace gets caught with them there, he could be evicted. I wonder how they get away with it. But then, who's really going to know, except maybe the roommate, and he wasn't there to ask."

"Even if those three are—were—living together, it doesn't tell us much," Brad said, "except that they were friends. Doesn't sound like Trace, or Lark, had any reason to kill their friend Spidey, let alone the paparazzo."

"Maybe not," I said, "but there's something those

two aren't telling me. They kept giving each other weird looks."

"Maybe they were in a three-way . . ."

I laughed. "In your dreams."

He raised a libidinous eyebrow.

"Do you think she's attractive? Lark, that is," I said, then regretted it.

"In a Joan Jett–slash–roller derby type way."

"Oh my God," I said, and left him alone to his fantasies.

There was still no sign of Delicia when I entered my office next door. Nothing new had been written on the message board. I listened to all the cell phone messages I'd received while I was out and found I had a number of requests for theme parties during the upcoming holidays. Could I do a "Gingerbread House Party" and contest for AAUW to raise money for women who want to go to college? Would I be available to host a "Toys for Tots" fund-raising gala at one of the local firehouses, with the firefighters dressed as "Fiery Hot Santas"? Did I have any time to work up a "Sixties Hippie Party" for the National Organization for the Reform of Marijuana Laws?

It wasn't November yet and the party season was already booking up. Who had time to search for a killer?

After two hours of nonstop phone calls scheduling parties, ordering props, booking venues, and reserving tents, tables, and chairs, I was ready to quit and go home—until Duncan and Delicia walked in.

"Where have you two been?" I asked, pushing back from my desk.

Dee looked at her entry on the in/out board. "*Uh* . . . with Duncan?"

I frowned at the two of them, standing there looking as guilty as Sylvester with a mouthful of Tweety. "Well, did you find out anything?" I assumed they'd been snooping around.

Dee sat down in her chair, while Duncan loitered against the door frame.

"Not really," Dee said. "Just—"

"Dee!" Duncan hissed.

"Give it up, Duncan," Dee said. "Presley knows. She's a psychologist, remember. She can almost read your mind. There's no sense in pretending we haven't been looking for Spidey's killer."

Duncan pressed his lips together.

"I told you guys—you specifically, Duncan—that I would do what I could to help find out what happened to Spidey and for you to stay out of it. And now I have two loose cannons to deal with—you and Dee."

"Sorry, Mom," Duncan said.

"Not funny," I returned. "I'm just saying, you're too emotionally involved in this. Let us—and the police— handle it."

"So what have you found out?" Duncan asked.

"I talked to a couple of people who were at the party—Jonas and Angelica."

"What did they say?" Duncan said eagerly.

"Nothing solid. Jonas is trying to protect Angelica. Meanwhile Angelica's worried about someone stalking her. You know they're seeing each other, right?"

Duncan's eyes widened. This was obviously news to him.

"And you know that Angelica's secretly married," I added.

This time his mouth dropped open.

"Duncan, you have to tell her," Dee suddenly said.

I looked at Duncan. He took another step inside and closed the door with a kick of his foot.

"What's going on, Duncan?" I asked.

He swallowed. "Spidey said . . . he said that actress, Angelica, she was into him. Said he was going to meet her in the cemetery that night, after the party was all set up and everyone was gone."

Now my jaw had dropped. "What?"

"He got a text from her. She'd been flirting with him all week, during the shoot. When he got that text, he was blown away."

"But I heard she flirted with everyone," I said.

"Yeah, I know. I saw her talking to a bunch of different guys, including Trace," Duncan said. "Everyone but Jonas. She didn't seem to even like him. And he pretty much ignored her."

"Yeah, well, that tells you something right there. When two people are trying to hide a relationship, they often go out of their way to act as if they don't care about each other. They're afraid they might let their emotions slip around each other unless they keep them tightly controlled."

"I still don't believe it." Duncan shook his head. "Why would Angelica text Spidey and ask him to meet her then?"

A light went on. "Duncan, do you know if the police found Spidey's cell phone on his body?"

"I don't know."

"His cell phone could contain all kinds of information that might help. It's better than a calendar, diary, and address book put together. I'll find out if the cops have it." I stood up. "Meanwhile, you two—cut it out, you hear? This is your last warning, or I'll . . . make a citizen's arrest."

Duncan grinned. It was good to see him smile. "For what?"

"For being a public nuisance . . . and posing as an officer of the law." As a matter of fact, Detective Melvin had threatened me with the very same offenses in the past. I moved to Duncan and gave him a hug. "Now, if you'll excuse me, I have some illegal police work to do."

I left them alone and headed back to Brad's office. "I need your help," I said, ignoring whatever it was he was doing.

"Of course you do," he said. "But I'm going to have to start charging you. Would you like to open an account?"

"Run a tab," I said. "I need to know if Detective Melvin found Spidey's cell phone and what's on it—last calls, dates, text history, everything. Will you call him for me? Please?"

"It so happens I'm meeting him at the police gym in a few minutes. I'll ask him then."

"Great, thanks." I started out.

"Hey, wait! Quid pro quo. Did you get anything new from Duncan?"

Apparently he knew Duncan and Delicia were back. I stepped inside Brad's office and spoke softly in case they happened to be in the hallway. "Duncan said Spidey got a text from Angelica the night he died, asking him to meet her in the cemetery after the party setup."

"Really? Sounds bogus to me," Brad said. "Why would a hot little actress like Angelica want to meet some skinhead movie extra—at night—in a cemetery—alone. You telling me Spidey fell for this crock?"

"I don't know. That's why I need to know what was on his cell. Was there a text? If so, did she send it? And if she didn't, who did it really come from?"

I leaned in and kissed Brad—part bribe, part lust. Not necessarily equal parts.

As for lust—could that be what was behind these murders?

Did Bodie also have a relationship with Angelica? They'd certainly crossed paths. And she seemed to be able to charm every guy around her. But Bodie? I highly doubted it. What had Brad called her? "A hot little actress." I wondered how Jonas felt about all her flirting.

Not to mention her husband.

Chapter 16

PARTY-PLANNING TIP #16

Bake a red velvet cake for your Vampire Party. You can find a recipe on the Internet, but the quick version is simple: just bake a white cake, add enough red food coloring to turn the batter a brilliant red, and then bake according to package directions. Frost with cream cheese icing and drip red food coloring droplets of "blood" on the top.

By the time I left the office, it was too late to do any active investigating, so I headed home. After feeding my cats and chatting with them about the high cost of cat food today, I settled onto the couch with a BLT, a beer, and my laptop. Brad called to say he'd be out late with Detective Melvin and would see me tomorrow. I couldn't complain, since I'd asked him to question the detective about Spidey's cell phone records.

But I missed his undercover work that night.

The next morning I showered, dressed in black jeans, a white shirt, and a black leather vest, ate leftover bacon and a piece of toast, and washed it down with a latte. I pulled out the guest list Lucas Cruz had given me for the Vampire Wrap Party. After looking up a few of the guests' addresses on my laptop, I Mapquested them and printed them out. The only address Cruz didn't have was for the paparazzo party crasher, Bodie Chase. I wanted to talk to Cruz and find out what the connection was between Angelica and Chase. Did Bodie know something about Angelica's flirtations—and think there was more behind that? A few Internet searches later I found his business ad: Hollywood Photos. It listed the types of photography Bodie offered: "Photojournalism, glamour/fashion/nude modeling photos, wedding photos, and Celeb for a Day," which, the ad explained, meant Bodie would follow you around the City for a day and take pictures of you as if you were a celebrity. Wow.

I dialed the office number, hoping to get a secretary or someone who could give me his home address. The phone answered on the third ring, and a male voice said, "Hollywood Photos."

"Yes, hi," I said. "I'm looking for Bodie Chase. Is this his place of business?"

"Yeah," the voice said, "but he ain't here. Can I help you? I'm his partner, Robby."

"Oh, well, I'm Presley . . . Chase, Bodie's sister. I haven't seen him in several years and wanted to come and say hello."

There was a moment of silence, then, "I'm sorry, Presley, but your brother is deceased."

"What? Oh my goodness," I said, hoping I sounded convincing in my grief. "When did he die? How did it happen?"

"*Uh*, well, he was killed," Robby said, in his slightly Southern drawl.

I tried to gasp. "You mean, like murdered?"

"Yeah, that's what the cops are thinking."

"I don't believe it!" I said. "Do the police know anything?

Robby's uncomfortable silence was the verbal equivalent of a shrug.

I paused for a moment, pretending to be overcome with grief, then took a deep breath and asked, "Robby, would it be possible for me to stop by his place and pick up a few things to remember him by?"

"He don't got much. The cops took a bunch of his shit—I mean stuff—but I'll look around the basement and see if they left anything behind."

"That would be wonderful, Robby. Thanks so much. Do you have a key to his place?"

"Yeah, me and him were roommates." He gave me the address. To my surprise, Bodie lived in the Tenderloin neighborhood of San Francisco, one of the poorest sections in the City. For some reason, I expected him to live in a more upscale neighborhood. Didn't paparazzi make big bucks snapping celebrity photos?

I hung up the phone, promising to be there within the hour. I gathered my things, told my cats to keep an eye out for any burglars, kidnappers, or mice—Cairo had caught a mouse a week ago and had brought it to me as a gift, which just made me wonder how many more there might be—then headed for the car.

Without stopping by the office to check in, I drove directly across the Bay Bridge to the Tenderloin, just north of Market Street. In the past, it had been referred to as Skid Row or "the Wino Country," since many homeless, drug addicts, and alcoholics congregated in the area. My mother once told me the name Tenderloin came from the days of vice, graft, and corruption in the City, referring to the "soft underbelly" of society. It was an area, she said, "that upstanding citizens didn't frequent." Except for the occasional musical or play at the Golden Gate Theater, my mother rarely brought me here. When we had to pass through the area, she pulled me along so quickly I thought my arm would come out of its socket. She never talked about the place, except to say, "Walk fast, look mean, and don't make eye contact."

Today the area was home to an eclectic collection of residential hotels, alternative sexualities, fenced playgrounds, halfway houses, and Southeast Asian families, many of whom were refugees during the late 1970s. It also housed the Asian Art Museum, City Hall, the Supreme Court, and the Main Library. In spite of gentrification— and being designated as a historic district—it still harbored a reputation for strip clubs, dive bars, assaults, gangs, drugs, prostitution, and homicides. The City hadn't ignored the area. There were plenty of social services, churches, and food programs. And for me there was a mystique about it, mainly because Sam Spade once enjoyed the nightlife in the Tenderloin.

But I wouldn't want to be walking down a dark alley at night without a good, loud party horn and some Silly String, in case of attack.

Basically, I was scared to death of the Tenderloin.

I parked in the Civic Center lot and felt safe enough walking along Market toward the Mason Street Hotel, where Bodie had apparently lived. Dodging pigeons on the sidewalk, I passed an eclectic collection of pawnshops, strip bars, and knockoff stores that alternated with Indian food restaurants, "gentlemen's clubs," yogurt shops, and the ubiquitous Starbucks. The pedestrians ranged from businesspeople in suits holding cell phones to ragged homeless people pushing grocery carts full of junk. One guy was urinating against an alley wall, between a barber college and a hostel, while another slept on the doorstep of a "Cameras, Wigs, and Loans" shop. I dropped a few dollars into empty paper cups along the way, enjoying the cleverer signs soliciting money—WIFE'S BEEN KIDNAPPED. NEED $1 FOR RANSOM; NEED MONEY FOR ALCÓHOL RESEARCH; I KNOW WHERE BIN LADEN IS HIDEN [sic]. NEED MONEY FOR AIRLINE TICKET AND FLAMETHROWER; and WHY LIE? NEED BEER.

The Polk Hotel was squeezed in between a Laundromat–donut shop and a Salvation Army store. From the outside, it appeared to be two rooms wide and six rooms tall, but I had a feeling it ran deep. Before I entered, I thought about something sad—the day my first kitten ran away when I was seven—and hoped the tears forming in my eyes would last at least until I spoke with the hotel manager.

I pushed open the once-glassed door that had been replaced with a wooden slat and iron bars. The door chimed inside the empty lobby, which was about the size of a large closet. A built-in, unmanned desk, flanked by a wall of pamphlets on one side and a worn leather couch on the other, greeted residents and visitors. I wondered how many "social visits" had taken place on that couch, and I shuddered.

As if the door chime weren't enough, there was a bell on the desk. I rang it several times, taking in the musty odor of God knew what—burned food, unwashed clothes, rat droppings. . . .

"Yeah?" A woman appeared from behind a shabby curtain, one of those Indian Madras wall hangings like my mother used to decorate her sixties parties. She wore a loose tie-dyed T-shirt over her ample bosom, gray high-water sweatpants, and her nails were painted black and white and decorated with tiny jewels. Her hair had been colored one too many times, in five too many shades, and ranged from gray roots to brown, red, and blond streaks. She could have been forty, but she looked sixty, no doubt in part due to the cigarette that hung from her magenta-colored lips. I had a feeling alcohol, drugs, and the absence of a good skin care lotion had done the rest of the damage to her lined, blotchy face.

"Hi," I said, almost forgetting about my fake tears. "I'm Presley Chase. Bodie's sister?"

She looked me over. "Yeah, sorry for your loss. You here for the rest of his stuff? I think Robby got it out of the basement."

I blinked, trying to hold back my surprise. Robby must have told her.

"Yes, that's right. The police didn't take everything?"

"Not much to take. Robby found only one box. He took it up to the room. You can get it from him."

"Thanks."

"Elevator don't work. Stairs are over there." She gestured with her cigarette. "Three B. Third floor. On the right."

I thanked her and made my way to the stairs. The smells grew more intense as I climbed each step. Marijuana. Clorox. And something that smelled like a dead animal.

My stomach lurched.

By the time I reached 3B, I was out of breath—not from the stairs but from the shallow breathing I'd done to keep from inhaling all the toxins I was sure were swirling around my nose. I knocked. No response. I knocked again, louder and longer.

The door opened to a man in a wife-beater T-shirt and boxer shorts, white socks but no shoes, and a five o'clock shadow. "You must be Bodie's sister," he said, looking me over.

I glanced at his boxers.

He chuckled. "Oh. Sorry. Didn't know you'd get here so fast. Just a sec."

He closed the door, then returned in less than fifteen seconds wearing a pair of jeans. He opened the door wide. "Come on in."

Did I dare? How safe was I in this place with a stranger whose roommate had been murdered? He could easily have been the killer.

"Uh . . ." I looked around for . . . what? A quick exit?

"Come on," he insisted. "I won't bite. And I'll leave the door open. How's that?"

I stepped inside and quickly took in the place, searching for anything I could use as a weapon if needed. Two beds on opposite sides of the room, one covered in a filthy, matted *Star Wars* comforter, the other an unzipped sleeping bag that had more stains than an auto mechanic's driveway. No bathroom. No mirrors. No objets d'art. But the walls were filled with enlarged photographs. I recognized a blurry Jennifer Aniston, a Madonna with her hand over her face, and a Britney Spears flipping off the person taking the photo.

A single box the size of a microwave oven sat on top of the *Star Wars* bed, marked "Bodie's junk."

"That's not his best work," the man said, indicating the photos on Bodie's side of the room. He extended his hairy hand, nails bitten to the quick. "I'm Robby Aplanalp, by the way. I'm a photographer too."

"Nice to meet you," I said, hoping I still had a little bottle of antibacterial gel in my car to cleanse my hand when I returned.

"Sorry about your bro," he said.

I said nothing, not wanting to complicate the lie. Instead I asked, "I wondered if I could ask you some questions about why Bodie was so interested in Angelica and Jonas."

"No idea," Robby said. He looked sincere, shaking his head. "I could tell he was on to something, but we didn't share stuff like that."

"What about Spidey, the young man who was killed?"

Robby shrugged. "I don't think he even knew that kid."

I decided to get to the point. "Robby, do you have any idea who killed him?"

"Hell, everybody," Robby said with a laugh. "Nobody likes us photojournalists. They call us paparazzi and say it like it's a bad word. But we're just trying to make a living like everybody else, you know."

I glanced around the hotel room. This didn't look much like a living.

He read my thoughts and sat down on his sleeping bag bed. "Most people don't really get what we do. They think it's all about the money. Sure, we want to make the big dollars for our snaps, hoping they'll appear in *People* or *Buzz*, or even on ET and TMI. And believe me, the payoff is huge for the right snap. But it's not just that."

"It doesn't seem to be about the glamour either," I said.

"Maybe we don't live the glamorous life that celebs do, but being on the fringe, we enjoy it almost as much as if we were living it. Voyeurs, they call us, among other things. But you know, it's really about the thrill of the chase, the adrenaline of getting up close and personal with these stars. Celebs forget. They wouldn't be stars without our getting their faces out to the public."

And getting in their faces, I thought. "So you do it to be close to the dream, even though you aren't really living it?"

"Pretty much. Plus the camaraderie among us photographers—even though we are in competition. We're all going after that dangling carrot that will get us a house in the hills, a Maserati, and a yacht in the Caribbean. Like Denny O'Connor. He's one of the top paparazzi in LA. A few years ago, he got a hundred and fifty large for a snap of Bennifer—Ben Affleck and Jennifer Lopez—*after* their breakup. That's the big score we're all after. The money shot. Can you imagine how much a rag would pay to get that first photo of the Brangelina breakup?"

"It sounds about the same odds as playing the lottery," I said. I nodded toward the box on Bodie's bed. "Do you mind if I look through his stuff?"

"Nothing much there, but be my guest. Cops took his cameras, film, all that shit—er, stuff. I'd forgotten about the box in the basement until you called. It's mostly pictures he couldn't sell. But it's yours if you want it."

The box was too big to cart to my car, and I wasn't sure I wanted to bring it back with me anyway, if it was contaminated with rat poop and whatnot. Instead, I opened the cardboard box and sifted through the papers and photos, placing them on the bed after looking at each one.

Robby had been right. There were mostly rejects—photographs that were out of focus or unusable in some other way. There were even a couple of nudes with blacked-out faces. I didn't recognize half the people, but others looked familiar, in spite of being obscured by hats, newspapers, hands, and big bodyguards. When I reached the bottom of the box, I found a dirty manila file folder, unmarked. I pulled it out and peeked inside, hoping I wasn't about to inhale some kind of lethal mold.

It was filled with legal forms. I held it up.

Injunctions?

"What's this?" I asked Robby.

He squinted, then said, "Oh yeah. Restraining orders. He's got a bunch of them. The latest one was for that Jonas Jones guy who's been filming that vampire movie over on Treasure Island. Bodie found out where he was staying in the City and started following him, hoping to get a picture. He had a hunch that guy was going to be a hot commodity as soon as the movie came out."

"Why was it buried at the bottom of the pile?" I asked.

"That's all stuff from last year, when Jonas Jones sued Bodie for spying on him."

"So Jonas got a restraining order against him?"

"Yeah. He said Bodie kept showing up every place he went. Even tried to get on to the set over on TI. But as I said, that was a year ago, about the same time

Lucas Cruz sued him too. The cops took all the stuff from this year."

I looked at the official paper. Someone had scrawled the figure "$50,000."

"Did he end up selling a picture of Jonas worth fifty thousand dollars?" I asked.

"Oh no. Just the opposite. Bodie got caught trying to photograph Jones with some woman at a café after he'd gotten the injunction. Jones called the cops and Bodie was arrested. He ended up having to pay Jones fifty grand."

Interesting. I wondered if the woman Jonas had been photographed with was Angelica. He had sued Bodie and won a large settlement. Maybe Bodie had held a grudge against Jonas and had come to the party to threaten him. Had he also been around the night before while we were setting up the party? Then how did Bodie end up dead? And what did this have to do with Spidey's death?

An even bigger question was: how had Bodie managed to pay Jonas such a large sum of money when it was clear Bodie had no money to speak of?

I replaced the photos in the box, keeping the file, and turned to Robby to thank him.

"So," Robby said, grinning, "you single?"

Chapter 17

PARTY-PLANNING TIP #17

Spill some blood at your Vampire Party to satisfy your guests' thirst for fluids. Get a chocolate party fountain and fill it with Bloody Marys. When it's time for dessert, clean it, then melt white chocolate, tint it red with food coloring, and let the guests dip ladyfingers into the flow.

This guy was full of surprises. Caught completely off guard, I mumbled, "Oh . . . *uh* . . . I . . ."

"McDonald's has a pretty good strawberry banana smoothie. Tastes like Jamba Juice, but it's cheaper. And they don't put all that organic crap in it. It's just down the street."

"Oh . . . goodness . . ." I checked my watch, then tapped Mickey. "I . . . have another appointment, and I'll be late if I don't get going. But thanks for the offer."

"You know, Bodie never mentioned he had a sister. Especially not a pretty one," Robby said, smiling at me like a schoolboy.

I'm sure I blushed from my nose to my toes as I made my way to the door posthaste, stepping over dropped clothing and some paper bags.

"He was full of secrets, that guy," Robby added, following me into the hall. His eyes narrowed. "I didn't even know he was invited to that film party the other night until I seen the invite. Probably didn't tell me 'cause he didn't want the competition." Robby forced a laugh.

I stopped in my tracks. "Bodie was invited?"

"Yeah, got a invite a day or two before the party. I know 'cause I accidentally opened it."

Yeah, sure, I thought. Accidentally.

"There was this vampire on the front with his cape open where you could read all the when-where stuff. Although it was kinda hard to read. Looked as though it'd been photocopied."

The invitations I'd designed and sent had been actual miniature coffins. Inside I'd placed a paper vampire with a folded black cape, just as he described. When the invitee opened the cape, they saw the party details written in glittery red ink. As Robby said, it sounded as if someone had taken out the vampire, opened the cape, and photocopied it. But why? Did someone want him at the party other than Lucas Cruz? Or did he get ahold of the invitation and photocopy it himself?"

"Do you still have the invitation?"

He shook his head. "He took it with him that night. Maybe the cops found it?"

Brad hadn't mentioned anything about an invitation, so I had a feeling Detective Melvin hadn't found it. And if it wasn't on Bodie, where could it be? Had the murderer removed it after killing him?

"You're sure you haven't seen it."

"Nope. It wasn't in that box of his stuff, right?"

"No," I said. "Will you let me know if you find it? It might help me figure out what happened to the . . . my brother."

I really needed lying lessons, I thought. I just wasn't good at this sort of thing. My mother could always see right through me when I tried, so I eventually gave up.

"Sure you don't want a smoothie? Maybe some fries on the side? I gotta cut down on my cholesterol"—he patted his gut—"but I'll bet you don't hafta worry about stuff like that."

"No, but thank you, Robby. You've been a big help. I have to run. Here's my card." I whipped out a Killer Parties business card. It had my name, Presley Parker, on it, but I'd let Robby assume Bodie and I had different last names. "Keep in touch."

I had just entered the dingy stairwell when I heard Robby call out, "What's Killer Parties?"

I pretended not to hear him and hurried down the stairs.

Just as Mother had taught me, I walked fast, looked mean, and didn't make eye contact on the way back to my car. Meanwhile, I thought about what I'd learned from Robby the roommate—that Bodie Chase had received a photocopy of the party invitation. From whom? I wondered.

So what did this latest piece of information mean? Someone had invited Bodie to the party—or at least let him know about it. Someone who had actually been invited and received the formal invitation, then photocopied it. Someone who probably attended the party and wanted Bodie there. But why? To stir up trouble? To give him a chance to find out a little dirt on the attendees?

Or to murder him?

When I reached my MINI in the Civic Center parking lot, I breathed a sigh of relief—I still had tires. There were no visible marks on the car, the convertible hood hadn't been slashed, and, when I checked, I found my laptop still in the trunk. I hopped in before someone decided to carjack me, and headed for the next person in the entertainment business who might have more information and perhaps might know something about the retraining orders—Gossip Guy himself.

As the San Francisco Bay Area correspondent to the Hollywood show, Ryan Fitzpatrick was a well-known personality in the City. He was the one who kept an eye and ear on our local celebrity gossip. San Francisco had its fair share of stars and scandals, rockers, and rehabbers. He reported his "facts" back to the *Gossip Guy* show via satellite, while sharing the items on the local news station. No doubt he had billions of followers on Twitter, Facebook, and his blog.

I pulled up to a soon-to-be-vacated spot on Van Ness, not too far from the TV station where he worked, waited for the Mercedes to drive off, and parked the MINI. Checking my guest list, I found Ryan's cell number and punched it into my iPhone. He answered on the first ring.

"Talk to me," he said, not wasting any time on greetings or salutations.

"Is this Ryan Fitzpatrick?" I asked, although I recognized his voice from TV.

"Possibly. Who's this?"

"Presley Parker, from Killer Parties. I'm the one Lucas Cruz hired to host the Vampire Wrap Party."

"Oh yessss," he said, suddenly more interested in talking to me. "You got something for me?"

"I may have. I wonder if I could see you. I'm right outside the studio."

"Sweet. I love it when news comes to me for a change. Just check in at the front desk and come on up. Third floor."

I hung up. That was easy. All you had to do was tell a reporter you had some news he might be interested in and he'd show you the red carpet. I wondered what would happen when he found out I didn't have anything—at least, nothing I would share with him. Hey, I've been thrown out of better places than a TV studio.

I stuffed coins in the meter and walked a few feet to the studio. The two glass doors were locked when I tried to enter. I heard a buzz, tried the doors again, and one of them gave. Inside, I was greeted by a uniformed security guard standing behind a tall reception desk. He pushed a pad of paper toward me as I approached.

"Hi, I'm Presley Parker, here to see Ryan Fitzpatrick."

"Sign in, please." He handed me a pen.

I did as I was told, filling in my name, my arrival time, what company I represented, and who it was I was there to see.

He pushed a visitor name tag toward me. "Fill this in. Return it when you leave." He handed me a black marker.

I printed my name neatly, peeled the back off the sticker, and stuck it on the front of my black vest.

The security guard pointed to the elevators with the pen. "Third floor."

I followed his directions and moments later found myself on the third floor. A narrow hallway led to a number of offices on either side. When I came to a room full of busy-looking people sitting at desks, I guessed this was the newsroom and approached a young woman who'd just hung up her phone.

"I'm looking for Ryan Fitzpatrick," I said to her. She pointed to a desk at the back of the room. I nodded my thanks and zigzagged around several desks to reach Ryan, passing several familiar faces I saw regularly on the news.

Ryan was on the phone when I reached him, so I took a moment to look around the inner workings of a TV newsroom. It looked much like any office—desks filled with computers, papers, knickknacks, awards, and family photos.

But the chart on the wall was what caught my eye.

A dry-erase board the size of a billboard covered most of one long wall. It was divided into grids with a black marker—the days of the week across the top, the numbered weeks along the left-hand side. Inside each grid square were what looked like the planned topics for upcoming news shows. They were written in varying colors, and I tried to decipher the code. I guessed that blue meant an interview, green was a restaurant review, purple was a local event, and red, a topical story. Today had been filled in with the blue words "Mayor," green words "Albona Ristorante," purple for "Exotic/Erotic Ball," and red for "Free WiFi in the City."

"Presley!" I heard Ryan call my name. I reluctantly pulled away from the fascinating board.

"The mayor's coming today?" I asked as an opener.

"I guess," Ryan said, apparently not interested in anything that didn't have to do with Hollywood gossip. He stood to greet me and I shook his hand. He wore his casual clothes, similar to those he'd worn to the party—jeans, T-shirt, and athletic shoes. The hoodie he'd worn hung on the back of his chair. "Come with me. Let's have coffee in the break room so we can chat."

I followed him back down the hall to a dimly lit room filled with food and drink vending machines, plus a coffeemaker. Budget cuts, I thought, disappointed not to see a catered café and mini-Starbucks on-site. Ryan poured himself a black coffee and offered me one. I took it with no intention of drinking plain black coffee. We sat down at an empty table—actually, all the tables were currently empty—and I took off my vest.

"So spill. Whatcha got?" Ryan said, jumping in. "Something about those two murders at your party, I hope."

"They didn't happen at my party," I said quickly.

"Whatever. Talk to me." He leaned in like a hungry wolf about to dine on an innocent lamb.

I sat back to give myself some space. "Actually, I wanted to find out something from you." If he thought I had something to trade, he was more likely to tell me what I wanted to know.

This time Ryan sat back too, stretching his legs under the table. "Oh, I get it. I scratch your back; you scratch mine. As long as it doesn't cost me. I spent my last dime on a tip that turned out to be bogus."

"You were at the party that night," I said, "so did you see anything that might indicate who killed that photojournalist, Bodie?"

Ryan tapped the table. "First of all, he was no photojournalist. He was a paparazzo, the sleaziest form of life in the news biz. Second, no, I didn't see anything. If I had, I would have put it in my segment. Now, what have you got for me?"

"You didn't like Bodie much then."

"No, I didn't like him. I told you, he was scum. And Lucas promised I'd have an exclusive. Bodie had no business being there. It was *my* story."

"Did you know anything about the injunctions Cruz and Jonas had against Bodie?"

Ryan blinked rapidly. This news had surprised even him. "What injunctions?"

I ignored his question as a thought about the time frame jumped to mind. "Wait—didn't you come to the party *after* Bodie had been kicked out?"

He blinked several times, and tapped his fingers more rapidly on the table.

"I . . . must have seen him on my way in. Or lurking around. Whatever."

"Whatever?" I said. A red flag went up.

"Look, what's this all about? I thought you had something for me." He stood, his face reddening. "I don't have time for this."

I remained in my seat and looked up at him. "Did you know that parkour guy named Spidey? The one who was killed the night before the party?"

"No, I didn't know him. How would I? I'm not into stupid stuff like those crazy people. And that girl with the long black hair—she's nuts!"

A red flag flapped. "When did you see the girl?"

Ryan flushed a deep red. "I—I don't know. When all those kids were running and jumping all around the cemetery at the party. There was a girl with long black hair. . . ."

Not the night of the party, I recalled. Lark had been there, but she'd had her hair twisted up into a spiky knot, and her face had been disguised by all that white makeup.

"You were there . . . ," I said softly.

He headed for the doorway, then paused. "What are

you talking about? Yes, I was there. I was invited, re-member?"

"No, you were there the night *before*, during the party setup and rehearsal. That was when you saw Lark, the girl with the long black hair!"

"So maybe I was. I'm thorough. Sometimes I check out the locations beforehand so I can get the lay of the land and find the best place to . . . pick up the dirt. But I had nothing to do with the deaths of those two guys, if that's what you think. If you're looking for someone with a motive, check out the person who's been right in front of your face. You can show yourself out."

The person who was right in front of my face. Whom did he mean? Ah. The one who'd had the confrontation with Bodie Chase. And the one who'd kept Spidey from coming to the party and seeing the object of his affection. The one with the temper, who might have a lot to gain from the publicity surrounding the mur-ders.

Lucas Cruz.

This, coming from a gossip reporter who appeared to have been at the cemetery the night Spidey was killed, but wouldn't admit it—and who shouldn't have been there.

Chapter 18

PARTY-PLANNING TIP #18

Set up a "blood bank bar" at your Vampire Party. Hang up IV bottle dispensers, each with a different type of "blood"—AB (red-tinted vodka), O (red wine), and V (red punch). Then let the guests dispense their drinks into large blood vials (available online!).

After seeing Trace in a towel, being hit on by Robby the roommate, and getting the boot from Ryan Fitzpatrick, I needed a break from crazy people. I hopped into the MINI Cooper and fled the hills of San Francisco for the quiet flatland of Treasure Island. I'd been neglecting my real job and was sure I had mountains of paperwork to catch up on and party arrangements to make.

I hadn't talked to Brad since last night and was eager to hear if he'd learned anything from Detective Melvin. Besides, I missed him. Jeez, what was happening to me? I was starting to sound like a lovesick teenager.

I spent the short drive mulling over the facts I'd gathered from my "interrogations."

Victim Number One: Spidey

- Spidey had been living with Trace and Lark at the dorm.
- Spidey had had a major crush on Angelica.
- Spidey had been killed in the cemetery the night before the party.
- Spidey had been texting and phoning Angelica.

So what did it all mean? The dorm? It could mean he had no money, no place to go. The texting and phoning? Could it be that Spidey was Angelica's stalker? No, she mentioned the stalker after Spidey died—unless someone picked up where he left off. So who knew he'd be at the cemetery late at night?

Victim Number Two: Bodie Chase

- Bodie hadn't made much of a living in the paparazzi business and was looking for the big score.
- Bodie had taken a picture of Jonas with a woman. Who was she? And was it significant?
- Bodie had been issued a restraining order demanding he stay away from Jonas Jones—and several others.
- Bodie had been killed the night of the party with the same shovel used the night before on Spidey.

So what did this mean? Was Bodie murdered because he was trying to get dirt on Angelica for that big score? Was it something worth killing him over? Where had he gotten the money to pay off Jonas Jones? And why kill him in the cemetery like Spidey?

With my thoughts racing, I found myself magically transported to the parking lot in front of Building One with little memory of the drive.

That was kind of scary.

I parked the MINI, then glanced around for Brad's SUV. It was not in its usual spot. I did see Dee's Smart Car, Duncan's VW van, and Berk's Cabriolet, and I was glad to know they were safe in their offices and not out hunting murderers—or being hunted by one.

"Hey, Dee," I said, waltzing into our shared office and slinging my purse onto my desk.

She looked up from a script she'd been reading. "Where have you been?"

I nodded toward the in/out board. "Says right there. 'Out.'"

"Very funny. Duncan's been in here a dozen times looking for you and driving me crazy. Meanwhile, your phone has been ringing off the hook."

"Sorry about that." I headed for the door, then paused and turned back. "Has Brad been in today?"

"I haven't seen him. But he's not my boyfriend, so I don't have a reason to keep track of him."

"Oh, now you're the funny one," I sputtered indignantly. "He's not my boyfriend. And I don't keep track of him. I just wondered . . ."

I left the sentence unfinished. I had nowhere to go with it, so why bother.

I stopped by Brad's office and knocked on the door, then tried the knob. It was locked. I assumed he was on a cleaning job. I was dying to know what he'd learned from Melvin and made a mental note to give him a call after I checked on Duncan. Entering the office next to Brad's, I found Berkeley fooling with his video camera and Duncan fiddling with his cell phone, which he'd taken apart. Pieces were strewn all over his desk.

Berk looked up when he saw me.

"Presley! Got something for you," he said, nearly leaping out of his chair. Before I could say anything to Duncan, Berk had me sitting in his seat and holding his video camera. "Check this out." He switched it on. My Vampire Party materialized on the small screen.

"Did you find something?" I asked as I spotted familiar faces and recalled the party scene.

"Just watch."

I did. Moments later I saw what Berk had intended me to see. While his close-up shot focused on a couple of partyers, in the shadowed background, I saw what looked like a figure ducking behind a tree, reminding me of the figure Brad and I had seen on the *Gossip Guy* footage, but from a different angle. The area was dark and details were difficult to make out—I couldn't see the person's face—but the body language was clear. Once again, the camera had caught someone trying to stay out of sight.

"That could be anyone," I said to Berk, a little disappointed at his minor discovery.

He handed me a still photo, enlarged from the

video I'd just seen. Protruding from behind that tree was a camera lens. Duncan leaned over to eyeball the picture.

"Wow," I said. "You think it's Bodie with his camera?"

"Who else could it be?" Berk said. I could hear the excitement in his voice.

"Maybe it was Ryan Fitzpatrick, the other paparazzo," I suggested.

Berk pressed PLAY on the video, and I watched the scene continue. There was Ryan in the foreground, holding his own video camera and panning the party.

So it wasn't Ryan.

Berk was about to turn off the video when my eye caught on someone familiar.

"Wait!" I said. There was Lucas Cruz again, only this time he was chatting with Angelica, who seemed to be hanging on his every word. She touched his arm, laughed at his jokes, even played with her hair while she talked to him. Was she flirting?

Then Cruz did something very strange. He turned his head away from Angelica and the small group he'd been entertaining, and looked into the dark cemetery. He froze for a moment, set down his drink on a nearby table, and abruptly walked out of the view of the video camera.

Just before the video ended, Lucas Cruz appeared to be headed for the figure hiding behind the tree.

I was speechless for a few moments. If it was Bodie, Lucas might have been one of the last people to see him. What had happened between the two men?

"Presley, are you all right?" Duncan said, pulling me out of a horrible fantasy where Lucas Cruz attacked Bodie in the shadows with a shovel and pushed him into the open grave.

"Pres?" Berk said.

"What? Oh. Sorry . . . I was just . . . never mind." I stood up. "Thanks, Berk. Really good work. You should apply for a job at SFPD in their photo forensics department." I turned to Duncan, who seemed to be putting the phone back together as if it were a 3-D jigsaw puzzle.

"What did you think of the video?" Duncan asked.

"Interesting," I said.

"Yeah, well, I got a call from Trace. He said you'd been over there snooping around. I don't think he liked it much."

"Really? Well, too bad for him," I snapped.

"Presley!" Duncan snapped back. "He's a friend of mine. I don't want you harassing my friends. Trace didn't kill Spidey, if that's what you're thinking. They were good friends."

I hesitated to tell him what I'd learned, but then I figured it couldn't hurt, and I hoped it justified my snooping. "Did you know Spidey was living in the dorm with Trace? I think Lark is staying there too."

"So?" Duncan said defensively.

"So, it's against the rules. It could get Trace kicked out of school if the RA found out."

"No one's going to tell the RA—besides you, maybe." He shot me a look.

I shook my head in dismay. "You really think I'd do that, Duncan? Give me a break."

His tense shoulders dropped. "No. But you seem to be hinting that my friends had something to do with Spidey's death. They didn't. Besides, they had no reason to kill that other guy—the paparazzo."

Unless Bodie saw something that Trace or Lark didn't want him to, I thought. Instead, I said, "You're right."

He took a deep breath and returned to working on his cell phone.

I leaned over and patted his shoulder. "You were right about Spidey having a crush on Angelica. Trace also said Spidey thought she liked him, because she flirted with him while he was on the set."

He said nothing, just kept fiddling with his cell phone again, as if trying to suppress his feelings. And what were those feelings? Anger at me? Concern for his friends? Deep-seated suspicions about . . . what?

"I told you," he finally said, fitting in a last piece and closing the case on the cell phone. "Spidey was clueless about girls. He didn't notice that she macked on every guy in sight. I don't think she took him seriously."

"Do you know if they met up?" I asked. "That night before the party, after the setup and rehearsal? They were both there. Maybe she agreed to see him after everyone was gone."

Duncan gave me a look that let me know I was as clueless as Spidey. "I really doubt it, Presley. A big star like Angelica, fooling around with a homeless dropout whose greatest aspiration was to do competitive parkour? Come on."

"He was good-looking, in a punk sort of way," I said.

Duncan looked at me and rolled his eyes.

There would be little sense in arguing with him. He was too biased to see the possibilities—that maybe Angelica did meet up with Spidey, the bad boy. Maybe she liked the thrill of being caught, or wanted to rebel against her husband, or to make Jonas jealous.

"Anyway," I said, changing the subject. "Anything new on the murders?"

"No, but I've got some ideas."

"Duncan . . ."

"Don't worry. Nothing that will get me into trouble." He turned on his rebuilt cell phone.

"What are you doing?" I finally asked.

"Pimping my cell phone."

"What?"

"I put in a listening device."

"What do you mean, listening device?"

"Something I got off the Internet. It's supposed to let me listen in when someone's talking and let me read their text messages. Even view their contacts list— stuff like that. It's called iSpy."

"You're kidding," I said, almost laughing. "You're hacking into someone's cell phone? You can't do that. It's illegal!"

"Using it might be illegal, but owning it isn't."

"That's a matter of semantics, don't you think?"

"Huh?" he said.

"Never mind. How does it work?"

"You install the software; then it uses GSM technology to listen in to other people's conversations."

"GSM?"

"Global System for Mobile Communications."

"Definitely not legal."

He shrugged.

"So how does it work?"

"You install it on your phone and you get a text message when your target gets or makes a call. Then you can listen in if you want, by calling a special number, which puts you into a disguised teleconference mode."

"What kind of special number?"

"A bridge, just like when you teleconference. Plus it comes with a GPS tracker, so you know where the target is."

"Okay, but since it's illegal to use it, what are you going to do with it?"

He didn't respond.

"Duncan?"

"I don't know yet. I'm just playing around with it."

Duncan loved electronic gadgets and was always on the cutting edge of the latest technology. He'd helped me host a Geocaching Party, using GPS devices to discover clues and hidden caches. But I had a feeling he planned to use this new gadget to help himself find out what happened to Spidey.

And that could only get him into a heap of trouble.

"Duncan, promise me you won't do anything illegal. At the very least, you could be arrested for wire-tapping or something. At worst, your so-called target could find out and . . ."

"And what? Kill me? I don't think so."

"Okay, Double-oh-seven. But be careful."

"Sure, Moneypenny," he said, implying that I was mothering him again.

Well, he was no Bond, I thought. He was more like Inspector Gadget. And if he tried to use that thing, he might get himself killed—just like his friend Spidey.

Chapter 19

Write some vampire-related quotes on tombstone-shaped poster board, such as, "One thing vampire children have to be taught early on is, don't run with wooden stakes."—Jack Handey. Then set them around the room to entertain your guests.

Anxious to hear what Brad had learned from Detective Melvin, I knocked again on his door on my way back to my office, hoping he might have sneaked in while I was talking with Duncan and Berkeley. No such luck.

I headed for my desk and sat down in my chair, my eyes glazing over as I surveyed the many party forms I'd already filled out for upcoming events. My phone light was blinking, no doubt signaling even more requests for parties, and I took the next ten or fifteen minutes to listen to them all. While I was happy to have the work, I felt a little overwhelmed.

One call got me especially excited—a request for a Wine Tasting Party in the nearby Wine Country, hosted by a friend of my caterer, Rocco Ghirenghelli, who owned a small winery in Napa. I called him back immediately and booked a time to chat with him about the details.

After I'd caught up on paperwork, I made another call to Brad Matthews. It was afternoon and I still hadn't heard from him. He must be as buried in work as I was, I thought. When he didn't answer, I left another message, asking him to call me. I hung up, thinking it odd that he hadn't at least checked in since last night.

To distract myself from worrying—and avoid work—I decided I needed to talk to Otto the grave digger, now that he'd been released from jail, and Angelica's mysterious husband. I had a hunch Otto knew more than he was letting on—after all, he was at the cemetery nearly all the time. As for Angelica's husband, there was something about that guy that didn't seem husbandlike. He was someone to check out. Of course, if I didn't answer the rest of these party requests, I'd soon be out of a job. But there would be time for that. Right now, solving the murders—and keeping Duncan out of danger—took priority.

Neither Otto nor Angelica's husband would be easy to find. I flipped a mental coin and decided to talk with Otto first, since he had "portended" the deaths. While I felt relatively safe going to the cemetery in the daytime, I wasn't stupid and didn't plan to go alone to a place where two men had been murdered. I'd hoped Brad could meet me there, but since I couldn't reach him, I went for plan B.

I turned in my chair. "Hey, Delicia, you busy?"

Dee, earbuds in place, was listening to music and mouthing the lyrics. She didn't respond.

I waved in front of her face. "What are you doing?"

"Trying to memorize this song," she said, popping out the buds.

"Are you auditioning for a musical?" I asked.

"Understudy for the role of Young Ethnic Female Performer in *Beach Blanket Babylon*." She framed her face and gave an exaggerated smile.

"How cool!"

"Yeah, *if* I get the job. They're looking for someone who can sing, dance, and act, as well as imitate cultural icons, like Beyonce and Condoleezza Rice. The benefits package is awesome."

"You're perfect for it!"

"I hope so. Sixty actors tried out, and I was one of nine who got a callback. Very nerve-racking, performing in front of Jo Schuman Silver and a bunch of other producers and directors. And I'm up against some pretty talented girls."

"So are you! You really have a shot at this. I'm so excited for you."

"Well, if I get the part, I'll be psyched. And if I don't, it was still fun to see Val Diamond rehearse. She's ridonculous!" Dee's face was flushed with excitement. I mentally crossed my fingers for her. "So, Pres, what did you want?"

"Oh, nothing. I was going to ask if you wanted to come with me to the cemetery to interview the crazy guy, Otto. But it's not important. You keep rehearsing. I know you're going to get this part."

"Thanks, Pres. You sure you don't need me?"

"No, I'll be fine." I picked up my purse and headed for the door. "And if you see Brad, will you tell him to call me?"

She nodded as she replaced her earbuds, but I could see her mind was already back on her song. I closed the door to our office to prevent further interruptions.

I debated whether to go to the cemetery alone or not, now that plan B had failed. Only stupid women go into dangerous situations alone. Like dark basements. Carrying faulty flashlights. Wearing only their underwear. On Halloween night. But I wasn't *that* stupid. And it wasn't Halloween night. I knew Otto was a loose cannon. He obviously had some kind of mental problem, probably due to alcohol. While I didn't think he killed those two guys—he had no motive other than to protect what he considered his property—he was still unpredictable and scary. And I was no match for his size and strength.

Damn it, Brad. Where are you?

I got into my MINI and drove home. There was no way I was going to drag Duncan back to the cemetery, and I was nearly out of options. I was about to give up on the idea of talking to Otto alone, when I had an idea. I pulled into my carport, hopped out of the car, and entered my condo. All three cats tried to trip me as I hurried down the hall. Either they really, really missed me, or they knew who buttered their cat food. I quickly fed them, gave each one a brief massage, and gathered a few party items from the closet before leaving and relocking the door behind me.

There was no way I was going into the metaphorically dark basement without protection.

Lawndale Cemetery looked deserted when I arrived at nearly four in the afternoon. There were no visitors or tourists that I could see. Being fall, it would be getting dark soon, and I didn't plan to stay beyond sunset. After parking on the narrow lane near the party site, I got out of the car, collected my party supplies, and locked the door.

"Otto?" I called out, stepping around several graves on my way up the slight incline to the pet cemetery. I remembered the trailer parked up there and wondered if the old man lived inside.

Every few steps I called out his name, not wanting to startle him. By the time I reached the ancient-looking trailer, I'd still seen no sign of Otto Gunther. I was about to knock on the rusting door, thinking he might be sleeping, or passed out drunk, or worse, when I heard a voice booming from behind me.

"Stop yer yelling!"

Talk about being startled—I nearly peed my pants. Tightening the grip on the two party props, I turned slowly, trying not to show him my fear.

"Otto! I was looking for you." He was standing inside a walk-in toolshed, holding a hand fork gardening tool. I smiled, hoping a flash of white teeth would let him know I meant no harm.

"What fer?" he said, baring his own crooked yellow teeth. "I already talked to the po-lice." He turned back to the toolshed and hung up the hand fork on a hook, in its black outlined spot.

"I'm Presley Parker. Do you remember me, from the party we were setting up the other night?"

He walked out of the shed, closed the door, and locked the padlock. Squinting, he took a step toward me and shoved a hand into the pocket of his filthy overalls.

Uh-oh. Was that a gun in his pocket or . . .

"I—I just wanted to ask you a couple of questions about what you saw last night."

"I didn't see nothin'," he barked. I watched as his hand gripped the object in his pocket.

I took a step backward and bumped into the trailer. Starting to panic, I raised the plastic pitchfork I had used for decoration at an Angels and Demons Party and held it like a spear. The three red prongs looked menacing—if you didn't look too closely.

Otto blinked.

I lifted my other hand with the canister and aimed at him. "Don't try anything, Otto. I have a weapon and mace."

Only I didn't have mace. I had a can of Spray Fake Blood. I'd bought a case on the Internet for the Vampire Party, then decided not to use it, since Cruz had his own art department and could whip up fake blood easily. I kept it because I figured it would come in handy one day for another party theme. The directions on the can promised "three different effects—bullet hole, dripping blood line, or blood spatter. Great for Shark Victim or Lizzie Borden costume." For now, all I cared about was the warning label: KEEP AWAY FROM SKIN AND EYES. MAY CAUSE IRRITATION.

Perfect.

"What the hell are you doing?" Otto said, eyeing my weapons.

"Protecting myself," I said, ready for any sudden attack.

Otto shook his head as if I were the crazy one, pulled a pack of chewing tobacco from his pocket, and walked around me to the trailer door.

I stepped back, ready to jab or spray.

He opened the door.

"Where are you going?" I asked, lowering the trident and fake blood. "Wait! I just want to talk to you."

He stopped on the top step, holding the door open, and turned to me. "With a pitchfork and mace?"

"I was just being cautious." Suddenly I felt ridiculous. Yes, I was alone in this cemetery with a giant of a man who had owned the bloody shovel that killed two people. But at the moment he didn't seem as crazy as he had the other day.

He started to go inside the trailer.

I stepped closer. "Can I ask you a couple of questions, Otto? Please?"

He paused. "Like what?"

Maybe Brad's hunch was right. "You saw something the night that Spidey got killed, didn't you?"

His eyes narrowed. "The owl portends—" he began.

"Cut the crap," I said. "There's nothing wrong with you a bath and a cup of coffee wouldn't cure. Tell me, what did you see?"

He smiled, a real smile, not a grimace. He knew the jig was up.

I smiled back.

"You want a beer?" he asked, still holding the door open.

"*Uh*, sure."

"I'll go git 'em. Find a seat. I'll be right back."

Thank God he didn't invite me into his lair. Of course, the alternative was sitting on a cold headstone that belonged to Fluffy or Cujo. I sat my bony butt on the largest headstone I could find—MAX. FAITHFUL COMPANION—and scanned the area for a quick get-away if needed. While Otto might be smarter than I originally thought, hopefully I hadn't gotten any stupider. "Always plan your exit strategy," my mother used to say. Of course, she was referring to escaping dull parties, but still, it was a life lesson I'd never forgotten.

Otto returned with two Budweisers and handed me one before taking up residence on a nearby dead-cat marker. I took a sip, he took a chug, and I gave the beer a few seconds to relax my tense muscles. "Thanks," I said.

"No problem," he replied. "Found them the other night after chasing off them grave-hoppers. They got scared and left them behind."

I wondered if that was how Otto got most of his liquor.

"You enjoy scaring people, don't you?"

He grinned again and took another swallow. This old guy was enjoying himself. "It's kinda expected of me, what with my living in a trailer here and looking the way I do."

"The city of Colma really lets you stay here?"

"Yeah. I do light maintenance for them, keep away vandals, stuff like that. It's quiet. My wife is here."

I was puzzled for a second. "Here?"

"Over there. Space four twenty-two. She was one of the last to be buried here. I like being close-by."

I nodded. It made sense in a way. "Have you been here for a long time?"

"A few years. I used to be a professor at Stanford. German literature. But I like the peace and quiet, the slower pace."

"Well, you had me fooled." I sipped my beer. "So, what did you see that night, Otto?"

"Okay, I'll tell you, but I don't want to get involved with the police again. I just want to live my life quietly up here, you understand?"

"I do."

"Okay, well, I saw those grave-hoppers and tried to run them off. They scattered—at least I thought they did. When I went back and checked, I heard voices. Two people arguing."

"A man and a woman?" I asked, thinking it might have been Spidey and Angelica.

"No. Two men. I couldn't make out what they said, and the argument didn't last long. They finally left, so I went back to my trailer and had a beer. Then I heard a thud. I looked out my window and saw somebody running. He ran by the Black Pond, threw something in, and took off."

The hairs on the back of my neck were dancing up and down. "You saw only one person running?"

"Yes. After I found out that kid had died, I wondered if the guy who ran off had anything to do with it, but the cops didn't think so. Not until that second guy got killed."

"Can you describe him?"

"No. He was wearing black, I think. That's it."

Everyone seemed to be wearing black that night.

"But you said he threw something into the pond. The Black Pond, you called it. Was it the pond we used at the party?"

"No. The duck pond, over there." He pointed to the left, the other side of where we'd held the party. I call it the Black Pond 'cause it's more of a swamp now. If you dropped something in there, you'd never see it again.

Wow, this was big news. The killer—assuming it was the killer—threw something into the pond. Evidence? The police never found Spidey's cell phone. Could that have been it?

"Did you tell the police, Otto?"

"No. I figured if they thought I was crazy, they'd let me go. But if I'd said I'd seen something, they'd keep me there forever, grilling me. I just wanted to get back home."

"Thanks, Otto. I appreciate this. You've been a big help."

"Like I said, I don't want to get involved with the police again. Besides, what's done is done."

"But you could be in jeopardy, Otto, if the killer thinks you saw something."

"I'm ready for him," he said mysteriously, then suddenly grinned. "And not with some toy pitchfork or can of spray paint."

I smiled. "Didn't fool you at all, eh? You didn't believe it was mace?"

"It said 'Spray Fake Blood' right there on the can. I can read, you know."

No doubt in five languages, I thought. I was starting to like Otto. After this was over, I'd have to do something to show my appreciation. Buy him a beer? Get him a haircut?

"What about the guy who was killed and tossed into the open grave that you discovered? Did you see what happened?"

"No. I was watching something on TV, had the volume up." He tapped his ear. "Getting to be hard of hearing, you know. I went outside for a smoke—my wife didn't like me smoking in the trailer. Funny how habits stay with you. Anyway, that was when I saw my shovel lying on the ground—the one from my shed. I guess I'd forgotten to lock it up. Then all hell broke loose. . . ."

He seemed lost in the memory. The fog had rolled in and the cemetery had gotten dark. It was time to leave. But I had one last question.

"Otto, what was all that stuff you said about 'trespassing on hallowed ground, disturbing the dead, the owl portends, death will follow'?"

He chuckled. "Oh that. People who come to cemeteries love that kind of mumbo-jumbo, superstitions and whatnot. I did a little theater in my youth so I like to give them a show. As I said, I scare off trespassers. Guess it didn't work with you and your party people, eh?"

"You pretty much scared the crap out of me."

He gave a satisfied nod. "Want to hear some more? If you count the cars at a funeral procession, you've just counted the number of weeks you have left to live. . . ."

"Stop! Now I'm going to have nightmares!"

Otto chuckled again, obviously enjoying himself at my expense. I considered giving him my plastic pitchfork. That old man had the devil in him. But I was glad I kept it. In spite of the moonlight, the walk back to the car in the foggy darkness totally creeped me out.

Chapter 20

PARTY-PLANNING TIP #20

If you decide to invite real vampires to your party, make sure they aren't immortal enemies. Not all vampires are alike, and include night-walking vampires, energy-feeding vampires, empathic vampires, and soul-sucking vampires. And for God's sake, never invite a werewolf to a Vampire Party.

Walking back to my car, I couldn't help but notice how quickly it had gotten dark. It must have been the plethora of eucalyptus trees that blocked out the usually gradual transition from day to night. The family-sized mausoleums were particularly haunting as they stood there silently, small stone houses filled with bodies. Some of the mausoleums seemed completely enclosed, with no visible entries or exits, but most had wrought-iron fences and gates to protect the long-term residents from being pillaged and plundered.

At the last minute, I took an impulsive detour to check out the Black Pond, only a few yards away. I got out my cell phone and used the flashlight app to guide the way and make sure I didn't trip on anything. When I reached the pond, it looked like a mud hole, about the size of a small swimming pool. It was so dark and dense, I doubted I would see my toes if I happened to stick my foot in, which I didn't plan to do.

If someone—say, the killer—threw something—say, the cell phone—into that pond, it would take a professional dredging service to find it.

I had a sudden thought. What if a body had been tossed in there . . . ?

Feeling goose bumps erupting all over my body, I turned back and hurried to the car, conjuring up images of every cemetery-related horror movie I'd seen. With my every step, I thought I saw movement where there should have been stillness.

Where was Brad when I needed him?

In fact, where was Brad, period? I was getting seriously worried.

Shifting into power-walking mode, I reached my car, fumbled with the keys—just like in the movies—and finally yanked open the door and scooted inside. After locking the doors, I punched Brad's number on my cell phone for the umpteenth time.

No answer, just straight to voice mail.

Did he have that many dead bodies to clean up after?

Or was he avoiding me?

Maybe that was it. He'd come to his senses, realized I had too much baggage to engage in a real relationship, and decided to "comfort" one of his grieving clients—the live kind, not a dead one. Generally I'm too distracted to become paranoid, but something gnawed at the back of my mind about Brad. Whatever it was, it didn't feel good.

I decided to swing by his house on Yerba Buena Island before going home, to see if he might have fallen or passed out or whatever. I pulled off the Bay Bridge and drove slowly over the curvy island road. Unlike Treasure Island, which lit up at night with houses and streetlights and few trees to block the moonlight, Yerba Buena Island was dark, thick with trees and sparse on house lights. I pulled up in front of the former living quarters of the big-shot naval officers, now deserted except for one. The homes might have been long empty, but they were still grand: two- and three-story Classic Revival houses, with crystal chandeliers, hardwood floors, and decorative wainscoting.

Brad lived as a caretaker in Admiral Bryson's home, just two houses away from the former Admiral Nimitz home, the grandest of all. I got out of the car and searched for visible warning signs that something might be amiss outside—an overstuffed mailbox, newspapers piling up on the porch, graffiti and vandalism. Everything seemed normal, including the front entry, which still sported the "Crime Scene—Do Not Cross" tape that Brad had strung up when he moved in to keep curious tourists from bothering him.

I walked up the gray steps and peered through the

windows. There were no lights on, no noise coming through the walls, no signs of life.

Then I remembered Bruiser.

Where was Brad's dog? Brad had sort of inherited a fluffy teacup poodle from a woman who'd been killed on a previous job. To my surprise, he'd kept the little purse pooch formerly known as Chou-Chou, renamed him Bruiser, and let the little guy even sleep in his—sometimes *our*—bed.

"Bruiser!" I called through the window. "Chou-Chou–Bruiser! Come here, boy!"

The dog usually came yapping to the front door at the first sign of a visitor, no doubt ready to attack at his master's command.

Not this time.

I walked around the outside of the house, looking for anything out of place, eventually giving up when I reached the front door again. That was when I heard a high-pitched scream.

I ran in the direction of the sound. It seemed to come from the street below where lower officers' quarters were. That was where Sansa Brien, a single mom, lived with her five-year-old son, Spencer. Spencer often dog-sat Bruiser, while his mother, like many enterprising single parents, worked from home. She ran a day care program for families living on YB and TI. Often when I drove to Brad's, passing her place, there were half a dozen children running around inside the fenced yard and screened-in porch.

"Sansa!" I called out when I reached the yard. Spencer and a little girl were playing with a baby carriage inside the enclosed porch while Sansa sat in a wicker chair, watching them. "Is everything okay?"

She looked up and grinned. "Hi, Presley. Sorry about the noise. Maile screamed when the dog almost escaped from the carriage."

I leaned over the chest-level fence and spotted Bruiser in the carriage. Oh my God. Wasn't that dog abuse? I wondered what the PETA people would say about this. However, Bruiser seemed to be enjoying being the baby. He was busily licking the little girl's hand.

So Bruiser was still at Sansa's. I knew Brad didn't like to leave his dog alone for long periods, so he took him to Sansa's day care when he was gone. Spencer was Bruiser's "primary caregiver," and Brad paid the boy for his services. It was a win-win for everyone, including Bruiser, who got more than enough attention.

Sansa stood up and pulled her sweater tightly around her as she approached the fence. "We were just about to go in. They love being on the porch, but even with the heaters, it's getting cold. I'm still waiting for Maile's mom to come get her. I guess she's running late."

"I don't know how you manage those kids all day long. I'd be in a coma after an hour."

She laughed. "Aw, I love it. It's like being a kid again and getting to play all day. Would you like a sand pancake? I think that's on the menu today."

Sand pancake. *Erp*, I thought.

"Listen, I won't keep you, but I see you still have Bruiser. Brad hasn't come back yet?"

"No. In fact, Bruiser spent last night here. I haven't heard from Brad. I usually get a call if he's going to be out late or on a job longer than expected. I tried calling, but all I got was voice mail."

Her words caused a chill to run down my spine. No sign of Brad since last night?

She must have seen the concern in my face. "You think something's wrong, Presley?"

"I'm not sure. But I'll call his friend, Detective Melvin, and see if he knows where Brad is."

"Well, let me know if I can do anything. Meanwhile, we'll take good care of Bruiser."

I headed back to my car with dread in the pit of my stomach.

Where the hell was Brad?

I called the San Francisco Police Department from my car and asked for Detective Luke Melvin. To my surprise, he took my call immediately.

"What's up, Parker?" he said, sounding rushed. I think that was a tone he cultivated.

"Sorry to bother you, Detective, but have you seen Brad today?"

"No, but then, I wasn't in charge of him today. I thought that was your job."

"Seriously, Detective, I think something's wrong. I haven't heard from him since he said he was meeting up with you last night. I checked his house. His dog sitter says she hasn't seen him either."

"Maybe he's busy cleaning up after dead people."

"Maybe, but I'm pretty sure he would have called at some point." I paused, waiting for a response. When none came, I asked, "Has anything turned up on the deaths of those two men? Something you might have mentioned to Brad when you saw him?"

"I told him about the DNA test. It came back positive for both Spidey and Bodie Chase. Confirmed that blunt force trauma led to their deaths. Also found a fake ID in Spidey's pocket, but no driver's license. The ID was for a dormitory at SF State."

The detective was full of news. He'd confirmed my suspicions that Spidey had been living in Trace's dorm room. But right now that didn't seem important.

"Did Brad say where he was going after he left you?"

"Said he was going to visit a friend. I assumed it was you."

"Any idea who else it might have been?"

"What's the matter, Parker? You think he's cheating on you?"

"Don't be ridiculous, Detective. If you know where he went, tell me."

"He said something about digging up some dirt on someone. Then he just took off."

"Digging up some dirt?"

"Something like that. When I mentioned that Spidey's wallet and keys never turned up, he got this look in his eye and made the reference to digging up dirt."

A chill shot through me. My hands started to tremble. "Detective, can you meet me at the Lawndale Cemetery? I think Brad's in trouble."

"What? Why the cemetery?"

"You said Brad went to dig up some dirt. I think he meant the cemetery."

"That's a big leap, Parker. Besides, why would he go back there? My officers covered that place."

"Maybe to look for something belonging to Spidey. Or maybe to see Otto Gunther . . ."

"We checked Gunther out and let him go. No evidence. He's harmless. Crazy, but harmless."

No one's harmless under the right circumstances, I thought. Maybe I was wrong and would have agreed with the detective after meeting Otto again.

"Well, I'm going there now. I hope you'll meet me. Something's seriously wrong. I feel it in my bones."

"Okay, okay. I'll see you there in . . . twenty."

"Thanks, Detective," I said.

The line went dead.

I drove like a vampire bat out of hell and reached the cemetery in twenty minutes. Traffic was light—most of the commuters were probably home already. I had a feeling I'd even beat Detective Melvin there—unless he used his bells and whistles.

I pulled up to the edge of the neglected cemetery, checked to make sure my car doors were locked, and glanced around for the detective's unmarked white car.

There was no sign of him—or any other car, not even Brad's SUV.

I decided to wait until the detective arrived before

getting out of the car and exposing myself to possible danger. I wasn't afraid of Otto anymore, now that I knew him better, but who knew who else might be around.

I hoped this was nothing more than a wild-goose chase, but I was beginning to panic about Brad.

The police had found Spidey's car, locked, but nothing inside except fast-food wrappers and some clothes. No ID. But had they found Bodie Chase's car? I didn't remember anyone mentioning it. Maybe the killer drove it off a cliff or into the Black Pond. Just because I didn't see Brad's SUV didn't mean he wasn't here.

But how was I supposed to find him if he was? My psychic abilities? A corpse's whisper? A bell-ringing coffin? I could always try screaming his name. But if something had happened to him . . .

This was nuts. Once again, I was about to make a fool of myself in front of the detective, who already thought I was a complete idiot. He'd probably take me in for a forty-eight-hour psych watch.

My cell phone rang, startling me. "Hello?" I said breathlessly.

"Presley, dear, it's your mother. Did I happen to give you the recipe for the pumpkin cake roll your grandmother used to make? I can't seem to find it, and there's this nice gentleman at the hotel here I thought might enjoy it."

"Mother, I can't talk right now. May I call you back?"

"Certainly, dear. But don't take too long. People around this place don't seem to last forever."

Her words made me shudder. I felt bad blowing her off. I promised myself I'd not only call her back, I'd help her make the pumpkin cake roll myself—when all of this was over.

I hung up the phone and held it in my trembling hand for a few seconds, wondering where the hell the detective was. I couldn't just sit here, doing nothing.

I had an idea and dialed Duncan's cell.

"Yo?" he answered.

"Duncan! You know that spy software you added to your cell phone?"

"Yeah?"

"Does it work?"

"Dude, I tried it out on Berk's and Dee's phones. It's awesome. Heard every word they said."

"Is it possible to use it to find someone, rather than listen in on their conversation?"

"Sure. I belong to a tracking service. I can tell where you are by just—"

I cut him off. "Not me. Brad. Can you find Brad's cell phone?"

"As long as it's GPS-enabled, I should be able to. What kind of phone is it?"

"A Droid." I recited the number.

"Hold on."

I heard him clicking away at his computer keyboard. "What are you doing?"

"Logging on to the tracking site. That'll give me a map and the location of the cell phone. Hold on. . . ."

Lights suddenly appeared in my rearview mirror as

I waited for Duncan to get back to me. A car slowly approached mine from behind. In the glare of the headlights and the surrounding darkness, I couldn't tell what kind of car it was, or who was behind the wheel. I broke into a sweat and double-checked the door locks.

"Duncan?" I whispered into the phone. "Are you still there?"

No answer. He'd put me on hold. Or had he hung up?

I glanced back at the car behind mine. The driver's door opened. I tried to make out the identity of the man who had stepped out of the car, but the headlights obscured my ability to see anything except an outline.

An outline that began walking to my car.

I hoped to God it was Detective Melvin.

Chapter 21

PARTY-PLANNING TIP #21

If you're a fan of the Twilight series, give your party room the look of a northwest forest, with gray crepe-paper clouds, a fog machine, and signs pointing to Forks, La Push Beach, and the Cullens. Or find a Transylvanian Gothic castle for your Vampire Party.

I grabbed the Spray Fake Blood container and held it with both hands, ready to bloody up whoever was approaching my car. Although it was locked, if the guy had something heavy, such as a shovel, he could probably bash the window in.

But I was ready for him.

Sort of.

The figure stopped next to the driver's side, his body blocking my view. I couldn't see his face, only his waistline, and even that was in shadows.

I held up the spray can.

The figure bent over and shined a flashlight in my face.

"Parker?" came a muffled voice through the window glass.

"Detective!" I practically screamed. I lowered the window. "Thank God!"

"What are you doing?" he asked.

"I was . . . waiting for you, of course." I tucked the Spray Fake Blood under the front seat.

"It looked like you were about to spray me. What's in the can?"

"*Uh*, mace. You know, just in case."

"Mace, *huh*. Never seen a can of mace that big. So, you wanted me to meet you here. I'm here. So what's this all about?"

I got out of the car. Now that the detective had arrived, my courage returned. I just hoped I wasn't crying wolf or the detective would never help me again.

My phone rang.

"Wait a second," I said. "Maybe that's Brad." The detective brushed off his tailored suit and tapped his Italian leather shoe while I took the call. It was not a good fashion choice for a cemetery, but then the detective always dressed as if he were about to appear on television rather than solve a crime.

"Hello? . . . Duncan! I thought I lost you! Did you call the number?"

One of Detective Melvin's eyebrows rose as he listened to my side of the conversation.

"Dude," Duncan said, "your reception is spotty. Anyway, I located Brad's phone. Get this. It's like, only a few feet away from yours. I checked yours too."

My skin went cold. "What do you mean, it's only a few feet away from mine? Where?"

"As I said, I'm getting a signal coming from the same place."

"Duncan, where, exactly? Be more specific."

"Hey, that's the best I can do. Look around. He should be right there. . . ."

The phone went dead. The signal was lost again.

I looked at Detective Melvin, who was staring at me.

"What's going on, Parker?" Melvin glanced around. "Who's here? Where?"

"Brad! Duncan tracked him using GPS and his cell phone. Brad's phone is here in the cemetery somewhere, supposedly only a few feet away from my own phone."

Detective Melvin flashed his light around the darkness. "I don't see anyone. Wait here. I'll have a look around."

I wasn't waiting for anyone, not even the detective. I held up my phone, stepped a few feet away, and punched Brad's number.

Nothing; there was only the sound of the eucalyptus trees rustling in the breeze.

I moved a few steps deeper into the cemetery and redialed. Nothing. I repeated the action, walking a few feet farther and pausing to listen for the sound of Brad's ring tone.

"Parker . . . ," Detective Melvin called out from the opposite direction.

"Quiet!" I snapped, temporarily forgetting I was talking to a police officer. I punched the number again. I listened. Still nothing. I kept moving past gravestones and mausoleums, listening until my ears ached.

"Parker!" he called again.

I froze. "Wait! I hear something! It sounds like music!"

The detective ran over and joined me. He listened and his eyes widened. I could tell he'd heard it too. It was the distant, muted sound of that irritating "Clean Up" song from the *Barney* TV show.

It was Brad's ring tone.

It was coming from only a few feet away, seemingly from inside a small mausoleum the size of a kids' two-story playhouse.

"In there!" I cried, running the few feet toward the fenced-in structure. The detective was right behind me. I yanked on the gate until I saw the chained lock.

While the gate around the mausoleum was old and rusted, the lock looked new.

Detective Melvin whipped out his radio, pushed a button, and spoke into the walkie-talkie. "Yeah, this is Detective Luke Melvin from SFPD. I have a possible two-oh-seven here, a man trapped. Request backup. Send an ambulance. And search and rescue." He gave the address and put the radio away.

"I can't open it," I said, letting go of the lock in frustration.

"I'll climb over," Detective Melvin said without hesitation. He hooked his expensive shoe in between two wrought-iron bars, stepped onto a crossbar, and hoisted himself up. He swung his other leg over and between a couple of mean-looking spikes that were just waiting to jab him. I almost couldn't watch.

Steadying himself, and no doubt offering up a

prayer, he grabbed hold of two spikes, swung his other leg over, then jumped down to the ground.

"That was fun," he said, brushing off his suit.

"Hurry!" I said.

The opening to the mausoleum was a metal door that also looked rusted by age and the elements. But if Brad was in there, then someone had managed to open it recently—and close it again.

There was a hole where the door handle would have been. It had either broken off at some point, or someone had cut it off. I felt sweat break out on my forehead, in spite of the cold.

Detective Melvin gripped the side of the door and tried to pull it open, but it wouldn't budge. He needed something to pry it.

I had an idea. "Hold on! I'll be right back."

Remembering Otto's toolshed, I ran up the incline. The lights were on in his trailer, so I headed for the door and pounded, calling his name. "Otto! It's me! Presley! I need your help."

Seconds later, Otto, wearing a bathrobe and slippers, opened the door.

"What's going on?" he said.

"My friend—I think he's trapped inside one of the abandoned mausoleums! We need something to pry open the door."

He blinked, probably not used to anyone wanting to borrow his tools in the middle of the night. "Come on," he finally said, and stepped down from the trailer onto the ground. I followed him over to his shed nearby and watched as he unlocked the bolt, then pulled open the door. Inside were enough tools to start a hardware store—everything imaginable, except a shovel.

He grabbed a small spade, a long two-pronged pry bar, and a hammer. He handed the hammer to me.

"Hurry!" I said, and led the way down the hill. We found Detective Melvin still trying to pull open the door to the mausoleum with his fingers, with no success.

Otto stopped abruptly when we reached the gate.

"Hold up," Otto said, eyeing the officer and shaking his pry bar at him. "You didn't tell me the police were here. This is the guy who arrested me."

"Otto, the detective is here to help me. I think my friend Brad is locked inside. Please. Will you help us?" I searched his rheumy eyes in the moonlight. Otto had obviously had a few beers.

"Outta my way," he said, in his cultivated-curmudgeon way. He tossed the tools over the fence, then hoisted himself over, much the same way the detective had done, only with less grace, wearing the bathrobe and boxers.

"Move!" he barked at the detective. Melvin was smart enough to know who was temporarily in charge and backed off.

Otto took the pry bar, stuck it in the crack between the door and the wall, and hammered it in as far as it would go. He began moving the bar back and forth. After several minutes of this, the door began to creak and then give.

"Grab that," he ordered the detective, nodding to

the small spade. "Use it at the bottom, while I work on the top here. Presley, keep the flashlight on the door."

Together they continued wedging the tools into the crack, slowly making progress at the opening. When they had enough of the door surface to grip, they took hold and wrenched the door open. It creaked again as it slowly gave.

Focusing the light, I strained to see if Brad was inside. The interior space was tiny, with barely enough room for one person to enter.

I shined the light on the floor.

There, on the cold cement floor, lay Brad, on his stomach, still dressed in his once-white jumpsuit. The top of the suit was caked with dark blood. So was Brad's forehead.

He wasn't moving.

Detective Melvin rushed in and knelt down, blocking the light.

"Is he alive?" I asked, tears welling in my eyes.

"Move the light!" he commanded. He felt Brad's neck for a pulse.

"Yes, but his pulse is weak. Looks like he's lost a lot of blood."

I heard sirens in the distance and wiped away my tears. It was chaos after that—a jumble of officers, paramedics, search-and-rescue guys—all moving to action to save Brad Matthews. The S and R guys used some kind of giant wire cutters and had the outer gate open in seconds. The paramedics stepped in next, and I caught snatches of comments—"head wound," "blunt force trauma," "blood loss," "start an IV." They lifted him onto the stretcher and carried him to the ambulance in a matter of minutes. I thought about asking if I could ride with him to the hospital but decided to take my car so I wouldn't be stranded.

I followed the ambulance to San Francisco General—there are no hospitals in Colma—praying that Brad would be all right. Hearing that he'd lost a lot of blood had shaken me the most. Thank God for Duncan and his gadgets, I thought as I raced along, trying to keep up. Thank God for cell phones. Thank God for Otto and his tools. Thank God for paramedics and S and R guys and police officers.

And thank God Detective Melvin believed me and met me at the cemetery. I owed him for that. I owed a lot of people.

When I reached the hospital, I parked in the ER lot and dashed inside, hoping I could see Brad in the emergency room and let him know I was there for him. A nurse told me I had to wait, so I finally wandered off to the ER waiting room, where I found Detective Melvin talking on his cell phone in spite of the sign that featured a picture of a cell phone with a red line through it. He hung up when he saw me.

"Heard anything?" I asked as I sat down one chair away from him.

He shook his head. "Nothing yet."

Tears welled up again. I hated letting Detective Melvin see me cry and tried to discreetly blot my eyes with the sides of my fingers.

"You really like the guy, don't you," Melvin said, sounding surprised.

"Duh," I said.

"Yeah. Matthews is a great guy. I've known him a long time."

"When he used to be a cop?"

Melvin nodded.

"So why did he quit the force? I mean, I know he accidentally shot someone, but why give up being a police officer?"

"You'll have to ask him," the detective said.

"Oh, it's the old Bro Code, eh?" I said, with a hint of sarcasm.

"Something like that."

These two guys really had each other's backs.

"Well, I can't just sit here and wait for news," I said, standing up. "I'll go crazy."

"You're not going back to the cemetery . . . ," Detective Melvin half asked, half warned me.

"No. Not tonight anyway. But I have to do *something*."

"Parker, let the police handle this. The situation is obviously escalating. You're in no position to help with this investigation. And you could be the next victim."

"I know," I said. "But there's one thing I can do right now."

"What's that?" the detective asked.

"Give blood," I said. I headed down the hall looking for someone who would take my O positive—besides a vampire. In light of everything, it seemed appropriate.

Chapter 22

I could never be a nurse or doctor, I thought as I entered the room. Just the idea of needles always caused me pain. I almost turned around.

"May I help you?" the volunteer at the desk said before I could chicken out.

"*Uh*, I'm here to"—I hesitated, and glanced around for an escape path—"*uh* . . . give blood."

"Great, you've come to the right place," the older woman said cheerily, as if I were stopping by for a spot of tea. "Have a seat. I'll need you to do a little paperwork first."

I sat, feeling my heart rate accelerate off the

charts. If anyone checked me now, I'd probably be admitted into the ER.

Calm down, Presley, I told myself, possibly out loud. *They're just taking a little blood, not bleeding you out.* My pep talk did little to ease my anxiety. I felt nauseated and dizzy, and I wondered if I'd faint right here at the desk.

Seemingly oblivious to my symptoms, the perky volunteer handed me a form that asked about my medical history, whether I drank or smoked, what I'd eaten recently, and so on. I stalled as long as I could, taking my time to fill out each question carefully and thoroughly. Finally, I had no choice but to give her the completed form while trying to keep the room from spinning. "Can I donate my blood to a specific person?"

"Yes, if it's needed and you're a match. Whom would you like it to go to?"

"Brad Matthews. He's in the ER."

After reading over the form, the volunteer looked up. "Are you all right?"

"Sure. Yes. Let's do this." I stood up. And wished I hadn't.

Sensing I needed support, she took me by the arm and led me to a reclining chair between two other chairs, both empty. Good. I didn't want to have to look at anyone else's needles or blood. A phlebotomist in a white lab coat came over and, after a brief greeting, began to feel my veins—which are pretty much nonexistent. Memories of being a kid and having a blood test for mono washed over me. Back then the nurse couldn't find a vein either, and kept poking and poking that needle until I finally swooned. My mother stepped up and demanded "an expert" or she was taking me home.

Where was my mother when I needed her?

The tech tied on a rubber tourniquet, cleaned my arm, tapped a few more times, and inserted the needle.

"Wow, you're good!" I said. I hadn't felt a thing. I was almost giddy with relief. "How much blood do you take? How long will I be here? Should I pump my hand?" Questions poured out of me as my blood seeped out through the tube.

"Just relax," the nurse said.

I tried to focus on something else—anything else. The two murders and Brad's close call jumped immediately to mind. Someone had tried to kill Brad! Why? Had he found out something that would incriminate the killer? Or had he just been in the wrong place at the wrong time? As soon as he was in recovery—I refused to consider the alternative—I'd ask him what the hell he'd been doing in the cemetery.

I thought about everyone I'd questioned—Lucas Cruz, Jonas Jones, Angelica Brayden, Trace and Lark, Otto Gunther, even Robby the roommate. I'd come up with bits of information here and there, but nothing that led me to the person who murdered those two men. The only one I hadn't talked to yet was Angelica's mysterious bodyguard/husband, but I still planned to, since he was closest to Angelica and the next logical step.

Finding the husband might be a challenge. He had to be with Angelica. Was she staying at the same hotel as Jonas? That was where I'd seen her last, before she fled for the church. I thought Lucas had mentioned that she had a place here in the City. He said she'd grown up here and returned whenever she had a break between auditions, commercials, and films. No doubt that would all change once the vampire film came out. She was destined to be a big star and no doubt remain in Hollywood.

Ten minutes later I was done giving my pint of blood.

After disconnecting me from the blood-sucking machine—I couldn't watch—the nurse handed me a cup of orange juice and a chocolate chip cookie. "Here you go," she said. "This will help your body adjust to your lower blood volume. In other words, keep you from fainting."

Still feeling light-headed, I crunched the cookie and washed it down with the juice.

She continued to recite the memorized spiel: "Don't do any strenuous exercise tonight. Drink plenty of fluids to rehydrate your body. If you notice any bleeding from the site that won't stop, call 911. Other than that, once you feel up to it, you're free to go. Thank you for your donation."

I got up slowly and gathered my purse and hoodie, feeling heroic, as if I'd just saved the world. I didn't know if my blood would go directly to Brad, but it was a good feeling, and I promised myself I'd do it more often, not just in an emergency situation.

I walked slowly back to the waiting room where Detective Melvin was reading a tattered *Time* magazine. "You're still here?" I asked, stating the obvious.

"Apparently," he said sassily, lowering the magazine. "How'd it go?"

"Fine," I said, showing him the bandage in the crook of my arm as if it were a war medal. "You should try it."

"I gave blood last week. They like us to wait a few weeks before coming back. I'm a regular."

Wow. The things you couldn't tell about a person just from his attitude. "Sorry," I said, regretting my flip comment. "That's great."

He shrugged off my apology.

"Any news?" I sat down next to him. He'd removed his tie and unbuttoned the top of his white shirt. His usually perfect hair was mussed. He almost looked . . . normal.

"He's out of the ER, in recovery. Head wound was pretty severe, but they cleaned and bandaged it. He's on meds now. Doc said he'll be all right, as long as there's no brain damage. We should be able to see him soon."

Brain damage. Oh God.

I settled into the chair, rolled my hoodie into a ball, propped it behind my head, and leaned against the wall. "Wake me if they say we can go in," I said, then closed my eyes and let the light-headed feeling take me off to sleep.

* * *

Someone was shaking my shoulder, trying to keep me from falling into an open grave. I jolted awake. "What?"

"He's awake," Detective Melvin said. "We can go in."

"Thank God," I whispered. I stretched and stood up slowly, then checked my watch. Two in the morning. "It's past visiting hours."

Detective Melvin smiled. This was the friendliest he'd ever been to me. "I have connections."

Yeah, the San Francisco Police Department, I thought. Good connection to have. I followed him to the doorway but, like a gentleman, he let me pass through first, then directed me to Brad's recovery room. The nurses smiled and nodded at him as we passed by. Either they knew him or they just thought he was attractive. He strode erect and nodded back, as if he expected such attention.

The light was dim and soothing in Brad's room, but the sound of a beeping monitor put me on alert. We entered quietly, as if our footsteps might hurt Brad's ears. He looked over when he spotted us and gave a half grin. I was startled by his appearance. The top and side of his head were wrapped in white gauze and tape, and he had stitches under his chin, protected by a large butterfly bandage. His complexion was wan— that might have been the lighting—and he appeared groggy, probably from the medication. But there was still a sparkle in his eyes when he saw me that reassured me there was no brain damage.

I moved to him and took the hand that didn't sport an IV. "Hi," I said softly.

"Hey," Brad mumbled with a thick tongue. He gave a slight nod to Detective Melvin.

"How you doing, buddy?" Melvin asked, towering over his bedridden friend. "Golf later?"

Brad sort of laughed, but winced immediately afterward and squeezed my hand.

"You're going to be all right," I said, stroking his hand. Platitudes seemed best at a time like this.

"How'd you find me?" he whispered through a raspy throat. I could tell it hurt to talk.

I explained what happened, how the detective had met me at the cemetery, what Duncan had done to help locate him, and how Otto had even contributed to his rescue. Brad blinked now and then as he took in the story and tried to process it. Unconscious for most of the time during the ordeal, he couldn't recall many details, so we filled him in as best we could. But there was still one unanswered question I had to ask.

"Brad, what were you doing in the cemetery?"

Brad frowned, then blinked some more, as if trying to pull out an answer from the deep recesses of his memory bank. "I . . . had a thought when I was with you, Luke. Let's see . . . you said something about Spidey's cell phone, wallet, and keys—that they never turned up. They weren't on his body, or near the crime scene, or in his car. I went back to see if I could find them."

It was probably in the Black Pond, I thought.

"And did you find it?" the detective said.

Brad took a slow, deep breath. "I figured he took his

things out of his pockets before they started jumping around. Probably put them somewhere safe near the starting point. Near his car."

"Why not just lock his valuables in their car?" I asked.

"Spidey drove a piece of junk," Detective Melvin answered. "When we finally found it parked out of sight at another cemetery, one window was broken. A door handle had fallen off. And the lock didn't work."

"He put everything in a backpack and hid it," Brad added.

"So did you find it?" I asked.

Brad gave another half grin. "It was tucked under a broken gravestone."

"Wow," I said, glancing at Melvin for his reaction. "What was inside?"

Melvin looked anxiously at Brad.

Brad's grin faded and he gave a heavy sigh. "No idea. Someone must have come up behind me, slugged me over the head with something, and taken it."

"Then dragged you into that mausoleum," Melvin added, "closed it up, and left you for dead. Wonder why they didn't take your cell phone."

"Don't know. Maybe he didn't have time."

"Must have been pretty strong to drag you over there and shove you inside," Melvin said. "Plus, he locked the gate with a new padlock. That takes planning."

I shuddered, remembering the fates of the other two cemetery victims. "Whoever it was must have been following you, Brad."

"Or maybe he just returned to the scene of the crime—looking for Spidey's backpack too—and saw me there," Brad said.

A nurse entered the room—she was way too young and way too cute. "I'm sorry, but Mr. Matthews needs his rest. I'm going to have to ask you to come back in the morning.

I squeezed Brad's hand, partly to let him know I would miss him, and partly to warn him to stay away from that nurse. He squeezed back, then gently caressed my fingers.

"Presley, be careful," he said. I could see he was starting to fade. "Someone knows you and I are snooping around, asking questions. You could be in real danger." He turned to Melvin. "Luke, keep an eye on her for me, will you?"

"You want me to place her in protective custody?" Melvin asked, pulling handcuffs out of his pocket.

"Very funny," I said, "although I wouldn't mind borrowing those cuffs. . . ." I shot Brad a wicked grin. He started to laugh, but the pain stopped him. "You rest up. I'll come see you tomorrow. Let me know if you need anything."

"Bruiser . . . I left him at Sansa's—"

"I know. He's fine. Spencer is taking good care of him. Last I saw him, he was dressed like a baby and was being pushed around in a carriage. I'll let Sansa know what happened. Now get some sleep." I leaned down and kissed him lightly on the lips, then turned away and left the room before he saw the tears in my eyes.

*   *   *

Detective Melvin saw me safely to my car in the hospital parking lot. He asked me to call him when I reached home and I promised I would, although it seemed unnecessary, and I was sure he wouldn't really want to be bothered. I figured he was just living up to his promise to Brad.

I got home in less than thirty minutes, with very little traffic, thanks to the early-morning hour. I pulled into the carport and headed inside my condo. The cats had been fed earlier, but they always acted as if they were starving, mewing and climbing all over me, so I refilled their bowls. Finally, I changed into my PJs and headed off to bed, exhausted from the emotional day and the physical bloodletting. I called the detective to say I was home safe, then flopped onto the soft mattress, wondering what had been in Spidey's backpack. It had to be something important to the killer, since he'd returned to the scene of the crime to retrieve it.

Or had he just been following Brad?

So what was it? Spidey's cell phone? If so, what had the killer tossed into the Black Pond the night Spidey was murdered? I'd forgotten to mention the pond to Detective Melvin, and I made a mental note to tell him in the morning.

Thank God it wasn't Brad at the bottom of that pond.

Hopefully it wasn't anyone else.

In any case, it was time for all this to end—before the killer tried again. But to end it, I'd have to figure out what Spidey, Bodie, and Brad had in common that would cause the killer to want to silence them. Other than their having been in the cemetery at one time or another, I couldn't come up with anything. Spidey had been there late, supposedly to meet Angelica. Bodie had been sneaking around there to find dirt on the stars, including Angelica. And Brad had been there looking for Spidey's backpack, which might have had his cell phone with incriminating phone messages from Angelica.

Angelica Brayden.

She was the only one—to my knowledge—with a secret that might jeopardize her career: that she was married. Was that really a big enough reason to kill people?

And would she have been strong enough to do it?

Maybe . . . with her husband's help.

Otherwise it had to be a man. Only a man would have had the strength to wield a shovel with such force and drag Brad to the mausoleum.

Like a bat that had lost its radar, I was flying around in circles, going nowhere.

Unless . . . it was someone who wanted to protect Angelica?

Chapter 23

🎈 *PARTY-PLANNING TIP #23*

Want to freak out your guests when they come to your Vampire Party? Wear colored—and creepy—contact lenses that temporarily change your eye color to red, yellow, black, striped, or even bloodshot!

I awoke from a dream about Angelica—she had fallen into the Black Pond—and it had scared the crap out of me. I had the sweaty forehead and tangled sheets to prove it. Angelica had to be the key to all of this. While I could find no real evidence, no solid reasons why I thought this, something in the back of my mind brought me to this conclusion. I'd learned to trust my instincts, whether it came to party planning or crime solving.

I grabbed my cell phone off the nightstand where I'd put it after talking to Detective Melvin the night before, and punched in his number. This time I got his voice mail.

"Detective, this is Presley. Listen, I forgot to tell you

something Otto Gunther mentioned to me yesterday. He said he saw someone throw something into one of the cemetery ponds the night Spidey was killed. He called the spot the Black Pond. He didn't see what it was, but I wondered if you could check it out. Meanwhile, I'm going to see Angelica. I think she's the key to all of this. Call me when you get this message."

I showered and dressed in black jeans and an old top I'd handed out at my Séance Party that featured a Ouija Board on the front. I wished I had a real Ouija Board that would give me the answers to my questions, but maybe the shirt would channel some clues. After feeding my boys and promising them some new cat toys when all this was over, I called Lucas Cruz.

"Presley," the director-producer said. He was either being psychic or had caller ID.

"Lucas, I need your help. Brad's in the hospital. He was attacked yesterday and left for dead—"

He cut me off with a gasp. "Crime Scene Brad? Is he all right?"

"He's okay. We found him in time."

"What happened to him?"

"He was hit over the head and stuffed into a mausoleum at the cemetery. Listen, I need to talk to Angelica Brayden as soon as possible. You mentioned she has a place in the City where she stays during her off time. Do you have her cell number and her address?"

"Oh my God. Who's next?" he said, his voice wavering.

"Lucas, do you have Angelica's information? I'm in a hurry."

"*Uh* . . . yeah, let me check. . . . She has a place on Post Street . . . *uh* . . ." He finally located the information and gave it to me. "Listen, Presley—"

I cut him off. "I've gotta run, Lucas. I'll call you later." I hung up before he could ask more questions, grabbed my purse and a bagel, stuffed my feet into a pair of black Vans, and fled the condo with my cell phone still in hand.

As I pulled onto the Bay Bridge headed for Angelica's place, I glanced at my cell phone lying on the seat beside me. I was dying to call the hospital and talk to Brad. Was it worth risking a ticket? "Heck yes," I said to myself. I checked my rearview mirror for any sign of a police car, then keyed in a search for the hospital number with my right thumb. If I got a ticket, maybe Detective Melvin could get me out of it. As if.

By the time I crossed the bridge, I was connected to Brad's room. The phone rang a dozen times without a pickup. He must have been indisposed in some way. I just hoped he was still all right. I'd make a beeline there as soon as I finished talking with Angelica.

I'd thought about calling Angelica first but decided a surprise visit would be better. I found a green parking space—twenty-minute limit—around the corner from the Post Street address and parked, figuring this wouldn't take long. And if I wasn't back in time, what was a ticket when one was trying to solve a murder case?

Judging from the number of windows, the ornate

cement building was four stories tall. Judging by the style, I guessed it was built in the late 1920s or early 1930s. I hurried up the faux stone steps to the iron gate that covered the door and searched for Angelica's buzzer. I rang it and waited for the door to open. Instead, a male voice said, "Yes?"

"Hi, *uh*, this is Presley Parker, from the party the other night? I have something for Angelica and happened to be in the neighborhood."

A few seconds of silence passed before the buzzer rang. I pushed open the gate and went in search of an elevator. Although there was no doorman, the Art Deco lobby was plush and featured marble floors, white columns, stamped tin walls, and a carved ceiling. The place murmured money instead of screaming it. I wondered how long Angelica had lived here, and why she still kept it if her plan was to go to Hollywood.

I stepped into the red-carpeted elevator that could probably hold maybe two thin people at a time, and listened to the grinding gears on the slow ride up to the third floor where Angelica lived. The door opened to a beige and blue carpeted hallway, with four numbered units. Each of the doors was painted to match the carpet. I located Angelica's place and rang the round bell.

A tall, lean man with dark skin opened the door. He wore gray sweatpants and a black T-shirt with a popular sports logo. Barefoot, he held something tightly in his right hand. A medicine bottle? I recognized him immediately as Angelica's bodyguard/husband.

"Hi, I'm Presley Parker." I reached out a hand. "From the party the other night?"

Stone-faced and ignoring my hand, he said, "Angelica's not home. I'll take whatever you have of hers and give it to her when she gets back."

This caught me off guard. "Oh, well, actually, what I have for her is some information." I tapped my head as if my news were locked up tight in my cranium. "I need to tell her myself. . . . It's kind of personal."

"Sorry. She isn't here, and I don't know when she'll be back." He started to close the door.

I raised a hand. "But, I thought you were her bodyguard," I blurted, even though I knew he was really her husband and was posing as her bodyguard to keep their marriage a secret. Best not to reveal too much too soon, I thought.

"Yeah," he said, shifting his weight, obviously uncomfortable with the question. His knuckles whitened around the grip of the bottle in his hand.

"If she's not here, then why aren't you out guarding her?"

"That's really none of your business. Now, if you'll excuse me . . ." He started to close the door again.

"Wait!" This time I stopped the door with my foot. I had a feeling this was a guy who wouldn't think twice about crushing my toes, but I hoped my Vans would soften the blow—and I couldn't let this opportunity slip by. "Listen, I think Angelica's in danger. I know about her stalker and I think he may be coming after her."

He pulled the door open again and frowned, his brown eyes darkening. "Where did you hear that?"

Before I could answer, a female voice called from behind him, "Roman, who's there?"

I couldn't see who it was, with the man named Roman standing in the way, but the voice was familiar. I ducked under his arm that held the door open and entered the room. Angelica stood in her bedroom doorway, her hair disheveled, bags under her eyes. She looked as if she hadn't slept in days. A rash filled her cheeks, and she had several bruises on her arms.

"Angelica!" I said, alarmed at her appearance. I had seen her only when she'd been fully made up, her skin like porcelain, her short blond hair silky and smooth.

She glanced at Roman. He gave her a stern look. "Angelica, go back to bed."

"What's going on?" I said, first to the bodyguard, then to Angelica. "Angelica, what's wrong? Has this guy done something to you?" I nodded toward the bruises on her arms.

"Roman . . . ," she whispered, as if running out of breath.

"Angelica, I'll be there in a few minutes," Roman said.

"Wait!" I said, moving toward her and blocking her view of Roman. "What's going on? Do you need help?"

"No . . . no. I'm fine, really," she said dreamily, her eyes blinking heavily. "Just tired. Roman's taking care of me."

"You're not all right," I said, growing alarmed. "Have you taken some kind of drug?"

She blinked slowly again. "I didn't mean to hurt him. I was just having fun, you know. It was supposed to be harmless flirting . . . but he took it too seriously. I didn't know how to stop it. . . ."

"Who, Angelica? Spidey? What did you do?"

Roman insinuated himself between us. "That's enough," he said. He took Angelica's arm gently and guided her back inside the bedroom.

I got out my cell phone and punched 911.

"Hang up," Roman said, appearing in the doorway.

"She needs a doctor!" I said. "She's obviously been drugged or beaten or something—"

"Hang up the damn phone and I'll explain." There was fire in the man's dark eyes.

I pretended to press a button as if hanging up, then dropped the phone back into my purse, hoping someone would answer and hear us. But Roman reached into my purse, pulled out the phone, and shut it down completely before setting it on a nearby end table.

He was good-looking, and smart too. More important, was he dangerous?

"All right, tell me what's going on," I said, backing slowly toward the front door.

"Sit down."

"No, thanks. I prefer to stand."

"Fine." He crossed his arms, still clutching the pill bottle. "What do you want to know?"

"First of all, I know you're not really her bodyguard. The two of you are secretly married."

He smiled as if I were a silly child. "You're right. I'm not really her bodyguard. But you're wrong about us being married. We're not."

Surprised, I asked, "Then what are you? Her Svengali? Her manager? Her . . ." I'd run out of options.

He looked at the pill bottle in his hand. "I'm her nurse."

I scrunched my face—not a good look for me—but I was thoroughly flummoxed. "Her nurse? Why does she need a nurse?"

"Angelica has lupus. She hired me to manage her health, give her her meds, and see that she eats right and gets enough sleep, while posing as her bodyguard."

Lupus. What did I know about lupus? Pretty much nothing.

"What's lupus?"

"Systemic lupus erythematosus is a chronic, inflammatory autoimmune disease," he said, as if he'd recited the information many times. "It affects the skin, joints, kidneys, and other organs. There's no cure, but it can be controlled. Occasionally it flares up, like today. Luckily she can afford a full-time nurse to help her deal with the disease."

His news had taken the wind out of my sails. I felt drained of energy. "How sick is she? I mean, can she work . . . ?"

"Angelica's case is moderate, except for the flare-ups. She gets rashes, bruises. Has headaches. Sometimes fever, achy joints, congestion."

Wow. She'd seemed perfectly normal at the party. Today she looked deathly ill. "How do you treat it?"

"Medication. Anti-inflammatories, steroid creams, antimalaria drugs, a bunch of others. Not all of the drugs work for her, or they have side effects. Sometimes it gets worse and she has trouble breathing. There's been some kidney damage. . . ."

"Oh my God," I whispered. "Why the secrecy? Why all the rumors that you're her bodyguard or that you're married?"

"Angelica doesn't want the gossip writers and paparazzi to find out. It could ruin her career. If anyone in the business finds out she has a serious disease, she may never work in Hollywood again. She wants to live as full a life as she can."

I sighed. It was a lot to take in. "Why did Jonas think you and she were married? She was having an affair with him, wasn't she? He said she told him she was going to quietly divorce you and marry him."

Roman sighed again. "I'm afraid she's told a lot of men that. Jonas wasn't the only one. As I said, she wants to live life to the fullest, and she doesn't want anyone to know about her health."

Whoa. I'd heard Angelica was quite the flirt, but I could barely comprehend all this. "She was stringing him along? And seeing other guys?"

"She did it mainly for the publicity. People love it when two stars from a film fall in love. It's big box office."

"Then why pretend she was married, and why pretend she wanted to marry Jonas?"

"Men seem to fall hard for Angelica. She makes each one feel he's the love of her life."

"But they're not."

"No. She pretends she's secretly married to protect herself, to give her that distance and keep the guy from getting too close. As for the men, they seem to love the role of protector, of illicit lover."

"Does she love Jonas at all?"

"I'm sure she cares for him," Roman said, "but as for being in love, I'm afraid not."

I thought about the video I'd seen of Angelica and Jonas. It appeared they'd been arguing. About what? Had she told him she wasn't going to leave her fake husband? Or had Jonas been upset about her flirtatious ways? As for the figure watching them from the shadows, it could have been Bodie, or even Roman. More questions arose.

"Does she really have a stalker," I asked, "or was that another lie?" I didn't know what to believe at this point.

"Yes, that part is true. She has a stalker. Someone has been sending her threatening texts and e-mails, and calling her cell."

"Have you told the police?"

"I wanted to, but Jonas said he'd find out who the

stalker was and take care of it quietly, to avoid any bad publicity. Angelica went along with it. Even though Jonas doesn't know about her having lupus, an investigation into her private life might be leaked, and she didn't want to risk it."

"Has Jonas figured out who the stalker is?"

"Not yet, but he says he's getting close. He said he took her cell phone to some computer expert who can trace things like anonymous texts and e-mails."

"Does he have her phone now?"

"I suppose. Meanwhile, I had to buy her a new one. I was just getting ready to set it up."

This was all too much. I stood up. "Well, thanks for telling me the truth, Roman. I'm sorry about Angelica."

"I trust you'll keep it to yourself."

"I'll do my best. But two people who are connected to her have been murdered, and I have a feeling there may be more. She could use a real bodyguard right now."

Roman nodded. "I'll do my best too." He showed me out, and I headed to my car, wondering if Roman had told me the truth. After all, he'd lied before. Maybe he really was keeping her drugged. I also wondered what Jonas's computer expert had discovered on Angelica's phone. As much as I wanted to check in on Brad, I felt I had to see Jonas—and find out what he'd learned.

I had a feeling if Jonas took the matter into his own hands and found himself facing the killer, he would end up like Spidey and Bodie Chase.

Chapter 24

As soon as I got back to my car, I did two things. First, I wadded up the ticket on my windshield and threw it on the floor of my car. Second, I called Jonas Jones on his cell phone, using the number I'd gotten from Cruz. I figured as long as I had the ticket, I could stay in the spot for as long as I wanted. After all, I'd be paying a hefty rent on the space.

The call instantly went to voice mail.

What did that mean?

He'd turned off his phone?

Or his voice mail was full?

I looked up the number for the Mark Hopkins Hotel and punched the instant connect link.

"I'd like to speak to Jonas Jones," I said to the operator who answered.

After a few seconds, she said, "I'm sorry. Mr. Jones has checked out."

"Are you sure?" I asked, surprised. I'd assumed he wasn't going to leave town until the killer was caught.

"Yes, ma'am."

"Did he leave a forwarding address?"

"No, ma'am."

Well, that's just great, I thought. *Now what?*

I punched Detective Melvin's cell number.

"Parker?" he answered.

"Hi, Detective. I'm trying to locate Jonas Jones. He's not answering his cell, and he seems to have checked out of the Mark Hopkins. Wasn't he supposed to stay in town? Any idea where he is?"

"Yep, and nope. He was told to let us know if he left town, so I'm assuming he must still be around. But as far as I know, he's not staying anywhere else."

"Can you find out where he is?" I asked.

"You telling me how to do my job, Parker?" he teased. At least, I thought he was teasing.

"No, Detective. I just wanted to talk with him. Will you let me know when you find him? I think he might be in danger."

"You think everyone's in danger lately."

"Very funny. It happened to be true in Brad's case. Besides, anyone could be in danger at this point."

"I'm well aware of that, Parker. That's why they made me a detective. I have an officer guarding Brad's hospital room, another one watching Angelica Brayden's place, one at Lucas Cruz's studio, one at Otto Gunther's trailer, and one who's supposed to be keeping an eye on Jonas Jones. Okay by you?"

I looked around for the cop who'd been assigned to watch Angelica's home but didn't see anyone in uniform. Maybe it was a plainclothes officer?

"Wow, I'm impressed," I said, impressed at how thorough the detective was being. And then I realized he'd neglected to send someone to protect me. Hadn't it occurred to him that I could be in danger too? Or didn't he care?

"Don't worry, Parker," he said, anticipating my concern. "We have someone heading over to Treasure Island to keep an eye on you too. I assume you're there now."

To keep an eye on me. That could be taken in a couple of ways, I thought.

"I'm on my way. And thanks."

"You're welcome."

"Oh, by the way," I added, "what about the Black Pond? Are you going to have someone dredge it?"

"We have a team out there now. Should know if they found anything of interest soon."

I thanked him again. He hung up.

I sat in the car a few more minutes, trying to figure out where Jonas might have gone and to guess which ordinary citizen nearby was actually an undercover cop. I wondered if Angelica knew where Jonas might be and thought about running back up to her place. But Roman had sent her back to bed. She didn't seem in any shape to answer questions. And currently she was without a cell phone.

Dead end.

Dead ends. The thought reverberated in my head. I called Brad—the nurse said he was sleeping—so I decided to drive to the cemetery and see if I could find out how the pond dredgers were doing. I figured I'd be safe enough with them around, especially if Detective Melvin had an officer there to keep an eye on Otto.

On the ride over, I thought about which of my suspects had police watching them: Lucas, Angelica, Jonas, and Otto. Did that mean he didn't suspect them? Of course, it also meant he could keep an eye on them in case they did something suspicious. I guessed Melvin wasn't quite as nonchalant about this investigation as I'd originally thought, especially now that his friend Brad had been assaulted.

I drove through the quiet cemetery and spotted three men hooking up what looked like a mini-houseboat to a long trailer flatbed attached to a large truck. The letters on the truck read "San Francisco Bay Area Dredging." Apparently they had finished and were about to leave. I parked, jumped out of the car, and walked over to the one wearing a pair of rubber overalls, covered in filth and mud. His red, weather-beaten face no doubt had stories to tell.

"Hi, I'm Presley Parker," I said, keeping my hands in my pockets. There was no telling where his hands had been. "I'm the one who asked the police to check the pond. Did you find anything?"

He gestured to a pile of sludge-covered garbage at the edge of the pond. "A bunch of plastic flowers, old teddy bears, some broken headstones, and a chair . . ."

A chair?

"And . . ." He pulled two small plastic bags from one of his deep pockets. Inside each was a muddy cell phone.

"Great!" I said. One of them had to be Spidey's. But whom did the other one belong to?

"I hope it was worth the cost," he said. "It ain't cheap."

I figured Detective Melvin would probably bill me.

"And it ain't pleasant," he added.

Yuck. Another dirty job, like crime scene cleaning, but someone had to do it. Luckily, not me.

"Are you taking the phones to the police right now?"

"As soon as we get back."

"I could do that for you," I offered.

He smiled, and the whiskers on his face stood up. "Sorry. Against policy."

I shrugged. I'd tried. "When will they be there?"

"Should be within the hour if we're lucky."

I watched as the truck and trailer backed up, then headed down the lane, pulling the dredger behind them. How long would it be before Melvin found out what, if anything, was on those cell phones?

With all my running around, the day had passed quickly. The fog had rolled in, and once again the cemetery was in the shadows of twilight. I hadn't eaten lunch and was starving. I figured I could grab a bite at the hospital cafeteria and eat while visiting Brad.

Just then I heard a noise coming from up the hill. I looked up and saw a light on in Otto's trailer. I decided to take a quick detour and hike up the brush-covered grade to see if he'd spotted any shady characters around the cemetery lately.

As I reached the top of the incline, I noticed the tool-shed was unlocked and the door was standing open. Hadn't Otto said he'd planned to be more careful about locking that shed after his shovel was used to kill those two men?

Maybe he needed a reminder.

I walked to the trailer and knocked on the door.

No answer.

No doubt he was doing his cemetery rounds, acting like the crazy person I'd once thought he was, making sure the dead were left in peace and the living didn't bother them.

"Otto?" I called out.

I heard a noise inside.

"Otto?" He had to be there. I knocked again.

My phone trilled. It was a text message from Detective Melvin. *Where are you???*

I started to answer, when the door to the trailer opened.

An officer stood in the narrow doorway, his hand

on the gun that was tucked into his gun belt. Unusually tan for the season, he was sporting a thick brown mustache and cop-style sunglasses, his brown hair visible under his police cap.

Sunglasses inside? At dusk?

I took a step back. "Hi, I'm Presley Parker. I came to see Otto."

"Sorry," the officer said, his voice low. "He's under police protection."

The door closed in my face.

I blinked. That was weird. I guess these guys were told to trust no one, not even a party planner like me. I got down from the bottom step, wondering what to do with myself now, when I remembered Melvin's text message. He wanted to know where I was—probably because I wasn't on Treasure Island under his officer's watchful eye.

I checked my watch. I needed to go to the hospital and see Brad before returning home and catching up on work. With the holiday season approaching, I was going to be flooded with requests for parties—hopefully none with another cemetery venue.

And there would be a cop at the hospital, just like there was here, so I'd be perfectly safe.

I started to return to my car when I saw the toolshed door open and remembered I'd meant to alert Otto. I could at least tell the police officer who was guarding him—or close it myself.

I peered inside. The tools were all lined up in their designated spots, except for the shovel that had been confiscated by the police. Still, there were plenty of other tools that could be used as murder weapons. I started to close the door, when I heard another noise—a crash—coming from inside Otto's trailer.

The hairs standing at attention on my arms told me something was wrong.

I thought about the officer. Why was he inside the trailer instead of outside?

And what was up with the Hollywood sunglasses?

I felt a cold chill in my bones.

I grabbed the first tool I could reach—the clawed hand fork—and dashed back to the trailer door. I hoped I wasn't too late.

I pulled out my cell and dialed 911 as I pounded on the door.

"Otto!" I yelled. "Are you all right?"

A muffled voice.

A thud.

Silence.

"Otto!" I pounded again.

The operator came on. An electronic voice said, "City and state . . ."

No! I had dialed 411, not 911!

The door flew open. The police officer, no longer wearing his aviator sunglasses, glared down at me.

Before I could react, he grabbed my arm and yanked me up and into the trailer.

I hit my head on something on the door frame of the small entry and fell to the floor, momentarily stunned. I closed my eyes to keep the room from spinning.

When I opened them, I found myself lying half under Otto's kitchen table, next to a pair of muddy boots.

The boots were attached to a pair of legs bound together with duct tape.

Otto.

I rolled over on my back and blinked, trying to clear my blurred vision and see Otto's face.

Another face leaned down close and grinned. The police cap was gone, along with the brown hair; it had been replaced by short black hair.

The thick mustache dangled from one side of the man's upper lip.

I knew I was looking into the eyes of the killer—the killer who was now pointing a gun at me.

The killer was Jonas Jones.

Chapter 25

PARTY-PLANNING TIP #25

*Here's a great photo op for your Vampire Party!
Build or buy a faux coffin, line it with red velvet, stand
it up against a wall with the lid offset, and have
guests photographed "sleeping" inside.*

"Jonas!" I cried, peering at him from under the table.

That I was stunned to see the young actor posing as
a police officer was an understatement, to say nothing
of his holding a gun. Was it a prop, like Raj's?

"What are you doing?"

Jonas bent over and reached for my foot to drag me
out from under the table. I kicked him off and scooted
back, tucking myself into a far corner among the cobwebs and tracked-in dirt, along with an old sock.

"Come out of there or I'll shoot Otto!" Jonas yelled
at me. He might have been acting, but the threat
sounded real. And Otto was in no position to defend
himself. Just before I'd hit the floor, I'd caught a glimpse
of him lying on the tabletop, not moving.

"They'll hear the gunshot," I said. Bent up under the table, I pulled my legs to my chest, trying to keep as far away from Jonas as possible. This was not easy under the small table, and I knew he'd come up with a way to get me out, sooner or later.

Jonas laughed. "Seriously? Who's going to hear it? There's no one around, remember?"

"The cops. Detective Melvin sent an officer over. He should be here any minute."

"Where do you think I got the uniform, Presley?"

Oh God. Had he killed the officer? He must have—he was wearing the cop's uniform.

And waving around the cop's gun.

How had he managed it? I wondered, then realized this was a cold-blooded killer who had no regard for human life. My heart raced; I broke out in a sweat.

"What do you want, Jonas? You can't just keep killing people."

"I've done pretty well so far," he said smugly. "Now come on out or you'll be the cause of this old man's death. You don't want that, do you?" Taking a knee, he waved the gun at me.

Although my body was racing with fear-induced adrenaline, my head was clearing. I remembered I'd had something in my hand when I knocked on the trailer door.

The clawed garden fork.

I felt around beside me and found it behind Otto's feet. Jonas shouldn't have seen me grasp the tool, ob-

scured by Otto's boots and the dark corner. I slid it behind my back and gripped it tightly.

"What happens if I come out? Won't you just kill
both of us?"

"Yeah," he said, laughing. "But it'll make things
easier. For all of us."

"Really? How so?" I asked, stalling for time.

"I have to set the scene," he said calmly. "Like all
good films, an actor needs a scene to make his role
seem real. I'm going to make it look like crazy old Otto
shot you, and then knowing he was finally going to get
caught for the other murders, killed himself, after setting fire to the trailer. At least, that's what the cops will
think after they investigate."

He gestured with his hand for me to come out.

I pulled back and tightened my grasp on the garden
tool.

"Your plan won't work," I said. "Otto doesn't have a
gun. Only a rifle."

"I know. That's why I'd prefer you come out so I can
shoot you with the rifle. But if I have to, I'll use the gun.
The police will just figure Otto wrestled it from the cop
they sent to watch him. I don't mind ad-libbing, but I'd
rather stick to the script. I am, after all, a director's
dream of an actor."

Sweat was trailing down my back. My forehead was
throbbing from the bump I'd taken, my hands felt
slimy around the hand fork, and my breathing had ac-
celerated to the point where I thought I might hyperventilate.

I had to distract Jonas if I wanted stay alive, even for a few more minutes.

"Why, Jonas? Why did you murder Spidey and that paparazzo? You're a talented actor, on the brink of stardom, I'm sure. Why ruin your career and your life?"

"None of that matters now. What matters is Angelica. We're destined to be together, and as soon as she divorces her husband, we will be. I couldn't let anyone like Spidey or Bodie get in the way of that." Jonas waved the gun as he spoke as if it were a theatrical prop. But I knew better.

"How was Spidey a threat? He was harmless!"

"Not really. See, he overheard Angelica and me talking that night about her leaving her husband and us running away together. He had a crush on her too— who didn't? But he came up to me later and threatened to tell the paparazzi about our plans. If word got out that she was actually married and fooling around with me on the side, I was afraid it would jeopardize my career, which, as you know, is just about to take off with this latest film. Call me old-school, but I didn't want to take the risk. He thought if he threatened me, I'd break up with Angelica and he'd have a shot at her."

Apparently he still didn't know that Angelica's so-called secret marriage was just a cover-up for her illness. And what he called "love" had actually become obsession.

"So you stopped him."

"I had to. I sent him a text from Angelica's phone, asking him to meet me—her—in the cemetery after the party setup. When he was alone, waiting for her, I sneaked up behind him and bashed him over the head with the crazy old man's shovel." He laughed. "It sounded like a pumpkin getting smashed."

"Then you took his cell phone and threw it in the pond."

"Yeah, you told the cops, didn't you. How did you know about that?"

"Otto saw you."

"I figured as much. I knew he must have seen something since he was around all the time. Crazy fool. I thought the police would nail him for the murders when they found the shovel. Instead, they let him go." He shook his head, disgusted.

"And you killed Bodie too."

"As I said, I had to protect Angelica. If it got out that she was married, and then I came along and was accused of being a home wrecker, it could ruin both our careers. I know this happens in Hollywood all the time, but I couldn't afford that risk. I mean, look what happened to Jesse James with Sandra Bullock. He'll never work in that town again. And Tiger Woods—"

"How did Bodie find out about you two?" I said, interrupting him.

Jonas sighed. "If I answer your questions, will you come out of there, or are you going to make me drag you out? You can't stay in there forever."

I nodded.

"Okay. Well, Bodie had been following Angelica—"

"Stalking her?" I interrupted.

"Not exactly. But he knew something was up between Angelica and me and wanted the dirt. When he confronted me, I told him I'd meet him after the party and tell him everything. . . ."

"Instead, you killed him too."

He shrugged as if it were nothing. "Had to be done."

Jeez, talk about a crazy person. Jonas was way more out on a mentally unbalanced limb than Otto. Meanwhile, I had to keep him talking and just hope the police eventually figured out one of their officers was down.

"Do you know who was stalking Angelica?"

"You said you'd come out."

"I will. I have a leg cramp from being all bent up. I'm coming."

"You'd better. Otherwise, I'll just have to shoot you." He said it almost pleasantly, which scared the crap out of me.

"Go ahead. Shoot me then."

"I have a better idea," he said, standing up from his squatting position. "I don't really need to work out all the details. Let the cops put together their own story. It'll be a real murder mystery." I could see only his legs and feet from my vantage point under the table. I wondered what he was up to. It might have been a trick to get me to come out, but I took the chance and inched forward, just enough so I could see more of his body.

He pulled out something small from his pocket, about the size of a Pez dispenser. I couldn't see his face, but I could see his thumb brush across the top of the object.

The tip caught on fire.

Oh God. A lighter.

I peered out farther, twisting my body, trying to see what he was going to do with the flame. I could only view him from the waist down. He reached over and held the lighter under the tattered window curtains.

They immediately caught fire.

"What are you doing?" I screamed.

He bent down and grinned at me. "What does it look like? I'm setting fire to the trailer. No worries. It'll all be over quickly."

Otto! I thought. Why wasn't he struggling or screaming? Was he already dead?

Rising up, Jonas took a step toward the door.

"Gotta run. But I'll be sure to bolt the door from the outside. That ought to keep the cops guessing."

It was now or never. I scooted out from under the table. "Wait! I have something for you!" I said, thinking of the trick I had used with Roman, Angelica's nurse. He hesitated, hand on the trailer door.

The room was filling with smoke. The flames had spread to the cheap wood veneer, sending even more sickening black smoke billowing throughout the place. I coughed.

"Too late, Presley. Angelica is all I need. Once I plant evidence that he did all this, she'll need me too."

He turned back toward the door.

"Jonas!" I screamed. I pretended to struggle to my

knees, trying to give him the idea I was too weak to do anything threatening. You don't have to go to acting school to know how to pretend.

He hesitated, turned, and looked at me, no doubt planning to give me one last debilitating kick—or shoot me.

I leaped up, raised the clawed hand fork, and swiped it viciously across his face with all the strength I'd acquired carrying heavy boxes of party supplies.

He screamed in pain and dropped his gun. It went off as it hit the floor. I brought the claw down on his arm fiercely, ripping the fabric of the uniform and scraping his skin. Blood streamed down his arm as he fell to his knees in agony. I spotted the gun within his reach and kicked it under the table. Since I had no idea how to use it, I figured it would be better out of circulation.

Curled into a fetal position, Jonas began yelling obscenities at me, spittle spraying from his lips with each word. He held his bleeding arm, letting blood run down the gashes on his cheek.

"You've ruined my face, you . . . !"

I didn't hear the names he called me. I had to see if Otto was still alive. He was slumped over the table, bound and gagged, a bloody gash on the side of his head.

I shook his shoulder. "Otto!"

He moaned.

I grabbed his overall straps and yanked, pulling him off the bench seat. He fell to the floor. The room filled with smoke and I couldn't stop coughing. I had to get us both out before we asphyxiated—or were blown to smithereens.

I opened the door and tried to push him out through the narrow opening, but the hefty man was a deadweight and wouldn't budge. I climbed over him and stepped down the stairs. Turning around to face him, I reached back, braced a foot on the step, took hold of his duct-taped legs, and, inch by inch, jerked him through the narrow doorway, down the steps, and onto the ground.

I glanced inside the trailer. Jonas lay on the ground, screaming, kicking, and batting at his pant leg, which had caught fire. I looked around for something to throw on the burning cloth—water, a blanket, anything. I finally spotted a cone-shaped flower holder stuck beside a dog's grave, snatched it up, along with a bunch of dirt, and threw it on Jonas's burning clothes, extinguishing the flames.

I was about to grab his feet when I heard the sirens.

Seconds later the area was swarming with police units. One of the cops jumped out of his squad car, ran into the trailer, and pulled a hysterical Jonas from the enveloping flames.

I don't think I'll ever forget the madness I saw in Jonas's eyes.

Chapter 26

Detective Melvin didn't look surprised when he saw Jonas's bleeding face and arm. He shot me a glance, nodded, then ordered his officers to cuff Jonas. He also called an ambulance for Otto, who lay on the ground, covered in a blanket to protect him from the chilly night. The duct tape had been removed from his hands, feet, and mouth, and the wound at the back of his head had been bandaged.

All that remained of the smoking trailer was a blackened shell. Firefighters had quickly put out the blaze, but the flames had gutted the interior.

"Otto?" I said gently.

He began to rouse and tried to sit up.

"Take it easy, Gunther," Detective Melvin said. "An ambulance is on its way."

Otto lay back down, turning his grizzled head to the side to avoid the wound. "Wha' happened?" he asked, slurring his words.

"You're going to be okay," I said. I briefly explained the ordeal we'd been through, and by the time I was done, the ambulance had arrived, lights flashing and siren screeching. The detective and I stepped out of the way of the EMTs and let them do their work. Once Otto was checked and tended to, he was carried to the ambulance and driven to the same hospital where Brad was still recovering.

Meanwhile, Jonas, his face, arm, and burned leg covered in bandages, made the trip to the hospital in another ambulance, accompanied by two police officers. He didn't even wave good-bye to me.

While officers went over the trailer and grounds with their flashlights and evidence kits, I sat down on a nearby pet headstone to catch my breath. Detective Melvin walked over, hiked up the legs of his slacks, and sat down on a headstone that read PETEY-BOY.

"You okay?" he asked gently.

"Yeah. Fine. Bumped my head. Probably have a couple of bruises, but I'm all right. How did you know to come?"

"The officer I assigned to keep an eye on you on Treasure Island said you never showed up."

"You were worried?" I asked, a little flattered that

the detective cared. Most of the time, he just found me irritating.

"Not really. You never do anything you're supposed to do. I figured you were snooping around some more. But when I didn't hear back from my officer assigned to watch Gunther's place, I knew something was going on."

I sat up, suddenly alarmed. "Did you find him—the officer?" My first thought was the Black Pond. I shuddered.

"One of my men did. Jones hit him over the head with another one of Gunther's tools, stripped him of his uniform, took his gun, duct-taped him, rolled him down the hill, then covered him with leaves. He has a pretty bad head wound, but he'll survive. Of course, he may not survive the ribbing he's going to get from the other guys."

I smiled weakly. Humiliation was certainly preferable to death. "Boy, Jonas sure was prepared."

"Yeah. As for you," Melvin said, "we found you through your cell phone."

"Duncan!" I exclaimed. "He used the GPS app again."

"He's a pretty smart kid," Melvin conceded. "Maybe he'd like to come work for the good guys someday."

"Yeah, he's pretty amazing," I said. "I'll put in a good word. Although he's not exactly the straight-and-narrow type. He kinda makes up his own rules."

"Well, maybe as a consultant."

Finally, I asked the question that had been burning in the back of my mind. "How's Brad?"

"Doing great. Should be out of the hospital in a day or two."

"Thank God. If you're done with me here, I'll head over there."

Detective Melvin stood up, then lent me a hand and helped me up. "See ya, Parker."

"See ya, Detective," I said, smiling. "And thanks for . . ."

"What? Rescuing you? No biggie. I do it all the time."

"You didn't rescue me! I was doing fine. But thanks for . . . taking the murderer off my hands."

"You're welcome. By the way, we were able to retrieve Spidey's messages. The second phone was Angelica's. Jonas must have tossed it in the pond too to get rid of the evidence of the so-called stalker."

I nodded, then beat him to the punch. "So you saw the text message from Angelica's phone asking Spidey to meet her in the cemetery after the party setup. Only that message was sent by Jonas."

"How did you know?"

Instead of answering him, I asked, "Did you find out who her stalker was?"

"Your friend Duncan figured out where the texts originated."

"And?"

"They came from Jonas's phone. Turns out Jonas Jones was her stalker."

Brad appeared to be asleep when I entered his hospital room. I tiptoed in and sat down in the lone visitor chair next to his bed. He turned over, fluttered his eyes open, and gave me his signature half grin.

"Hi," I said softly.

"Hey. Where you been?"

"Oh, here and there. You've been sleeping a lot. I didn't want to disturb you."

Brad shot me a glance with his bloodshot eyes. "You've been chasing a killer, haven't you, Presley Parker?"

I shrugged, thinking if I hung out with this man much longer, I wouldn't have any secrets left.

"So, did you catch him?" He reached for my hand. His felt dry and cool.

I filled him in briefly, then said, "We'll talk about it more later. Right now, we need to focus on getting you out of here."

"Doc says I can go home tomorrow. But I may need a little private nursing care for a while. Maybe one of these peppy nurses can come home with me."

I started to slap his hand, then gave it a good squeeze instead. "*Uh*, yeah, maybe not. But I'm glad to see your sense of humor is coming back."

"Actually, I talked to Luke. He told me you saved Otto Gunther's life."

"Big mouth," I said.

"Who you calling big mouth?" came a voice from the door.

I turned to see the detective standing in the doorway.

"My man!" Brad said, his voice hoarse.

"How's it hanging?" Melvin responded.

I loved guy talk.

"Pretty good. Only hurts when I play golf."

"Nurse! Keep those drugs coming," Melvin pretended to shout out the door.

"So, you heard Nosey Parker almost got herself killed? Until I rescued her, of course."

"You did not rescue me! And don't call me that."

"Yeah," he continued, "you were about to asphyxiate and be burned to a crisp in a flaming trailer."

"But I didn't, did I? I got out, and so did Otto."

"That she did," Luke admitted to Brad. "But you might want to keep her out of the toolshed and away from sharp objects in the future."

"What's he talking about?" Brad asked, his eyes beginning to droop.

"I'll tell you later," I said. By the time I finished the words, Brad had nodded off.

"Did you learn any more from Jonas?" I whispered to the detective, not wanting to disturb Brad. "Or why he was stalking Angelica?"

"He was trying to get her to rely on him for protection by threatening her with an imaginary stalker. He wanted to prove that her husband-slash-bodyguard couldn't take care of her the way he could. It was his way of bringing her closer to him and making her more dependent on him."

"Wow. He was pretty delusional, wasn't he," I said. "Is Otto all right?"

"Yeah, I just came from there. The head wound is fairly deep, but he'll be fine. Did you know the guy taught at Stanford? Read it in his file."

I smiled, not surprised at all. "I'll have to look in on him. He helped a lot, you know."

"Yeah, so now what are you going to do with yourself?" Melvin asked.

I looked at him.

"Other than party," he added, smiling. "At least try to stay out of trouble, will you?"

"Don't worry. I'm going straight to Brad's house and get his room ready for proper nursing care. I don't want him bringing home any of those cute young candy stripers to give him a sponge bath."

Detective Melvin laughed, a rare occurrence.

"Besides," I continued, "I learned something from hosting this Vampire Party."

"Yeah, what's that?" Brad said groggily, his eyes fluttering open again.

I turned to him. "Anyone can pretend to be anything if they just get the right costume."

And I had the perfect Naughty Nurse costume for tending to Brad.

How to Host a
Killer Vampire Party

Vampire Parties are all the rage, thanks to books, TV shows, and movies such as Twilight, *True Blood*, and *The Vampire Diaries*. Whether you're on vampire Team Edward or werewolf Team Jacob, a fan or barmaid Sookie Stackhouse and vampire Bill Compton, or favor good/evil vampire brothers Stefan and Damon Salvatore, you can host a Night of the Living Dead party to celebrate a birthday, Halloween, or the latest vampire episode.

Invitations

Lots of vampire-related party supplies are available, but you can easily make your own invitations and personalize them to your theme. For a coffin invitation, fold a sheet of black construction paper in half. Draw the shape of a coffin on the paper, making sure one side of the coffin is on the fold. Cut out the coffin and, using a sparkly pen, write "Do not open until midnight" or "Open at your own risk" on the front. Or you can type it up on the computer using a spooky font, print it, cut it out, and glue it to the front. Next, find a picture of your favorite vampire on the Internet or in a fan magazine and copy it for each invitation. Open the coffin and glue the picture on the right-hand side. On the opposite side, write the party details. For added fun, cut out drops of "blood" from red paper and place them in the envelope. Or add a set of vampire teeth.

Costumes

Ask your guests to come as their favorite vampire—or werewolf—past or present. When they arrive, offer them face paints, vampire teeth, and vials of fake blood to add to their costumes. Make simple capes out of black fabric and hand them out to your guests.

Decorations

Create a gothic atmosphere with helium-inflated black and red balloons. Tie the balloons onto furniture, to backs of chairs, and float them to the ceiling. Turn the lights down and light candles, or string holiday lights around the room. Replace regular lightbulbs with black lights and red bulbs. Make a giant coffin using a large appliance box. Paint it black, add a string of garlic or a wooden cross to the top, and place it in the center of the room to use for setting out snacks. Place vampire fangs, garlic, and plastic bats around the room or hang them from the ceiling. Cover your mirrors and black out your windows. Set the table with a black cloth and bright red paper products. Use vampire teeth as napkin rings. Make a centerpiece using a glass bowl, fill it with red-tinted water, and float black candles. Make some personalized tombstones from cardboard or foam, and write epitaphs on them for each guest. Set them around the room. Play Clair de Lune, Muse, and Coldplay music in the background.

Games and Activities

Team Trivia

Divide guests into two teams and have them answer trivia questions about vampires and such from Twilight, *True Blood*, or *The Vampire Diaries*.

Quote the Vampire

Write down quotes from vampire books or shows and have guests try to identify the speaker.

Vamping Vampires

Write down scenes from your favorite vampire film, book, or show, and have guests act them out for one another to guess.

Vampire Shirts

Let guests make their own T-shirts with their favorite vampires or sayings on them. Print pictures of vampires and sayings on iron-on paper using the computer, and then let guests iron them on and decorate with glitter glue, sequins, and other embellishments.

Vampire Videos

Watch videos of your favorite vampire films or TV shows. Don't forget the originals, such as *Dracula*, or the popular *Buffy the Vampire Slayer*.

Refreshments

Serve lots of red-colored food to satisfy that thirst for blood—red licorice, sliced red peppers, strawberries, red apples, red salsa with red tortilla chips, french fries with ketchup dip. Ask the bakery to tint a loaf of bread red, then make sandwiches with red jam. Cut out bat-shaped cookies, bake them, and spread with chocolate icing.

Offer a variety of red-colored drinks for the vampire guests, such as tomato juice, cranberry juice cocktail, red punch, red sports drink, etc. Freeze gummy worms in red water to make ice cubes for the drinks.

Make a coffin-shaped or tombstone-shaped red velvet cake, covered with chocolate icing.

Favors

Give the vampires plastic teeth, black capes, fake blood, posters of hot vampires, face-painting makeup, videos of the shows, or other vampire-related gifts—lots are available!

Read on for a sneak peek of the next exciting
installment in Penny Warner's
Party-Planning Mystery Series.

Coming from Obsidian in September 2012.

PARTY PLANNING TIP #1

*When hosting a wine-tasting party, remind guests to
use all five senses—eyes for clarity and color, nose
for intensity of bouquet, palate for taste, tongue for
texture, and ears for the sound of "Mmmmm. . . ."*

"I'll drink to that!" my office mate on Treasure Island,
Delicia Jackson, said after my work-for-hire chef, Rocco
Ghirenghelli, set down a freshly decanted bottle of the
Purple Grape winery's two-year-old merlot.

"You'll drink to what?" I asked her as I watched
Rocco pour the maroon liquid into a glass etched with
the words "California Culinary College." The wine
licked the inside of the glass as it spiraled like a whirl-
pool to the bottom.

"Ignore her, Presley," Rocco said, raising an eyebrow at Dee. "She'll drink to anything."

Delicia stuck her tongue out at him. That was the kind of relationship my two event-planning assistants shared with each other.

Rocco, rarely out of his "chef whites," was dressed in khaki slacks and a brown button-down shirt. He handed the glass to me. "Don't chug it like you usually do."

"I don't chug my wine!" I said. "I'm just not pretentious, like some of those wine snobs."

"There's a big difference between gulping and tasting," Rocco said. "I want you to really *taste* this wine. You have to know these things when you host that upcoming winery event."

"I know," I said defensively. As I reached for the glass, I had a sudden flashback to my college days— days of wine and chugging. Admittedly I could have used a few pointers if I wanted to carry off this prestigious party Rocco had snagged for me. I lifted the glass by the stem, like I'd been taught by the *Wine Goddess* cable television show, then swirled the contents as if I knew what I was doing. Bringing the glass to my lips, I inhaled the "bouquet."

It smelled like grape juice. Really good grape juice.

"Okay, now savor it as you take it in," Rocco said, as Dee looked on, frowning.

"I love it when you talk dirty to me." I grinned mischievously. Rocco blushed the color of the red wine. Even his balding pate turned rosy.

I took a sip, swishing the liquid over my tongue and palate.

Dee giggled. "You look like a fish."

"Don't swish it," Rocco demanded. "It's not mouthwash. *Taste* it."

I swallowed.

"So. What did it taste like?" Rocco asked, both eyebrows raised in anticipation.

"*Uh* . . . kinda fruity, kinda spicy. A bit of a woody aftertaste." I'd learned some of the lingo from the TV show.

"Excellent! You've got a good palate, in spite of your tendency to guzzle wine as if it was tap water. All right, now hold your glass up to the light. What color do you see?"

I studied it a moment. "Dark maroon."

Rocco nodded. "Good. Now inhale it and tell me about the aroma."

I took a quick whiff, then a deeper inhale. "Definitely fruity. Like grapes."

Rocco sighed and ran a hand through his thinning hair. Apparently "fruity" and "grapes" weren't the descriptive words he was looking for. "Okay, this time, take a sip and let it rest in your mouth for a few seconds. Notice if it's tart or sweet."

I took a second minimouthful, let it "play" over my palate, and said, "Both."

Out of the corner of my eye, I saw Dee pulling the bottle of wine toward her.

"Is it rich or lean?" Rocco asked. "Velvety or smooth? Silky or sticky?"

I set the glass down, causing it to clink against the desktop. "I don't know, Rocco. It tastes like wine. Red wine. How am I supposed to enjoy it if I have to think about it?"

Rocco rolled his eyes, exasperated with his wine-disabled student.

Behind his back, Dee was about to pour wine into her empty coffee cup.

He snatched the bottle from her hand. "That's a sixty-dollar bottle of wine!"

"Come on!" Delicia said, holding her cup out like a street beggar. "Pour a couple of dollar's worth in here. I want to get my *drink* on."

Rocco ignored her. To me he said, "Well? Do you want this job or not?"

"Of course I want it! A wine-tasting event in Napa, with a food-pairing from the California Culinary College? Anyone would kill to do an event like that. I promise I'll study up on wines before the event."

Rocco's face softened. He looked somewhat satisfied, until he no doubt realized that my definition of *studying* wine was essentially the same as *drinking* wine. "All right, I'll let my sister, Gina, know. I've really talked you up, so don't let me down."

"I won't, Rocco. I swear. Thank you. I owe you."

With the wine bottle in hand, Rocco walked out of the office, leaving me to drool over the plum job he'd risked his palate and reputation for. His sister, Gina, was an instructor at the CCC in Napa and had been asked to cater some amuse-bouches—small bites—from her bestselling cookbook of the same name at a wine-tasting party. Her longtime friends Rob and Marie Christopher were hosting the event at their up-and-coming boutique winery, the Purple Grape, to announce their newest merlot. They were hoping to make a splash with this inexpensive but hearty wine, and thought presenting it at a special tasting would be the best way to launch it.

And I was the lucky party planner who got to put it all together.

I was not only looking forward to planning the event; I was also excited about spending a few extra days in the world-famous California wine country. I planned to indulge in a spa treatment, maybe take a balloon ride, and hopefully enjoy some personal time with my "boyfriend," Brad Matthews—if he could get the time off. As a crime scene cleaner, he never knew when he'd be called to clean up after a messy homicide, suicide, or accidental demise. Unlike a party, death had a way of arriving unplanned.

I'd also decided to take my mother along. She could always use a getaway from her care facility, and had mentioned she had an "old paramour" who lived in the Napa area. I just hoped her early-onset Alzheimer's wasn't playing tricks with her mind again.

"So, Dee," I said to my friend, who was still holding an empty coffee cup. Even pouting, she looked adorable in a ruffly white blouse, short black skirt, and red peep-toe platform heels that raised her from a short five feet to a towering five three. "How'd you like to play the Wine Goddess, like that girl on TV?"

She sat up, grinning. "Sweet. I'll wear a big flowered skirt and a puffy peasant top and put on a crown made from grapes and—"

I nodded as she continued the seemingly endless description of her planned costume. Sounded like something out of that old *I Love Lucy* episode where Lucy and Ethel stomp grapes for a laugh. My mind wandered further as I thought about how I might use my other part-time crew members for the wine-tasting event. Gamer/computer whiz Duncan Grant could DJ and help out with the entertainment I'd planned, which included grape stomping, barrel rolling, and of course, a wine-tasting contest. Berkeley Wong, rising indie filmmaker, would videotape the event for my Web site. And I could always use TI security guard Raj Reddy. You never knew when you might be dealing with intoxicated guests, especially at an event like this.

As for Brad, I'd bring him along for personal use.

The six of us, all with offices on TI, had become friends over the past year. Everyone seemed to enjoy helping out at my bigger events—but then, who wouldn't want to go to a cool party *and* get paid? Amazingly, after several recent headlining functions, my Killer Parties event-planning business was growing like a well-tended grapevine. Good thing, since the rent was rising on my office space, my condo, and my mother's care facility.

When Delicia's motor finally ran down, I asked her to book a few rooms for the crew at a bed-and-breakfast near the Purple Grape.

"Seriously?" she asked, lighting up again. "You're comping our weekend?"

"Of course," I said, feeling magnanimous. "That's one of the perks you get when you work for a party planner like me. Besides, the Christophers have offered my mother and me a room at their 'villa,' but I'd like to find a place nearby for you, Duncan, Berk, and Raj."

"What about Brad? You shacking up with him at the winery—in front of your mother?"

My mother was no prude. She'd had a series of love affairs in between marrying five husbands. In fact, even now as her Alzheimer's slowly progressed, she seemed to be getting more . . . amorous. She apparently had an endless supply of paramours.

I wasn't a thing like my mother in that department. I'd had one long relationship with one of the professors at San Francisco State, where I'd taught abnormal psychology. But I dumped him when I found out he'd been cheating on me with a cliché—one of his students. When the university had dumped me—budget cuts—I met Brad. He was the only other guy I'd really been with since then. And I was taking that relationship very slowly.

"*Hmm,*" I said, "that could be awkward. I was planning to sneak him into my room. But maybe you should get him a room, too, just in case."

"I'm on it!" As an underemployed actress, Dee spoke mostly in exclamation points. "This is going to be so off the hook!"

With the party only a month away, much of the preliminary work had been done, but I still had lots to do. I pulled out the Killer Parties planning sheet I'd been working on and read over the entries under the who, what, when, where, and why sections. That was the fun part—brainstorming ideas to match the theme and then watching it all come to life.

Ahhh, a wine-tasting party in Napa, an "adventure" for my mother, and a romantic weekend with Brad. I couldn't wait to get my party on.

I spent the next few weeks juggling the wine-tasting plans with several other parties I'd been hired to do, including a "Come as Your Favorite Author" party—a fund-raiser for the San Francisco Library—and a "Red Hat Funvention" for a group of women who wore red hats and purple outfits and liked to party. By the end of the month I was more than ready for a peaceful break in serene wine country.

Early Friday morning I picked up my mother at her care facility. Although the party wasn't until Saturday, I'd been invited to join the Christophers and Rocco and Gina for a preparty dinner at the California Culinary College, and meet a couple of their neighbors. Brad couldn't make it, so I'd asked if my mother could join us.

"Oh, Presley, dear, I'm so looking forward to this," she said, after I stuffed her two suitcases into the minibackseat of my MINI Cooper. I pulled up the directions on my iPhone's GPS, we fastened our seat belts, and off we went for what I hoped would be a tasty and relaxing evening, with lots and lots of wine.

The sixty-mile drive passed quickly, thanks to my mother's tour-guide lecture about the Napa Valley. As a native San Franciscan, she knew the history of nearly every place within a three-hour radius. The breathtaking view of mustard fields and perfectly aligned vineyards offered eye candy, along with rolling hills, fields of wild flowers, and wineries in every style of architecture, from modern to medieval. My mouth watered as I thought about the bottles of wine those vineyards produced.

"Presley?" I heard my mother say, and retreated from the recesses of my brain. "Are you listening to me? You were such a distractible child with your ADHD, and you haven't changed."

"I was listening, Mother," I lied. "You were talking about the history of Napa." I'd heard the speech before during the several trips we'd made over the years when she had hosted her own parties there. My mother, the grande dame of San Francisco café society, had planned events for such resident luminaries as the Smothers Brothers, Pat Paulsen, and Francis Ford Coppola, who all had wineries in the area.

"So, as I was saying," she continued, "when Prohibition came along, it hurt the industry terribly."

While she talked on, I thought about the evening ahead. Although Rob and Marie had meant for it to be a thank-you evening, I figured it would give me a chance to go over last-minute changes and nail down final details, as well as make sure Rob would be donating a percentage of the money he raised selling wine at the event to my charity of choice. I'd picked Alcoholics Anonymous this time, since my third stepfather had died of the disease and it seemed appropriate.

But most of all, I looked forward to another preview of Gina's amuse-bouches. Everything sounded better in French. Merlot, cabernet, chardonnay . . .

". . . then many of the wineries shut down," I caught Mother saying. "But after the Second World War, they picked up again, and that was the beginning of those big monopolies like Napology that now produce large quantities for less money."

Rocco had mentioned something about how the large wineries were changing the Valley, causing "rumblings" from the smaller boutique wineries as well as from environmental groups. "Rob said there have been protests," Rocco had told me, "from a group called the Green Grape Association. They've been complaining about all the special events, the noise and traffic, the crowds and litter. They claim these events are harming the environment."

"Are they protesting smaller wineries like Rob's?" I'd asked, thinking of the Purple Grape.

"They're going after any winery that isn't green enough to suit them."

Rocco had mentioned a woman named JoAnne Douglas, president of the Green Grape Association. He said Rob had called her a "fanatic" for her radical methods in trying to stem growth in the valley. Although she owned a neighboring winery, she had not been invited to the party like the other neighbors.

". . . and today," Mother said, interrupting my thoughts again, "more than five million people visit the three hundred wineries here."

The personal audio tour stopped when we pulled up to the Purple Grape estate. Mother was finally speechless—thank God—as she gazed at the Tuscan-style mansion nestled in the Napa hills and surrounded by rows of vineyards.

"My goodness," she whispered. "We're staying here? I feel like I'm in Italy."

Before I could comment, a tall, good-looking man in jeans and a dark blue golf shirt appeared at the double-front doors a few yards from the circular driveway. He smiled pleasantly and waved, then started toward us, following a stone path that wound through an impeccably landscaped flower garden. Noting his graying temples and his lean but muscular shape, I guessed him to be a young fortysomething. Out of habit, I checked his shoes as he reached the car. Brown leather Ferragamo loafers. Italian shoes to match the villa?

"Welcome to the Purple Grape!" he said, opening my mother's car door. "You must be Presley," he said to me, "and this must be your charming mother, Veronica."

He lent her a hand to help her out. She blushed—I thought she might swoon—and fell instantly in love. I recognized the symptoms.

"Yes, I'm Presley, and this is my mom. You must be Rob. Thanks so much for putting us up at your beautiful home." I took in the sprawling single-level house, from the red tiled roof and wrought-iron fence, to the circular fountain surrounded by four marble statues of children wearing crowns of grapes and holding goblets. The place was breathtaking. I almost swooned myself at the thought that we'd be staying in such an incredible home. As I started to open the trunk to retrieve my small suitcase, I heard someone call, "Rob!" from the house.

A woman came running toward us from the home. She also wore jeans, plus a champagne-colored knit top. Her dark hair was swept up and caught by clips. On her feet were slip-on black leather flats—Clarks or Rockports—simple, practical, comfortable. But unlike Rob, the look on her face wasn't at all pleasant.

Rob's smile turned to a frown as she approached. "Marie? What's wrong?"

Marie's flushed face and wild brown eyes made me tense up. *Uh-oh.* All was not well in Napa's Camelot. It probably had something to do with the upcoming event. Such was my party karma.

"It's JoAnne," she said, breathless from the short run to my car. Even though she was in her early forties, I doubted this trim, attractive woman was out of shape. No doubt stress was causing her to hyperventilate.

Rob sighed, and his shoulders drooped. "What's she done now?"

Out of the corner of my eye, I saw two other people appear in the doorway of the house. A woman—blond, younger than Marie, wearing tan shorts, a tight tank top, and leather sandals—was leaning against the doorjamb, her arms crossed in front of her midriff. I wondered if this was the JoAnne they were talking about. Next to her stood a man, nice-looking, thirty-something, dressed in a black suit in spite of the warm spring weather. I couldn't make out his shoes from this distance, except that they were black and probably expensive, judging by the suit.

I thought I saw a look pass between the two of them.

"She says we have to cancel the party!" Marie cried.

"What?" Rob said, shaking his head. "She can't do that. There's no way—"

"Yes, she can!" Marie said, cutting him off. "She's threatening to call the police!"

Great. The party hadn't started and already the cops were involved. I had a feeling the fizz in this event was already starting to go flat.